I0691207

SHARP ABSENCE

KATE ANDERS

BOOBERRY BOOKS

Editing by: My Brother's Editor

Cover by Murphy Rae

ISBN: 979-8-9855717-0-7 (eBook)

ISBN: 979-8-9855717-2-1 (Paperback)

Library of Congress Control Number: 2022902916

To Moe

Always my biggest supporter, you never had any doubts that I could do this.

For that and so many other reasons I can't wait to spend another 17 years with you.

PROLOGUE

"MY SHARONA" BY THE KNACK

My body comes to consciousness abruptly at the crack of thunder. It takes a few moments for me to open my eyes because everything just feels wrong. Confusion floods my thoughts and an unexplainable feeling of panic. But the real motivator to get moving and open my eyes is the fear that is pumping through my blood. In fact, in this moment, fear is the only thing I'm a hundred-percent sure of.

My eyes take longer than they should to open. It feels like when you sleep way too long and they are caked closed. Only the sensation is different, almost sticky.

Even in the dark, I can tell my vision is blurry. A flash of light illuminates the area in front of me but it takes a while for me to realize it is lightning, gone as quick as it comes, leaving behind only the confirmation that my vision is a hot mess.

Before I even feel the pain, I feel pressure. My head feels like it's heavy, but oddly, it's mostly a full sensation at the top of my head with a fullness that makes me think my face might be swollen. But the strangest pressure is coming from my chest. It feels like someone is sitting on my chest, but oddly, there isn't any pain or discomfort from the pressure on my back.

Bringing my hands up to my face to see if it is in fact swollen allows my body weight to shift, bringing a sharp jerk of whatever is across my chest, startling me.

"What the hell?" I murmur to myself while bringing my hands down to my chest and find a strap across my chest holding me in place.

I'm upside down. How the fuck am I upside down? Well, that explains all the pressure I'm feeling, my face probably looks like a tomato with all the blood rushing to my head. With that figured out, I go back to trying to figure out what's wrong with my eyes, and sticky is exactly the right word. My face is wet, all over wet. But not all of it feels like water, no, some of it feels thick and sticky.

My pinkie finger brushes up against something embedded in my face, and the pain is startling. It kind of feels like when you step on a pebble and it gets stuck on the bottom of your foot, except different, sharp. It takes a few seconds to get a purchase on whatever it is and pull it out of my face, which only unleashes more sticky liquid down, or rather up, my face. Blood. It's blood.

Another flash of lightning lets me see my rosary pooled at what is apparently the roof of my car, to be exact. I'm upside down in my car.

How the fuck did this happen?

There's a hole where the memory should be. The only things left behind are panic and fear. Trying to rationalize that it makes sense I would be afraid if I was about to be in a car accident doesn't really work. Something tells me it's more than that. The more I think about it, the more I think I shouldn't be in this car.

My vision is finally starting to clear up or maybe my eyes

are just getting the opportunity to adjust to the pitch black, so I decide it's time to go.

Fumbling around trying to find the release to the seat belt takes more time than I would expect, I guess being upside down really messes with the way your brain perceives your physical location. As soon as I hit the release, though, nothing happens. The mechanism doesn't pop out and my weight is still resting on the seat belt, keeping me attached to the seat.

"Think, think," I whisper.

The door. I should try the door next. As soon as my arm starts to cross over my body, I feel this sharp and sudden overwhelming pain. It feels like someone is wrenching my arm out of the socket. The pain is so intense and sudden that I start to get dizzy and feel like I'm going to pass out. Clutching my arm against my chest, I try to hold on to consciousness while realizing how much trouble I'm really in.

A few seconds pass before I realize I have a knife in my glove box that I could use to get out of the seat belt.

There's no way I can reach the glove compartment with my left hand, so with the only option being my injured right arm, I take a deep breath and push through the pain. Tears start welling up in my eyes and a cold sweat breaks out along my skin as I finally feel my fingers wrap around the cold steel of the knife.

I take another deep breath, knowing what comes next is bound to hurt just as much.

It's not like the movies where I could just swipe through the seat belt and suddenly be free. No, it's a lot harder than that. I've been hanging upside down for who knows how long, I'm clearly injured, and my body is quickly getting weaker and weaker the longer I'm in this cold and wet car. What must have been minutes pass by as I struggle to saw my knife through the tightly woven fabric of my seat belt.

The last swipe of the knife has me propelling down to the

roof of my car with no way to catch myself. The shock of hitting the roof echoes through my body and leaves a wake of pain in its path.

I should be feeling better about this. I'm making progress. But honestly, I only feel worse.

My body hurts worse than when I woke up and I feel way more panicked now that I am free than I did when I was pinned down. It doesn't seem logical.

I let myself just lie on the roof for a few minutes before I realize that my body is starting to shake and my teeth are starting to chatter against each other. The urge to take a nap is starting to take hold and the fear I had been battling up until this point starts to take a back seat.

Get up. You have to get up. I lift my head up to look around. I know I just heard a voice, but I can't see anything. And the only thing I can hear right now is music coming out of my radio. I think I imagined it. Either way, it feels like good advice.

Rolling over takes time, as I try to protect all the areas of my body that are aching. The palms of my hands keep landing on top of little pieces of glass I assume are from the windshield, I think a few have actually embedded themselves into the skin. When my hand finally hits the cold wet grass, it's startling.

I no longer want to sleep and the fear is starting to take hold again. I'm still on my hands and knees as I make it out of the car and look around.

Now that I'm out, I can tell I obviously crashed, and the lighting is better so I can get a better idea of what's going on and where I am. Even with more light, I'm struggling to figure out which direction to go, I see headlights coming toward me and that's when everything in my body shifts.

A cold sweat breaks out against my skin and my heart starts pumping harder and I can feel my pulse in my ears. I probably have a head injury and my body is definitely battered and bruised, but I know I can't head toward the road and those lights.

There is no doubt in my mind, not even a little, that I need to move in the opposite direction.

I start dragging my body toward the tree line, at first feeling the wetness of the grass saturate through my jeans even more before I'm able to get into an upright position. I give thanks that I didn't wear flimsy shoes, my leather boots did a good job protecting my feet in the crash, and I get the feeling I'm going to need that protection as I start hobbling into the trees.

I risk a quick look back when I see the lights stop moving next to my upside-down car.

The only thing I know for sure is that whoever this person is, they are in a car similar to mine and that in no way should I call out to them for help.

I start moving faster into the woods, trying to be as quiet as I can, hoping beyond all hope that whoever was in that car didn't see me limping into the woods.

But I don't have that kind of luck. I hear the door slam shut, bringing about a second wind I didn't know I had in me.

The woods are densely packed, which I'm grateful for because I'm having trouble keeping myself both upright and moving forward. I keep tripping over roots or things on the ground, mostly because my legs feel like they are made of cement and it's hard to lift them high enough to get clearance. I keep my left arm as outstretched as possible to keep finding trees to hold me upright while I keep my right arm tucked into my side, trying to protect the shoulder from being jostled any more than it has to be.

I quickly pause to catch my breath, letting me hear someone starting to enter the woods behind me.

Fight, flight, or freeze. I've heard about it a million times. My body wants to freeze, to simply stay still to avoid the pain. My brain, though, is screaming, *RUN*.

Knowing there is no fight in me, I start moving forward as quickly as I can. Even knowing I am being chased, I can't help but to chance a look back. I can't even tell where the tree line begins, let alone make out the shape of a body.

I finally start building up a hobbling rhythm as I stumble through the woods. I know I'm making too much noise. I know I am probably the easiest person in the world to track right now. The grunts alone are leaving a sound trail to follow as I stumble around.

Fuck, I don't even know which direction I should be running, just that I should be running.

And that's when I hear it. A voice. It's close to me and moving closer.

I wasn't fast enough.

I wonder how many before me weren't fast enough.

CHAPTER ONE

"CHEERS (DRINK TO THAT)" BY RHIANNA

"Come on, Kenz, you can't just spend the rest of the year hiding out in our apartment," Clara whined at me.

"I don't know why you are pushing this. You hate going to parties," I replied.

"I know, I know. I do. I totally hate these things. Like a lot. But it's not fair, babe, you did nothing wrong, and yet you're holed up in here acting like you were the one who has something to be ashamed of."

I sigh.

"It's not that, Clara. It's just, what's the point? Clearly everything I thought about basically everyone in my life except you was wrong. It's just easier this way. I'll just keep my head down and before you know it, we both will have graduated and we can start our lives away from all this bullshit."

She's not wrong. I am acting like I'm the one who did something wrong. But honestly, what else am I supposed to do? I thought I was going to marry that jerk. I spent three-plus years being Collin's girlfriend. I thought our friends were *our* friends. Clearly, I was wrong. All it takes is Collin "upgrading," while we were still together and somehow, I end up the bad guy? I don't think I will ever understand how I was the one who walked in on him railing her from behind, and I still ended up being the villain in the story.

Well, that's not true. I totally understand how it happened. Chanel. The world's most vapid narcissist on the planet, who Collin apparently worships now, has made it her life's mission to paint me as an unstable lunatic who just can't let Collin be happy. Frankly, I could not care less at this point. Do I hope they both get herpes? Sure, who wouldn't? But am I sitting around plotting how to get the guy who couldn't keep it in his pants back? Fuck no. And seeing as how no one except Clara stood beside me, well, why bother with them either?

"I don't know, Clara. It seems like a lot of effort for literally no payoff."

"Look, we don't have to stay long, just in and out. It's our senior year. We have less than five months left before this is all over. Do you really want to look back in twenty years and think about how you wished you had stood tall and not let some trashy mean girl chase you out of your college experience?"

"Jeez, when you put it like that!" I throw my hands up in exasperation.

"YES! Success!" Clara twirls around in circles in the middle of our living room. "I knew I would win!"

"Yeah, yeah, yeah," I say while shaking my head.

"Time to get ready to party!"

The stink eye I send Clara's way must get through to her because next thing I know, she's bringing over a bottle of tequila and pouring us shots.

"Look, we'll go in, head nod at all the right people, and then we can run by Starbucks and get you your favorite hot choco-late and park ourselves in front of 10 *Things I Hate About You* and forget about all this." We clink and take our shots. "I just hate seeing all this happening to you. You used to smile every day, and now you just keep your head down."

"Fine. I'll go get ready. But you have to dress up. If I have to do this, so do you." I look her up and down and notice the clasp of her locket has made it all the way to the locket, so I reach out and fix it. "There. Perfect."

Clara smiles at me. "Deal."

Ringing coming from Clara's pocket startles me, making Clara laugh out loud. She silences the ringing while holding her stomach, giggling.

"Man, it's so easy to throw you off your axis," she says through her giggles.

I can't help but laugh with her, 'cause she's right. I startle quicker than anyone I know. We both head to our rooms to get ready for what is sure to be a torturous party that honestly neither one of us really wants to be at.

THE THIN STRIP of light under the door flickers as people keep walking back and forth. I can still hear the music thrumming through the walls as everyone else not hiding in a dark closet has a great time. Seriously, how do I always get myself into these situations? The past three months it's like I have been trying to have every awkward college experience all in a condensed time period.

If we're being honest, I haven't exactly hidden in a closet since I was like five and playing hide-and-seek with my brother. Five-year-old me had a good reason for being in a closet though, twenty-two-year-old me has no good reason. Except maybe cowardice. What can I say? There was someone already in the bathroom and Clara had just stepped away to grab us a drink. There was literally nowhere else to go.

Chanel and Collin walking through the door like they were

some sort of bizarre college royalty, just triggered every instinct in me to flee. So, flee I did, right into this here closet. The worst part of this whole mess is that there really is no good way out. I see three scenarios. One, someone opens the closet door and I have to explain why I'm standing in a dark closet surrounded by winter coats. Two, I try to sneak out but since it's a crowded college party everyone notices, and once again I'm the girl in a dark closet obviously hiding from her ex. Three, I sit in this dark hole of a closet and reevaluate my life choices while I wait for this party to be over so I can sneak out.

I should have known that with the luck I've been having lately, there's no way I'm getting out of this unscathed. If it was quieter, I probably would have heard the knob turning on the door, but since I was reevaluating my life choices, I wasn't exactly paying attention. Which probably accounts for why instead of standing awkwardly in a closet when the door opens, I basically fall out of the closet, knocking over some unsuspecting frat guy.

And wouldn't you know it? My luck holds true.

"Ugh, Collin, isn't that your ex?" The whiny voice that is Chanel rings in my ears. God, she could give *The Nanny* a run for her money. "I told you she was following us!" She literally stomps her feet like an addle-minded toddler.

By the time I look up, I realize her shrieking has captured the attention of basically everyone in the room. Joyful.

"Yeah, Chanel, I'm totally following you, 'cause you're just so fucking awesome I can't control myself," I say while I roll my eyes and try to stand up with some dignity.

"SEE! She admitted it! I knew she was stalking me! You heard it, right, Collin? Everyone heard it! She's a stalker!" She shrieks even louder during round two.

She can't be serious, right?

I shift over toward Collin and I just can't help myself. "*This* is the upgrade? The bleach must have killed her last brain cell if she couldn't catch on that that was sarcasm." After I dust my jeans off, I look back at him. "I'm pretty sure you're the scum of the earth, and I kind of hope your penis falls off, but even I think you could do better."

And she's back to stomping. "COLLIN! Are you going to let her talk to me that way? Oh my god, oh my god, first she's stalking me and now she's insulting me to my face!"

I'm not really sure how to interpret the look Collin gives me. He doesn't actually look mad. I don't know, I just know I can't think about it. I have to get out of here. This party was a bad idea.

"Aw come on, baby, let's not let this ruin our night, it's our anniversary," Collin pleads while looking around the room, clearly wanting this scene to end. Lucky for him, Chanel is kind of like a squirrel, easily distracted.

"Six entire months, Boo Bear!" she exclaims.

Wait. Hold the phone. Quick math says... What. The. Fuck.

"You have got to be fucking kidding me." If looks could kill, Collin would be dead. Body smoldering on the ground, dead.

"Uhhhh..." Collin looks like a deer in headlights.

"*It was only the one time, baby, a mistake. You know I love you.*' Yeah right, Collin. I knew you were full of shit, but seriously, you were *dating* her for three fucking months while we were still together. How did that work, exactly? Did she know you were talking about our wedding and our lives together or were you just feeding bullshit to both of us?"

"What is she talking about, Boo Bear?" Chanel pouts.

"You know what? I don't care. There is literally nothing either of you could ever say that I want to hear." Walking away has never felt so good until, of course, I feel a hand wrap around my arm.

"Wait, Kenz, you don't understand, it's not like that—"

"It's exactly like that, Collin. And I need you to hear me right now, like, really listen, okay?"

His pitiful nod of defeat is enough for me.

I look him dead in the eyes and say, "I really hope your dick falls off."

Clara enters my peripheral vision and grabs my hand.

"How's about we get that hot chocolate?" she asks with a smile.

And just like that, I know everything is going to be okay.

"I CAN'T BELIEVE the nerve of that guy," Clara scoffs as she plops down on the couch.

"I know, right!"

"I'm sorry about making you go to the party tonight. I guess I really didn't think it through. I should have known they would be there."

"Nah, you were right. I can't keep avoiding them. And I'm not the one who did anything wrong. It was *three* months. Three. Months. I can't believe there was actually a time when I was considering if I should forgive him. I actually bought the bullshit he was feeding me about it being a one-time thing." Embarrassment flows through me. "And then for him to turn around and dump me in a fucking Starbucks like I was some kind of inconvenience for him... I just. I just don't know him anymore. Maybe I didn't ever really know him."

"No, honey, you knew him. This Collin, this version of him, I don't recognize him. Everything changed when he started getting close with his grandfather, you know that. This isn't on you. This is all on him. And you *know* he is going to wake up one day and look in the mirror and hate himself." She says it with such certainty that I can't help but believe her.

"Yeah, you're right. It just sucks. Like, I'm not still in love with him or anything, but we had plans. And now I look for what comes next and I have literally no idea. Everything is so up in the air. What kind of job I want? Am I going to stay in school? Are we going to keep being roommates now that Collin and I aren't moving in together anymore? I feel like I know nothing anymore."

"But that's exciting! You can do anything you want now! Sky is the limit. You don't have to plan your life around what Collin wants to do. Think about it, you were planning on getting a job and supporting you guys while he went to law school. What a waste that would have been."

"So true." She is so right. I can't help but wonder how much of myself I was planning on giving up. Hell, how much of myself I did give up in my relationship with Collin.

"You can do anything, Kenz. Anything at all. If you want to stay in school, do it. Do you want to go out and get a job? Do it. If you wanna run off and join the National Guard, do it. Literally do whatever makes you happy, just make sure you stick around." Clara reaches out and grabs my hand with a giant smile on her face. "Because of course you and I are going to stay roommates. You and I are the real deal. Sisters for life."

I can't help it. I throw myself on top of her and give her a giant hug.

"Sisters for life," I agree.

"But if you decide not to stay in school, maybe we should look for a new apartment. A fresh start, you know?"

"A fresh start." I smile at her. "Sounds just about perfect."

CHAPTER TWO

"WHAT'S UP" BY 4 NON BLONDES

"**K**enzie!" is the first thing I hear when I wake up. Well, wake up is a strong description. More like startled. I reach for my alarm clock and oh my god, why is Clara yelling at me at 5:45 in the morning?

"WHAT?" I yelled back.

I can hear her stomping through the living room and toward my room.

"You left the door unlocked!" Clara exclaims as she knocks my door open.

I shake my head to clear the cobwebs from my brain and replay the night before. Nope, I definitely locked the door. "What are you talking about?" I ask.

"The door, Kenz. It's unlocked. *You* left the door unlocked last night. Anything could have happened! Seriously, Kenz, how could you be this irresponsible?" Clara looks like she is about to cry or start foaming at the mouth. Either way, it's not a good vibe first thing in the morning.

"Clara, chill. I swear, I locked the door last night. I remember turning the lock 'cause it pinched my finger like it always does, and it fucking hurt," I tell her.

"Yeah, but you didn't lock the dead bolt. *Anything* could have happened!"

"Okay, fine, I forgot the dead bolt, but it's not like I left the apartment completely open to the apparent serial killers and arsonists that are running the halls of our building."

"This isn't a joke, Kenz."

"Yeah, no I get that, Clara. You're acting insane. This is clearly not a joke," I tell her, really getting pissed off. "If you are so concerned with the lock being locked before we went to sleep, you could easily have walked by the door to make sure everything was good. Besides, it's not like I did it on purpose, and you know it."

"That's not the point. It's dangerous. We are two young women who live alone with no protection. You can't just go around not taking our safety seriously."

"Look, I don't know what's wrong with you right now, but enough. It's 5:45 in the fucking morning. We were up super late last night, and I really don't need this kind of attitude this early in the morning for something that clearly wasn't intentional or even completely accurate. I promise to double-check the lock every night from now on, okay?" I basically yell back at her.

"There is nothing wrong with me, Kenz, but clearly you don't seem to care about our safety." And with that, she turns and slams my door behind her.

IT MIGHT BE JANUARY, but the sun seems to have missed that memo because it's brighter than it's been all winter. Of course, on the one day I forget to bring my sunglasses with me. I blame Clara. It was not a good way to wake up this morning, and I have been off-kilter ever since.

I'm finally back home from class, and I couldn't be happier to be back home since I am literally covered in an iced latte, thanks to the aforementioned sun. If the sun hadn't been blinding me, I would have seen Chanel and her cronies approaching, and I would have been able to move out of the way before one of her flying monkeys "tripped" and basically dumped her brand-new iced latte all over my favorite shirt. And of course, somehow it was my fault for being there. Chanel better count her lucky stars, because if I wasn't already running late for class, I definitely would have made a scene. And after last night's party, I have no shame, so the scene would have been epic.

Thankfully, Clara's car isn't in the parking lot, so at least I know I will get some peace and quiet once I get inside.

Making my way up the stairs, I hear Mr. Peterson's door open. Great. It's like he sits by his window watching the parking lot so he can always be in the hallway when any girl comes home. He is literally every creepy stereotype you can think of: his off-putting smell, that he doesn't seem to recognize that your eyes aren't on your breasts, complete inability to recognize personal space so when you try to pass him in the hallway, he always makes physical contact. But of course, when you say something to apartment management, he is so seriously confused about how we could complain about him going through the public hallway to get to his car. So ridiculous.

I take a deep breath as I reach the top of the stairs, a valiant effort not to breathe in his off-putting smell. Of course, he is standing right by his door, clearly waiting for me to make it to the second-story hallway.

"Lookin' good, Kenz," he says while leering at my breasts. Seriously, how does he know my name? I pause and stare right at him.

"Are you fucking kidding me?" I challenge him.

"What? Is it some kind of crime now to tell a pretty girl that she looks nice today?" he says with a smirk.

"Oh, is that what you were doing? 'Cause it seemed more

like you were leering at a twenty-two-year-old's breasts, and considering you're an unkept man in his, what, sixties? It's fucking creepy."

"Oh look, another feminist bitch who can't take a compliment." He sneers at me.

"Yep, that's me, just another bitch who doesn't want to be stalked by a creepy old guy," I retort. I plaster myself up against the wall and gesture for him to move past me.

"Oh no, you go first," he says with his creepy smile making a reappearance on his face.

"No, no, I insist," I tell him, fully aware my resting bitch face is on point.

The smile on his face falls and I watch him try to work through in his demented mind how he is going to "accidentally" bump into me when I'm literally plastered up against the adjacent wall. That's right, asshole, there is no way in hell I'm going to let you get your jollies today with an accidental boob graze.

He scoffs as he finally walks past me.

I can't help but to mutter, "Checkmate," under my breath as he passes by. I haul ass to my door and once I'm inside, I can't help but hear Clara's fanatical voice about the damn dead bolt, so I double and triple-check it just to be sure. Thankfully, it's one of those dead bolts with a key, so I don't have to worry about Clara not being able to get in when she comes home from class.

Time to get this coffee off my clothes, and with any luck, a shower to reboot and start this day over.

Hours later and I've got music vibrating the walls, while I work on yet another paper analyzing the ever so tedious *Waiting for Godot*. It never fails. Every semester, I always end up with one professor that wants to take a closer look at *Waiting for Godot*; I mean, what's wrong with Shakespeare? Bright side, I can write this paper in my sleep.

So, while I have the minimum required amount of brain cells working on this train wreck of a paper, the rest of me is fully engaged in '90s radio. What can I say? I love the '90s.

So, of course, it's when I'm in full chair-dance mode singing "I said, Hey, What's goin' on" that Clara returns home. Not that I notice at first, no it's not until I am using my hand microphone to belt out the lyrics that I hear the laughter near the front door.

So what do I do? I turn the music up, stand up and keep belting out the lyrics as I make my way over to Clara, who is at this point doubled over in laughter.

When I finally finish sashaying my way over to her, I can't help it. I pass her the invisible hand mic, which she, of course, accepts.

Next thing I know, we are both standing in the entryway under the glow of our Christmas lights belting out "Hey, yeah, yeah," at the top of our lungs.

When the song ends, we are both giggling and smiling at each other. This right here, in this moment, is why Clara isn't just my roommate or my friend, she's my sister. The fight from this morning, long forgotten. This is the girl who always has my back, calls me on my shit, and is always down for a '90s song break.

"Sorry about this morning," she says to me a little sheepishly.

I bump her hip with mine. "Eh, no biggie. I had a run-in with creeper Peterson on the way home from class, so I get it," I tell her.

"UGH!" she grunts as she throws her bag down on the couch before turning back to me. "I hate that guy. I have never once introduced myself to him, but he's been all kinds of up close and personal with my tits. And what's the deal with him always seeming to know shit about us? How in the world would he know I was a computer science major? The other day he wishes me luck with my interview. Like, how would he know I was going to an interview?"

"Did he wish you luck, or your boobs?" I ask.

"My boobs, of course. I think I could have literally just had my head cut off and he wouldn't notice. Nothing exists for this guy above the collarbone."

"I know. There is something seriously wrong with that guy. I talked to the guy in the front office, and they were all, '*Oh that's just Mr. Peterson, he's getting up there in age, I'm sure he didn't mean to bump into you,*' like really?"

"Ugh. Anyway, how was class?"

"It was okay. I got in late to my first class and, of course, the prof decided to just stop talking midsentence and stare at me until I sat down. Pretty sure I need no more embarrassing moments," I groan.

"Yeah, I heard."

Great, it's already around campus. Chanel can't waste an opportunity to spread more drama around campus, especially about me.

"It's funny," I tell her. "I made it three and a half years at this school not having a single rumor or embarrassing event get spread around campus, and now it's like every other day."

"It's just Chanel, she's an evil genius at manipulating social life on campus. Imagine what that girl could accomplish if she didn't use her powers for evil." Clara sits next to me on the couch and puts her arm around me. "You know you're going to be fine, right?"

"Yeah, I know. After all, how many times can someone dump iced coffee on someone before everyone knows you're doing it on purpose?" I joke.

"So true," she says midgiggle.

"What about you? How was class?" I ask.

"Eh, you know, same as always," she replies, kind of avoiding the question as she heads to the kitchen. "Not much to report."

"Really?"

"Yep, nothing exciting." I can hear her rummaging around in the kitchen.

"I'm surprised," I say. "I normally can't shut you up about your classes." Laughing, I say, "Not that I know anything about what you talk about. I'm normally confused two minutes into your explanations. And don't even get me started on coding. If I can't learn Spanish, there is no way I am ever going to learn how to code."

"It's not that hard, Kenz. Once you get the hang of it, you don't really even think about it anymore. You develop your own style of coding. Some people's styles are so recognizable I could tell you who wrote it just by looking at it."

"Yeah, that's my problem. If the rules are so broad that you can recognize someone's coding style, how the heck am I ever going to get it?" I ask. "I like rules for language," I say, gesturing to myself. "That's why I am an English major. Lots of rules."

"Yeah, 'cause it's not like there aren't tons of exceptions in English, or like someone's writing style isn't super identifiable in English," Clara says, rolling her eyes.

"Okay, okay, you're totally right, I cave. But I'm still never going to learn how to code, and don't even think about mentioning algorithms" —I point at myself— "*English major*. No math. I barely made it through mathematics for liberal arts majors. Your math makes me want to crawl into the corner of my bedroom and cry myself to sleep."

"You make it sound like torture." Clara laughs.

"Because it is!"

"You are so ridiculous," she says, shaking her head. "Don't

go knocking on math. I'm loving my topological data analysis class this semester."

I throw my head back and pretend to snore.

Clara throws a dish towel at me and I duck just in time to avoid getting hit in the face.

"What? I don't even know what that means!" I see Clara open her mouth to explain and I rush to interrupt, "I wasn't saying I want to understand!"

"Fine, fine, fine, stay in the dark. You realize that computers run the world, right?"

"Of course I do, which is why I always say thank you when Alexa turns my lights off when I ask. When the machine rebellion begins, they will remember I was always on their side and very polite," I say matter-of-factly.

"Oh my god, you are seriously insane."

"I'll have you know I am a fucking delight," I say, crossing my arms.

"Of course you are."

Ringing sounds from the living room.

"We seriously need to get different ringtones. I can never tell whose phone is ringing," I tell Clara as we both head back to the living room in search of our phones.

"Please, your phone never rings," she retorts.

"I have cultivated my lack of a ringing cell phone, thank you very much. After years of research, I have found if you never answer phone calls, or return voice mails with anything other than a text, people will eventually learn to only text you," I tell her.

Not my phone ringing.

Clara finally digs her phone out of her bag and silences it.

"See, you don't even want to talk to whoever that is, but I bet they will call back," I say, pointing at her phone.

She rolls her eyes and says, "I think someone has been giving out the wrong number or something. Nobody is ever on the other end or they ask for someone else that isn't me." She shrugs. "It's easier to just not answer."

"Exactly."

Clara looks back down at her phone. "Well, I guess I should probably get to work on my machine learning project." She grabs her bag as she heads through the living room back toward her room.

"Machine learning! And you think I'm crazy because I think machines are going to take over the world one day."

CHAPTER THREE

"GRAVITY" BY JOHN MAYER

"I got it!" Clara yells out from back in her bedroom. I barely catch my cup of hot chocolate from spilling, being startled when Clara keeps yelling, "I got it, I got it, I got it! Kenz, I got it! Can you believe it?"

"The internship?" It's literally the only thing that she could be talking about, but hey, she's excited, so I'll play along.

"YES!" she screams. "I can't believe it. I knew I had a chance, but they really picked me. Out of everyone, they picked me! I never get this lucky."

"Clara, seriously, you work your ass off more than anyone I know. It's not luck. Of course they knew you were the perfect choice for the position," I tell her.

"I know, it's just, I dunno, I didn't have a great feeling about it." She shrugs.

"Why not? I thought you told me the interview went really well?"

"Well, yeah, it was fine, but you know how it is. You always second-guess if you answered the questions the right way. And to be honest, it was a bunch of dudes in suits at a conference table grilling me. I can talk to a nerdy guy with tattoos on his arms, but suits. No way. They make me nervous, and this was a roomful of suits," she explains.

"Really? I've picked you up from lab like a million times and not even the professors wear suits. It's like a convention of how comfortable can we get." I laugh with her at the visual.

"Yeah, I know, but you try sitting in the same chair for over twelve hours a day, staring at a screen trying to write code to get the machine to do something that seems like a simple task only for it to result in an error message. Believe me, being comfortable is important. I know people who have spent hundreds, even thousands, of dollars on a top-notch computer chair."

"Now that doesn't surprise me at all. I don't think I have ever sat in a truly comfortable desk chair in my entire life."

"So true." Clara tilts her head to the side and starts fiddling with her locket. "Do you think they will have nice chairs at their office? I mean, the internship is a lot of hours."

"It's a multimillion dollar company. I'm sure they are better than the sixty-buck chairs from Walmart, but probably not by much."

"Ugh, you're probably right." She shakes her head. "I don't care, I got the internship! And that jerk from class, Preston, is going to have to eat his words."

"Oh, right, that guy." I cock my head to the side. "I take back everything I just said. He's the one guy in four years of seeing you in computer labs who actually wears pretentious clothes. Does he starch everything he owns because, honestly, it looks like his clothes wouldn't bend to let him sit down?"

"Oh my god, YES!" Clara doubles over. "You can smell it too! I never considered that starch had a smell, but you know when he comes into a room because of the smell." She laughs. "He came back from his interview and was so sure that he got the internship."

"Of course he did. He seems like one of those guys who

couldn't possibly imagine why anyone would ever choose anyone but him."

"Yep, exactly. He was bragging about how he talked to the executives about where he buys his favorite ties. Honestly, when he was talking about it, all I could think was if they give this pompous jerk this internship, then I definitely don't want to work for them."

"But they didn't. They picked you, 'cause you're exceptional and they know it."

"Do you know how many doors this is going to open for me after graduation? I have almost five months to work on some major projects that I can put on my resume. It's basically a guarantee that I am going to get hired on at one of the big tech firms around here when I graduate. And you know the pay is going to be kick ass. Just think of the apartment we'll be able to afford. No more creepy Mr. Peterson."

"Man, for that alone, I think we should totally celebrate. Dinner tonight, we could go to the Melting Pot. I know how much you love melted cheese."

"Really?" Clara bounces up and down with excitement.

"Of course, my treat. Honestly, Clara, you deserve this so much. I am so proud of you," I tell her with a quick hug. "You are going to do amazing things, Clara Tomas."

"CLARA," I call out from the living room. "The reservation is at eight. We gotta go! Hop to or no cheese for you!"

I pause as I am putting on my watch and listen for Clara, but I hear nothing at all. What is she doing? I walk over to her bedroom and her door is just barely cracked open. I tap it and it swings open a few more inches.

I see Clara sitting on the edge of her bed, silently crying.

"Clara?"

She looks up at me, and I can see the path her tears have taken down her face. My heart breaks a little for her in this moment. I can see her fiddling with her locket again, and I can tell that this is one of the few times that she has opened the locket.

"You okay?" I ask, already knowing the answer.

Clara sniffles a little and looks down at the pictures in her locket.

"Yeah, I'm okay, I'm just..."

"Hey, it's okay. It's a big day. It's only natural that it would bring up big feelings for you," I tell her, hoping that it brings her any kind of comfort.

"I know." She looks up and smiles weakly at me. "I just miss them so much. I barely even remember my dad, but my mom... I just miss them."

"Of course you do!" I move over to her to sit next to her on the bed.

"We talked about what it would be like so many times, you know?"

"You and your mom?" I ask.

"Yeah." She pauses, looking down at the picture of her mom in a field of flowers. "She was so excited about me going to college. We spent so much time sitting at the kitchen table mapping out what my plans were going to be." She smiles. "I remember her asking me what my dreams were. If I could do anything when I grew up, what would it be? Sky's the limit kind of stuff." Clara laughs a little. "I thought she was crazy, but she wouldn't let it go. So I made up my dream job, and she just sat there and listened. She asked questions and helped me flesh it all out, and when I finished, she just turned and looked at me and said, 'let's make it happen.'"

I reach over and grab Clara's hand. "She sounds amazing, Clara."

"She really was. She would have been so excited about this

internship. It was on the list of pie in the sky dream steps so I could make all my 'when I grow up' dreams come true."

I don't know what to say at this moment. I don't recognize myself in Clara's life. She had this amazing mother who was so supportive and actually wanted to know who her daughter was growing up to be.

My mother checked out long ago. Sometimes I wonder if my mom even remembers my birthday anymore. Clara's mom is the mom I used to have until everything changed when I was eight. Now I have these strangers who look so familiar but don't seem to see me at all. If my mom died, I would be sad, of course, but it wouldn't crush me. When Clara's mom died, she fell apart. Sometimes she still does. They were best friends. They loved each other, cared about what each other wanted in life. If my mom dropped dead tomorrow, literally nothing about my life would change. At all.

I say the only thing that comes to mind. "I'm so sorry, Clara. I wish I could have known her. She sounds amazing."

"This is all I have left, you know," she says, holding the locket. "It doesn't seem like much, but really, it's everything to me. Especially on days like today. It feels like my mom and dad are both with me, you know? Like they were there when I got the news about the internship, like they are somewhere watching over me having their own little celebration that my dreams are all coming true."

I squeeze her hand again. "Of course they are with you, the way they loved you, Clare Bear. There is no way they would be anywhere else but watching over you."

"I hope you're right."

"Of course I am. I'm outstanding like that. I know all kinds of neat stuff," I joke, trying to get a little smile out of Clara.

"Of course you are," she retorts as she rolls her eyes.

"You okay?" I ask as I nudge her with my shoulder a little.

"Yeah, sometimes a girl just needs a good cry," she tells me.

"You know what a girl needs after a good cry?" I ask.

"Melted cheese and unlimited bread?" She perks right up.

"Uh, yeah. Can't forget about the melted chocolate and unlimited Rice Krispies too."

"You can keep your Rice Krispies. I'm all about the brownies."

"Ugh, no. Brownies dipped in chocolate? I'm sorry, that's just too much for me. You can keep your brownies."

"Deal. But we split the strawberries."

"Of course."

I reach over and pull her into a big hug.

"I'm so proud of you Clara, you're going to do amazing things, and I know without a shadow of doubt in my mind that your mom is more proud of you than any other mother in the history of moms."

Clara laughs. "You know there are people out there that cure diseases and discovered how to make insulin and many other amazing things, and you think my mom is the proudest? I haven't even done anything yet," she exclaims.

"Yeah, but you will. And if your mom is anything like you, she would throw down with any of those other mothers to tell them how great her baby girl is."

Clara pulls out of our hug with a smile on her face and the sound of laughter coming out of her. "You're right, she totally would."

"Damn straight." I nod my head once for emphasis. "Come on, chick, let's get us some cheese."

THE SOUNDS of the restaurant are picking up. I can hear the people over in the bar area laughing and talking. I can't help but try to remember the last time I went out like this, to a nice restaurant with friends and laughter. It's been a while.

Probably since the last time things were good with me and Collin.

Clara is right. I used to smile. He made me smile. But hearing those voices coming from the bar, the way the sounds of their laughter carry across the room, I can't help but wonder when the last time I had that was? Sure, I joke around with Clara, and honestly, she's the only reason I laugh or smile at all anymore. But before, when Collin and I were still together, and I thought I had my life all mapped out, did I laugh like that? Was I happy? Or was it all just an illusion I was building? A desperate attempt to make sure my life didn't end up like my childhood, filled with a quiet desperation just to be seen and bone-chilling sadness that never seemed to let up. I hate to admit it, but it might have been an elaborate illusion. But was it always that way?

I had butterflies in the beginning. I remember them. And he was funny, always with a sarcastic quip. We had a similar sarcastic style back then. We would play off of each other for hours; I remember that feeling of happiness. When did it all change? Was it all just Collin? Or was some of it me?

"Earth to Kenzie," Clara says while waving her drink in front of me, "You okay?"

I sit up straighter in my chair. "Yeah, of course, just thinkin', no bigs," I tell her.

"You sure? You looked about a million miles away," she says.

"Totally. I promise. Besides, tonight is all about you and celebrating," I tell her, trying to change the subject.

"You know, just because we are having a fancy dinner because of me, doesn't mean we can't still talk about you."

"Yeah, I know, but your thing is way more exciting than mine."

"You thinking about Collin?"

"You know, I hate that you can do that," I tell her, already gearing up to be frustrated.

"Read your mind?" she asks with a smile.

"Yes," I say right back.

"I'm your best friend. We are basically sisters. Of course I can read your mind."

I just stare back at her.

"It's not that hard, Kenz. It's not like things have been easy the last couple of months. Everything with Collin is a shit show, and not just because of him. Besides, it seems like Chanel's mission in life is to torment you."

"It's not that," I try to explain when she looks like she is going to challenge me. "No really. It's not so fresh anymore and I can't help but wonder if I was actually happy with Collin."

"You were. For a while." She pauses. "But if I am going to be honest, even before everything blew up, something changed. I know I keep saying that you used to smile before, and it's true you did... but it was more than that."

"I used to laugh."

"More than that, too. You were excited about the future. You used to talk about graduating and the life that you were going to build with Collin. Constantly talking about how much you loved his family, and holidays, and tons of other stuff. And then you didn't anymore. You talked about what you were doing next week, and what Collin said, or what Collin wanted to do. You let all the *future* stuff go."

Sitting back in the bench seat, I really think about what Clara is saying. I can't find any fault with it. I did used to be excited for the future. The family I was so excited to become a part of and build with Collin. Everything kind of changed last summer, when Collin started spending a lot more time with his grandfather at his law firm. It was all image, what other people thought of us, and being the most important person in the room. I hated it. What's wrong with wearing sweats or leggings to class? Never in my life have I worn more than a few swipes of makeup unless it was some kind of formal event, and suddenly Collin was using words like *homely*.

"You know, if I am being honest, I think things with Collin were ending, even without Chanel. It's like he turned into this person I don't really know anymore. The future I thought we were building was suddenly looking a lot different, and it wasn't really one I was sure I wanted to be a part of."

"You know that's okay, right?" she asks.

I shrug my shoulders.

"No, Kenz, I'm serious. It's okay for you to change directions. To not settle for someone who won't make your dreams come true. You deserve happy. Real happy. Not someone else's version of what happy looks like. I'm not saying it's going to be easy, or that you won't have to work for it; but I am saying you don't have to stick with something that isn't giving you what you want."

She's right. I know she is.

"I think I would do so much better with everything if they weren't just hanging around everywhere I go. I want to just move forward. Sometimes it's really hard figuring out what comes next when my past just keeps popping up just to knock me down when I'm not looking."

"Yeah, well, Chanel's a bitch. She's one of those women who get the entirety of their self-worth from making other people feel bad about themselves and whose arm they are hanging off of." She downs a big gulp of her pink drink. "It's sad when you think about it."

"It would be more sad if she wasn't directing all her nonsense toward me," I retort.

"Word."

"Oh my god, Clara, you have to be the last person on earth who is still saying that." I laugh.

"Just be glad I didn't say word to your mother." She says it so matter-of-factly before she burst into laughter. Of course, I follow right behind her.

Just then, I hear John Mayer coming out of her purse.

"Is that 'Gravity?'" I ask as she digs around in her bag for her phone.

"Yep! You said you wanted different ringtones," she explains.

"Yeah, but John Mayer?"

Clara stops digging and stares right at me as "Gravity" keeps coming from her bag. "Do. Not. Dis. John. Mayer."

"Okay, okay, I'm sorry, John Mayer's great." Clara side-eyes me. "I'm serious. 'Slow Dancing in a Burning Room' is a musical masterpiece."

Clara narrows her eyes some more. "You're poking fun, aren't you?"

"Just a tad," I say as I pinch my fingers close together as she finally pulls the phone out of her bag and silences it. "You could have answered it, you know," I tell her.

"I know, but tonight is all about us." She smiles. "Well, us and cheese," she says as she picks up another piece of bread and dives in.

CHAPTER FOUR

"I TRY" BY MACY GRAY

I really love my major, I swear I do, but lately, not so much. It's weird that I feel that way now, when the countdown to completion is almost up. I don't know, maybe it's because I saved the classes I was least excited about for this last semester and now I am stuck reading and writing about literature I just don't like. I never realized how much longer the research takes and how long it takes to read something when you legitimately don't like the subject.

And I can feel myself slowing down with every passing minute as I work through other people's academic articles trying to find the right quotes to put into my paper. No, it's worse than that. I can feel my head fall down toward my chest before jerking upright because this shit is literally putting me to sleep. Note to self, next time I can't sleep, do this.

"Yes!" Clara declares. We're both in the living room working on school crap, but she looks all kinds of relaxed spread out on the couch with her laptop in her lap, propped up by a million pillows, while I am sitting in one of the smaller corner desks we have in the room. I swivel in my chair to get a full on look at her.

"Progress?" I ask.

"Yep." She smiles at me while removing her headphones. "That error message I have been getting for days finally stopped popping up. I thought I would never program my way out of that mess, but I finally did."

"That's because you're a genius," I tell her with a laugh.

She giggles and throws a pillow, which misses by a mile.

"Seriously though, with any luck, the rest of the project will proceed at pace and I won't have any major issues. I'm still on my schedule—"

"Self-imposed schedule," I interrupt.

"Fine, yes, self-imposed schedule. I was really getting worried that I was going to get stuck at the beginning and have to change all my plans."

"But you didn't," I remind her when she sounds annoyed.

"Yep, so right. So I think what needs to happen now is that we should take a break. Because while I am super excited and feel like I just won a million bucks, you look like you're going to pass out on top of your laptop. Well, that or take a baseball bat to it."

"Am I that obvious?" I ask.

"I told you not to take all those classes in one semester. You spread it out, one crap class per semester and then it hurts less." She tells me so matter-of-factly.

"See, I figured it was more like do it all at once and it will be over faster." I hang my head. "I was wrong. Clearly. I feel like I am pulling my own teeth out while listening to polka music on repeat."

"Wow, now that's a visual." Clara laughs at me. "Come on, let's take a break. We can head over to grab some coffee, and maybe this time it will actually stay in the cup."

She actually has the audacity to wink at me. Of course, I have no other choice but to reach over and grab the pillow she threw at me earlier and send it hurling back toward her.

"HEY!" She laughs. "If you can't laugh at yourself, you're never going to make it in this world," she tells me.

I stand up from my chair and stretch out, feeling the burn in my muscles loosen and elongate after being stuck in that chair for the past three and a half hours.

"Fine, but I'm not ordering coffee," I tell her with a hard look.

"You have never ordered coffee. In fact, I'm not even sure you have ever even tried it before."

"It smells. I don't eat or drink shit that smells bad."

"Coffee does not smell bad!" The offended tone completely takes over. "Coffee is the nectar of the gods, it smells like heaven and productivity."

"Trust me, you don't even want me to tell you what I think it smells like." I grab my car keys and head to the door. "Coming?"

"I really want to say something snarky about not wanting to hang out with a coffee heretic, but I really want some coffee, so yes, I'm coming. But hold on, I need to save all of this stuff to my cloud."

"Seriously? I'm sure you already saved it on your computer, and we are only going to be gone for like a half hour," I tell her. She really is obsessive about this stuff.

"Yes, I have to. Literally anything could happen while we're gone."

"What? You think crazy Mr. Peterson is going to come steal your laptop?" I look at her like she's nuts.

"You never know! Besides, you've been working on that paper for hours, what if you tripped and fell and broke your laptop? Which is not out of the range of possibility since you trip and fall over nothing all the time. You're gonna wish you had a supercool cloud backup so you don't have to end up rewriting your paper from hell," she lectures.

"Yeah, okay, come on, let's go."

She closes her laptop and starts toward me. "One day you are going to wish you were as cool as me with my cloud."

"I'm sure I will."

I'M ALREADY SITTING in one of the corner booths with my hot chocolate in hand, while Clara is standing at one of those stands making her coffee perfect with all the little add-ins they have. I swear, the best part of a hot chocolate is you don't need to add anything to it to make it great. It's already perfect and ready to go as soon as it hits your hands. Plus, it's not a half bad hand warmer.

Clara finally finished and plops down across from me in the booth.

"So nice to be out of the house," she tells me.

"You get out of the house every single day, Clara. It's not like you're being held hostage in there." I laugh.

"Yeah, I know, I just like a change of scenery. Well, that and a fantastic cup of coffee." She smiles as she takes a sip. "Yep, it's perfect, totally worth the trip out."

"You're such a dork. But you're right, it was definitely time for a break. I was going a little crazy in there."

"I could tell. So tomorrow is Monday, anything we need to figure out for next week, any big plans or anything?" Clara asks while playing with her stir stick.

"I don't think there is anything that needs to be figured out. Did you see that notice about the complex coming to check on everyone's heaters and swap out filters and stuff?" I ask.

"Yep, I don't have class during our scheduled time on Thursday, so I figure I will just hang out at home that afternoon. That way, we don't have some stranger in our place by themselves."

"Perfect. I'll try to be there too, but my last class ends like right as our window starts, so I might be a little late."

Clara shrugs. "It's cool. I'll be there either way. It probably really only needs to be one of us. So nothing else?"

"I've got the career counselor tomorrow." I fiddle with the lid of my hot chocolate. "To be honest, I'm actually kind of nervous."

"You made the appointment? That's so great. I'm telling you, this is just what you need. For the last three-plus years, you've had an idea what the future looks like and a plan to go along with it. This is the perfect first step to making your new plan. The *YOU* plan."

"I'm sure you're probably right, but why am I so nervous about it? Like seriously, every time I think about it, I feel like I am going to break into a cold sweat."

"Hmm, I gotta think about that," she says as she stares into her coffee like it's going to give her all the answers. About a minute passes before she jerks up and exclaims, "I got it!"

I can't help but smile. She really is one part crazy, two parts genius.

"Alright, let's hear it."

"You're nervous because now you have to make a choice. And it's an all-you choice. Last time you had a plan, you made it with someone else, with Collin, and the two of you were planning out what the *two* of you wanted. Those choices didn't work out, so now you are starting over, and you don't want to make the wrong one," she explains.

"I really don't want to make the wrong choice. I don't want to be one of those people who hate their jobs for forty years and are miserable every step of the way." I sigh. "I've had enough miserable to last me a lifetime."

"Worst case, let's say you pick a job you hate, you can totally change careers, people do it all the time. There's a guy in one of my classes who is in his midforties, and he's great. One of the greatest in the program. And he's done nothing with computers for work. He has this really refreshing perspective and different way of thinking than everyone else in the class, and he seems so excited to be starting something new. So worse case, you regroup and pick something else."

"You make it sound so easy."

"I'm sure there are a lot of logistics to figure out, but you love making plans, all that color coding, and just think about the to-do lists." She wiggles her eyebrows at me like she was talking about a hot guy and not my obsession with organizing.

"Okay, you're right, that part doesn't suck. I just wish I picked a major that has a straightforward job trajectory. Think about it, you're going to graduate, and you already know all the tech firms here that are going to be trying to recruit you guys, and that's not even considering nationwide."

"True."

"I'm going to graduate and besides talking about going into teaching, there isn't really a set path forward. I think every adviser I've had has always talked about going into academics or how every company needs people with communication skills. Not exactly super helpful, you know?"

"I get that." She pauses. "I know you and Collin had talked about you teaching while he went through law school. Is that something you are still considering?"

Was I ever excited about teaching? The genuine answer is no. I have wanted that elusive family unit for so long that the job part was just one tiny part of making my dreams come true. Teaching was going to get us through Collin's time in law school, and then in a few years, we would talk about having kids. I get lost in that picture in my head about how I am going to be the best mom, how I'll go to all the parent-teacher meetings, drive them to all their soccer practices, always carrying a cooler of snacks in the back, how I will always listen to my kids when they tell me about their days, and help them build their science fair project. Basically, everything I missed out on.

I was so busy planning out how my kids would never go to bed hungry, or forgotten at school for hours, that I never really even considering if teaching was something I really wanted. And now, thinking about it, it doesn't really feel like me. Teaching the same novels year after year to a bunch of high school students that don't really want to read the books in the first place doesn't really feel like fun to me.

"No. I can't really see myself going into teaching," I finally answer her honestly.

"Well, see what the career counselor says tomorrow. This is literally her job. I'm sure she will have a lot of ideas for you to consider. Maybe she can even set you up with an internship somewhere so you can get a feel for something before you graduate."

"That's true. I never really thought about getting an internship." I already felt myself feeling less anxious about this whole thing.

"Plus, if you still don't know what you want after the meeting tomorrow, there is always grad school. And with your undergrad, you could go a ton of different directions with that. Buy yourself a little time before you enter the real world?"

"I have mixed feelings about staying in school. I love learning, always have. It's been my sanctuary since I was a kid, so obviously I'm not opposed. But I also don't want to keep going just to keep going, you know?"

"Totally. You want to have a goal."

"Exactly. You still planning on doing grad school part time?"

"Definitely. I'm about positive I'm going to get a job off of my internship. I don't think they have ever not offered to an intern before, and the company has a reputation for being very accommodating of continuing education, so yeah, definitely.

All the really cool classes don't even start until you get to grad school level."

"This is going to end up being another conversation about high-level math, isn't it?"

"Nah, not unless you want it to be, because if you want to talk about high-level math, I can certainly accommodate that desire."

"Nope, nope, totally good. But thanks for the offer." I smile at her with a small laugh. "What about you though, anything important going on this week?"

"I'm probably going to be at the university all day tomorrow. We have a guest speaker coming into my machine learning class and they said he normally sticks around all day to answer questions and look at people's projects and stuff. I'm going to soak that up, spend every second picking this guy's brain," she explains.

"You look like one of those fangirls talking about a boy band," I tell her. "Who is this guy?"

"He's one of the Google engineers working on AI. So basically, he's a subject matter expert with my dream job. Plus, if he could give me some feedback on my project, I'm sure it will be amazing. He has this reputation with the teacher as being really helpful to the students. Most of our guests that we get either don't know how to communicate with young people and their talks are more like corporate sales pitches, or we get people who are closer to our age bracket and revert to college students as soon as their talk is over."

"Makes sense. So basically the long and short of it is I am on my own for lunch and dinner tomorrow," I tell her.

"If you wanna grab lunch on campus, I can totally carve out some time for my bestie."

"I think I can manage that. We could go to the smoothie bar; that way you can get your peanut butter fix and grab like a flatbread or something."

"That works perfect. I'll meet you there after your appointment. What time do you think it will end?"

"She said in the email to expect to spend at least forty-five minutes in the office going over all the options, so let's say around one? Give me time to get over there from her office."

"Perfect." Something catches Clara's eye up toward the front of the store.

"What's up?" I ask her since I'm facing the back of the store.

"Don't look now, but evil nemesis just walked in."

"Great. I swear to God if I end up with a latte on my clothes again, she's going to end up with the plastic surgery she always dreamed of," I tell Clara.

Clara tries and fails at suppressing a snort.

"Don't draw attention!" I hiss at her as I sink down into the booth a little more.

"You aren't hiding from her, are you?" Clara whispers.

"NO! Of course not. I'm just not inviting trouble," I hiss back. "Well, that and I'm trying really hard not to go to jail."

Clara once again snorts, but at least this time she muffles it a bit.

"As soon as she gets to the counter, I say we make a run for it," Clara says. "After all, spending the afternoon bailing you out of jail doesn't seem like the best use of my time."

"Aw, you're so sweet." I roll my eyes. "I'm down with that plan. Let me know when she makes it to the counter. I'll just be here working on my invisibility spell."

"Oh my god, and you say I'm insane!" Clara whisper-yells at me.

I watch Clara's face as she tracks Chanel around the coffee shop. I haven't seen Chanel yet, but I definitely hear her. That high-pitched laughing sound she makes that is sure to upset every dog in a five-mile radius. She can't really think that it's cute, right? She can't be that delusional, can she?

"Alright, I think we are good, just don't make any sudden movements," Clara whispers.

"Why? Is she like a T. rex and can only track us with movement?" I joke.

"Don't make me laugh! I can't sneak out of here if I'm on the floor," Clara hisses at me.

We both slowly start grabbing our bags and sliding out of the booth. It's not until we are both standing up next to the booth that our eyes catch and we can't help but burst out laughing. This is ridiculous. We are seriously hiding from this bimbo like little middle school kids and not like the adult women we are.

Clara grabs my hand and starts pulling me to the entrance while still laughing her ass off. Just as we are crossing the threshold, I hear Chanel once more.

"It's her! It's her! Look, I told you, guys, she stalks me everywhere I go!" Man, the pitch on her makes my eardrums feel like they're going to explode.

Clara looks out at me once we are outside. "Does she really believe her own shit? How does someone stalk someone else by already being somewhere for a half hour and then leaving when you arrive? Isn't that more like avoiding stalking?"

"Ah, but you, my friend, are using logic, and I don't think God was dealing out a lot of logic skills when he was making Chanel," I tell her.

"True, he really broke the mold when he was making her, huh?"

"You said it, not me."

CHAPTER FIVE

"WHERE IS MY MIND?" BY PIXIES

I've always hated when people bounce their leg up and down while sitting near me. It's distracting and honestly sometimes it makes me kind of dizzy. It's like nails on a chalkboard for me. Yet, here I am sitting in an uncomfortable chair made of easily cleaned fake leather, bouncing my leg up and down, waiting for the career counselor to call me back.

I know I shouldn't be this nervous. Yesterday's conversation with Clara really made me feel so much better about the situation. But now it's a day later, and I can't help but have all those feelings of anxiety rush back. I guess the long and short of it all is that I feel rudderless. My whole life, I have always had a direction to go in. When I was little and life was still on the more normal side of things, it was all about getting validation and attention. I wanted to be the perfect little girl that my mom could brag about to the other moms. I craved the phone calls from my dad while he was on deployment where I could tell him about my solo at the dance recital or how I got an A in math, just so I could hear him tell me he was proud of me. Even after everything changed, I kept all those goals. After my brother died, no one really cared what I did or how great I was. There was no more "Way to go, Kenzie," or "I'm so proud of you," followed by my dad's signature hair ruffle. In the end, my goals changed to getting away from the train wreck that became my family.

I worked my butt off to get into a good college, and when Duke gave me a scholarship, I couldn't have said yes faster. This was the plan: leave my dumpster fire of a family behind and carve out a new life for myself with the family I made on my own. I really thought I had it all figured out, like everything just started falling into place once I got to Durham. At first, I couldn't trust it, but then I thought I deserved this. After everything, I deserved things just working out for me.

And now here I am waiting for some lady to call me back into what is sure to be a cramped office with stale air, so we can discuss my life plans. Because right now, I have no life plans.

"MacKenzie Sharp?" An older woman is standing in her doorway staring down at a file that probably boils the last four years down to one sheet of information.

"Yep, that's me," I say while I plaster on a fake smile and stand to follow her back into her office.

"Have a seat." She gestures to an equally uncomfortable-looking chair as the one I just vacated. "I see here you are an English major?"

I nod.

"Well, since you are here, I assume you aren't interested in going into teaching?"

"Uh, well, it was the original plan. But um, well..." I stumble around my words trying really hard not to just blurt out that the guy I was supposed to marry cheated on me and blew up all my plans and now I don't know what I want to do with my life.

"That's okay, plans change. It's what college is all about. Finding your path." She smiles at me kindly. "So why don't you tell me of any ideas you have or maybe what made you pick this major and we can go from there," she says encouragingly.

"Okay. I can do that. Truthfully, I just liked my English classes best. When I was taking my core classes, the English ones were the ones I looked forward to," I tell her.

"What about the classes stood out to you?"

Shrugging, I'm not entirely sure I have an answer for her. I just liked them. I love reading, I always have. It's always been my escape from the shit show that was my world.

"I guess it's because I really enjoy reading..."

"Okay, that makes sense. Have you thought about perhaps doing something with reading or with books?"

I just kind of sit there and stare right at her. She puts down her paperwork, takes off her glasses, folds her hands together and looks right at me. I feel like I'm in the principal's office.

"Look, MacKenzie, there are a lot of options out there, but I need some kind of direction. A lot of English majors go into communications. You learned a lot about how to communicate in writing, you can handle research and constructive criticism, these are all valuable skills at companies. But if you aren't looking for a communications-type job, then none of that matters. If you want to look at something having to do with reading or writing, we could look into the publishing side of things, like editing at a publishing house or maybe being a technical writer. Then, of course, there are the options that require more schooling, like perhaps trying your hand at law school or even a degree in the library sciences. You probably have a lot of skills that would serve you well in both those careers."

The silence that comes after is deafening. Do any of these ideas just jump out and grab me? No. Not even a little. Although the idea of hanging out in a library all day and getting paid for it seems like something I could easily get behind. I wonder how much longer I would have to go to school to be a librarian.

"The librarian thing doesn't seem horrible... how would I go about that path?"

"Well, not horrible is not exactly what I would call a ringing endorsement. But it would be another two years of study for a master's degree. So you would need to get in all of your applications pretty soon, and you also need to consider that we don't offer that degree at this university, so you would need to find a different university to attend for that degree plan."

"Oh."

"Don't worry, you still have weeks before applications are going to be due, but you will want to get started now, depending on the requirements that the school has." She swivels in her chair and starts pulling out all these pamphlets from behind her and stacking them on her desk. "And if you decide you don't want to continue on with your education, you just let me know and we can take a hard look at something in publishing, I'm sure we could find you an internship or some-thing to get you some experience before we send you out into the workforce." She says it like a joke. She stands up and gathers all the paperwork before reaching out to hand it to me.

"That's it?" I ask, honestly kind of surprised. It's been like maybe twenty minutes since she called me in here and I don't feel any less lost than I did when I walked in. I feel more over-whelmed.

"Well, I think you have a lot of thinking to do, young lady." I hate that. "Plus, you are going to want some time to go over all the information I have for you here," she says while moving the papers closer to me, almost forcing them into my arms. I have no choice but to take them. "Now if you have any more ques-tions, don't you hesitate to call my office and make another appointment," she says as she is already opening the door, showing that it's time for me to go.

"Um, okay? I guess thanks." I stand up and walk past her, wondering how this was in any way helpful.

I TOLD Clara I would call her when I got out of what turned out to be a nightmare appointment. Then again, I also told her it was going to take like an hour. That's what the confirmation email said. I look down at my phone and see it has been exactly twenty-two minutes. There is no way Clara is going to be expecting me to be done this soon.

"Fuck it," I whisper to myself. I'll just call her, give her a heads-up I am early and start heading over to the smoothie place.

I open up my favorites on my phone and click on Clare Bear. A picture of her in pajamas with a funny party hat laughing pops on the screen while the phone rings. And rings. And rings. Nothing. She was super stoked about that dude from Google coming to talk, so maybe she's just distracted.

I've got plenty of time to kill, so I decide to just walk over to the smoothie place to get some exercise and consider everything I heard in the last hour. It's lunchtime, so people are out and moving in droves. I stick to the right side of the sidewalk and cross my fingers that I don't run into anyone I know on the way.

That meeting was a total joke. But it gave me a lot to think about. I don't know if I really want to keep going to school for another two years. I definitely don't want to go to law school. That was always Collin's thing, never mine.

The idea of spending my days inside a library actually sounds kind of nice. I love libraries, and research, and the smell of old books. But I'm sure librarians don't spend a lot of time reading books while they are on the clock. Plus, I'm having flashbacks to middle school and having to learn the Dewey decimal system. Do they still use that? It gave me nightmares back then. What can I say? I have always hated numbers, any kinds of numbers, so not my thing.

I guess she was right though; I have to choose between getting some kind of job in an office where I sit there and do communications. My new nightmare is that it's some sort of euphemism for social media manager. To this day, I have never figured out how to use Twitter. I've never even downloaded Snapchat or WhatsApp let alone do I know how to use them. Are they even the "cool" apps? I don't know.

Shouldn't this be easier? Shouldn't I know what I want to do now? I guess the idea of working in a publishing house sounds like a fun idea. Or maybe an agent's office. Reading manuscripts, helping get new authors published. I wonder if the money is any good? I'd probably have to leave North Carolina. Leaving the state isn't something I'm sure I'm ready for.

It's comfortable in North Carolina. Clara is planning on sticking around here and we have already talked so much about staying in our roommate situation. Yeah, I definitely don't want to move.

I get jostled off the sidewalk by a group of jocks who are throwing a ball around while walking.

"Watch it," I say with my resting bitch face in full effect.

They look mildly chagrined as they continue by me. Maybe I should put my phone in my bag. I didn't pay for the insurance on this sucker, so if it breaks, I'm fucked. I slip the phone into one of the side pockets of my messenger bag before continuing on.

I can see the sign for the smoothie place off in the distance. Do I want to be a business owner? How hard can it be to open up a franchise? No. That sounds horrible. And like it probably includes a lot of numbers. Also, I know nothing about business. Moving on.

I could write? Journalism seems like it would be super hard

to get my foot in the door, but the research aspect seems like it could be fun. I love digging into a good story and looking up more information. I think I might need a journalism degree for that.

Thankfully, it doesn't look like too many people decided on smoothies for lunch today; it is winter and smoothies are more of a morning thing around here. After I order my tropical smoothie, with a hint of chocolate, of course, I head over to the tables to check the time. It's a lot closer to when I told Clara my meeting would be over, so I give her another ring and let her know I'm already here.

When I finally dig out my phone from my bag, I see a missed call from Clara. Great, those morons who think playing catch on a public sidewalk made me miss her call. She left a voice mail.

"That's weird," I mutter to myself. No one ever leaves voice mails anymore, and certainly not Clara. She knows I never listen to them. Maybe things are going great with the Google guy and she wants to stick around instead of meeting for lunch.

I push the button to listen to the message and put the phone up to my ear.

At first, I hear nothing. I slide my finger over the volume button and turn it all the way up. That's when I realize I can hear Clara breathing. It's a butt dial. Of course it's a butt dial. I'm just about to pull the phone away from my ear when I hear her voice.

"Hey, MacKenzie. I know we're supposed to meet for lunch but, um, some stuff came up and I just..." She trails off. Something about her voice sounds wrong, like she's crying but trying to hide it. "I'm really sorry about missing lunch. You know how much I hate canceling plans... Look, um, there's something really important I need to talk to you about tonight. I should have talked to you about it earlier. I just, things have been really crazy for you and I didn't want to pile on. Anyway, it's important, so tonight, okay? Love you."

There is this extended pause in the recording, like she didn't hang up right away. In fact, it's just dead air for like twenty seconds before she hangs up the phone.

At first, I don't know what to make of it. So I call her back.

No answer.

I call again.

Straight to voice mail.

I can feel my heart rate speed up in my chest. She never turns off her phone. Not after her mom died, she had turned her phone off that night and missed the last call her mom ever made to her before she died. She even leaves it on when she gets on airplanes, just in case, she always says.

I try one more time. Straight to voice mail.

I grab all my stuff but leave my smoothie behind. As soon as I exit the shop, I think about where I am going. Should I head to the apartment? Or maybe I should go over to where Clara's classes are. She sent me her schedule at the beginning of the semester so I would know where to find her in case of an emergency. If I walk over to where her classes are, I get farther away from my car, but if I go to my car, I'm going to have to fight traffic if I decide to check out the classrooms.

I don't know why, but I have this feeling in my gut that I should go home. It was too quiet on the recording. Last night, she had talked about being in the lab all day. There is no way it would be that quiet if that's where she was.

I start power walking back to my car and start praying that nothing is actually wrong and I'm just being paranoid.

~

I'M sure I broke more than a couple of laws getting from campus to the apartment complex, but my brain is not firing on all cylinders right now. The bad feeling that has been in my gut for the last twenty minutes only seems to grow. I keep trying to tell myself that I'm being ridiculous. Nothing is wrong. She didn't even say anything was wrong in the voice mail, just that she wanted to talk about something and that she was going to miss lunch.

I'm blowing this completely out of proportion.

As soon as I park, I swing my door closed with a slam that, under ordinary circumstances, would have made me cringe. I'm pounding my way up the stairs so quickly that Mr. Peterson doesn't even have time to get out into the hallway before I'm already passing him to get to my door.

"Not today," I mutter as I pass him.

I struggle a little at first to get my key in the lock. My panic is making things difficult. It's not until I slide my key into the dead bolt that a sense of dread really takes over. It's not locked. I left super early this morning to spend some time in the library. Clara left after me. She for sure would have locked the dead bolt.

I take a deep breath, feeling the air inflate my lungs almost to where it gets uncomfortable. I can do this.

Nothing.

Everything looks the same.

It's quiet in the apartment. I can tell just from stepping through the door no one is home. I peer through the kitchen. Everything looks fine. I move toward my left to check out the living room. Looks exactly the same as when I left this morning.

No, wait.

Clara's obsessive pillow pile she uses on the couch, gone. I look over at the desk she uses on the left side of the room. There isn't anything there. Nothing at all. Clara leaves her stuff all over the place all the time, and she's never been accused of having a clean desk; probably not once in her entire life.

But this desk, it's not just clean. It's empty. I don't know how I know, but I do.

Clara's not here.

And that feeling in my stomach, the one that feels like someone has punched me in the stomach, is telling me she might never be here again. God, I hope I'm wrong.

CHAPTER SIX

"FOREIGNER'S GOD" BY HOZIER

There's a third option no one ever talks about. When a person experiences an extreme event, especially an unexpected one, the influx of stress puts the body into the fight-or-flight response. A phrase basically anyone who is an adult would know, it's so drilled into you. But the third option is where I find myself.

Freeze.

It's a strange feeling. I know something terrible is going on, and I know in my head that I should be running around trying to solve this problem, but yet I don't. I stand here in this living room, just staring at the empty desk. I have probably looked at this desk a thousand times without even realizing it. But in this moment, it's all I can do. Stare.

The dark-brown stain on the wood. The stain in the right-hand corner where one of Clara's pens leaked onto the desk and we could never manage to get rid of the stain, no matter how many home remedies we tried. Even the absence of items is causing me to fixate. Where is the rock, paper, scissors, lizard, Spock coffee mug that I got her for Christmas last year that she keeps all her pens in? The purple notebook where she jots down every errant thought is gone.

And here I am, just stuck.

Staring.

There are no answers to be found in the quiet. The sounds from the heating seem to be lulling me into an even deeper trance.

I've heard your life flashes before your eyes when you are about to die, but right now I feel like I am rewatching a movie in reverse at high speed of every interaction Clara and I have ever had. The story of our friendship.

Until one memory hits home. We had just moved into the apartment after a year together in the dorms. It's late at night and we are both sipping on hot chocolate and sharing stories of our childhood. She's the first person I ever opened up to about what happened to destroy mine. I remember like it was yesterday breaking down and telling her about how my brother died, how my mom was running late and decided to pick me up first since I was younger and my brother was in high school and old enough to wait by himself. How he decided not to wait and got in the car with a friend for a ride home instead. I told her all about what the flashing blue and red lights looked like when we drove past the accident right in front of the school. That I remembered thinking how sad it was when I saw the paramedics loading a body into the ambulance with a sheet over it. And then, of course, the moment my mom found out it was my brother under that sheet. How life just changed in that one instant. I lost my brother, my best friend; but I also lost my mom. She never really came home after that afternoon. Sure, her body still lived in that house, but she was never the same, and neither was I.

It's the jolt I finally need to come out of my frozen state.

I can't lose Clara.

I can't lose the one person who I consider family in this world.

Dropping everything onto the couch, I finally get my wits back and start to search through the apartment. It's the little things. Things no one would notice that I start to catalog in my brain.

The empty desk.

The missing pillows and folded lap blankets.

A couple of photos missing from the walls.

The shishi statues that used to be on the window frame.

As I walk toward the back of the apartment, I notice that the door to my room is closed, something I know I did not do, because I basically never close that door unless I am going to sleep. Clara's door, though, the one that is habitually closed unless she is in there, is wide open.

I take a deep breath, trying to steel myself for what I might find when I enter into this room.

Stepping into the room, I realize that I didn't really know what to expect, but it definitely wasn't this. There is nothing to write home about.

All the furniture is still there. It looks like one of those apartments you would go and look at that comes furnished, no personality and no bedding. It's the lack of bedding that springs me into action. With every drawer that I open to find it empty, I can feel my hope that this is just a misunderstanding dying in my chest. By the time I get to the closet, I can tell I have been holding my breath for too long. It's empty too.

I'm ashamed to admit I don't really know where to go from here. My first instinct is to ask Clara what she thinks we should do next. Doesn't really work in this situation.

Being in this room is somehow suffocating, even though it is the emptiest room in the apartment. I quickly move back toward the living room, making a dive for my phone, which has wedged itself between two couch cushions.

I click on Clara's name again and pray for a ringing.

My prayers are unanswered. Straight to voice mail.

A million thoughts run through my head. Do I call the police? What would I say? Maybe I should retrace her steps this morning. Or maybe I can find a number for one of the people in her class and see if she was there this morning. Was I the last person who saw her?

There's no way she could have just left because of me, right? It's not like we had issues, or that she was planning on moving out and just neglected to tell me, right? She literally just told me yesterday that she would be at the apartment on Thursday for when the maintenance guy comes to do a check on the heater. Clara's also the first one to call me on my shit. The first one to tell me when I am being irrational or silly, or on rare occasions that I've been mean or rude. She wouldn't just leave. At least not without telling me.

Besides, this isn't just leaving or not coming home one night from a frat party, this is a straight up pack everything I own and find a new place to live kind of thing. Doesn't seem right to me. Nothing about this seems right to me.

Since I can't figure out what my next step should be, I decide the best option would be to think like Clara. If Clara came home one day and I wasn't there, I basically moved out in the span of just a few short hours, and my phone was going straight to voice mail. What would she do?

Clara has always been the logical one of the two of us.

First things first, Find My Friends. We linked our iPhones through the app, I should be able to find her last location on the map. I pull up the app and wait for the spinning circle to show me where she was last located.

It's from this morning, in the apartment. It's almost two o'clock now, so the last time she registered on the app was almost six hours ago. A lot can happen in six hours.

"What's next," I mutter. "Come on, Clara, tell me what to do."

I glance over at her desk, still wishing I would see her sitting there working on yet another mathematical application.

I still maintain Clara would never just up and leave, certainly not without telling me first.

"A note." She had to have left a note, right? That's the only thing that makes any sense. I run as fast as I can into the galley kitchen to where we have a message board on the wall where we leave notes for each other.

Rapidly I check to see if there is anything new. Sadly, the only thing I see on there from Clara is a note where she wrote the lyrics to "Be Optimistic" from Shirley Temple. She used to sing it to me whenever I was down in the dumps, and after one particularly bad encounter with Chanel, she left the lyrics up on the board to cheer me up.

I reach up to take it off the board, but I can't bring myself to touch it. No, it stays where it is.

Defeated, I move back to the couch and look down at my phone. Maybe another listen to the voice mail wouldn't hurt, maybe I'll hear something I missed when I wasn't surrounded by the noise of a food place.

As I run through the voice mail for a second listen, it's not the words I am listening to. It's the space in between. The long pauses she left along the way. It's quiet wherever she is. I don't hear any voices in the background, no ambient music piping through the speakers of a coffee shop. Just quiet. I can hear her breathing, it's a little bit labored, but it sounds like she has been crying, so it makes sense that her breathing pattern would be a little bit heightened.

It's not until the end of the voice mail that I notice something. She didn't hang up the phone call until long after she finished speaking, and I almost started to reply to the message before I heard something quiet in the background, it sounded like a voice.

A man's voice maybe. I don't know, it's too far away to tell.

I replay the whole message again from the beginning, hoping I get something more on this third pass-through.

Definitely a man, one word. I think he says, "done." But that's it, that's all I hear. He's so far away from the mic on the phone that I can't even make out anything special about the voice, like if it is one that I would recognize.

She wasn't alone. That's something, at least. Not that I know who she was with. Honestly, the only guys she really ever talked to were the guys in her classes, they sometimes had study groups, but she never really socialized with them outside of that context.

Either way, I think my best move from here is a mass text, anyone who knows Clara whose phone number I have in my phone I am going to send a message to.

"Has anyone seen Clara? She was supposed to meet me for lunch and didn't show up, and now I can't seem to find her. She's never late to anything, as you guys all know, so I just wanted to see if anyone has seen her just to make sure nothing happened. Let me know ASAP. Thanks xx, Kenz," I whisper the words as my fingers fly across the keyboard, typing in my desperate attempt to find answers without sounding like a lunatic.

It takes a few minutes but the answers start to come in. All variations on the same theme.

No Clara.

HOURS HAVE PASSED by and while I have spent more time on my phone than I have in the last week, I am still no closer to figuring out what is going on. I'm beginning to think I am out of options when it comes to sitting at home and figuring this out from my couch.

Pretending that Clara actually decided to up and move out of the apartment without telling me, I think about all the steps that she would have had to take in order to move into a new place. She would obviously need a different place to go to but seeing as how she is super introverted, there is no way she is moving in with someone who wasn't on the group text where everyone already agreed that they haven't seen her. So she would have had to get her own place, she certainly could afford it, but she would still have to fill out an application and the landlord here would probably know, right?

Finally, a place to start.

Throwing my phone in my pocket and grabbing my messenger bag, I rush toward the door, only locking the bottom lock. When I find Clara, she can yell at me about the dead bolt, until then, I'm in a hurry.

Mr. Peterson is already standing in the hallway, leaning up against the wall with his arms crossed over his chest. I have no idea how he always manages to know when someone is leaving their apartment but he always manages to be out in the hall.

I decide to ignore him and keep moving forward with my mission to get to the landlord as quickly as possible before they close for the day at four thirty.

"What, no snarky remark today?" Mr. Peterson sneers.

Fed up with the way this day is turning out, I can't help but stop and take out my frustration on the creep from across the hall.

"I don't have time for your shit today. You know what? I never have time for your shit. No one does. No one wants to deal with you, we just have no other choice," I yell at him. "Oh, and just so we are perfectly clear no one here buys into your bumbling old man act, we all know it's just an excuse to be able to touch us without getting into trouble. We are *all* sick and fucking tired of this bullshit."

"Is that right?" he responds. "And what exactly do you think you can do about it?" he taunts.

I start to open my mouth to argue with him when it hits me. He is *always* out in the hall whenever anyone is in the hall. Coming or going. Never fails.

Time to tone it down.

"Look, I'm sorry, I'm just having a really shitty day. I apologize," I say, trying my very best to look contrite.

"Uh-huh." Clearly, he isn't buying it.

"Have you seen my roommate?" I ask. "You've seen her before, tall, skinny, long brown hair, wears glasses?"

"The nerdy Mexican," he says, his eyes almost daring me to get angry.

I clear my throat and clench my hands into fists, trying my hardest not to react.

"Uh, yeah, sure, that's her. Have you seen her today?"

"Not since this morning, she was in a big rush, already out and down the hall when I made it out to check on all the commotion."

"The commotion?" I ask, so hopeful that he might actually know something.

"Yeah, girl was dropping crap all over the place. And muttering to herself. You know you got to be careful about doing that kind of thing in public, people will start to think you are crazy carrying on like that." He starts to ramble.

So basically nothing. Well, maybe not nothing, I'm the klutzy one. It makes sense for someone to notice that I was dropping things all over the hallway, I do it all the time, it's why I carry a messenger bag, before I was dropping my purse all the time. Not Clara though, I've seen her carry like fifteen small items at once and never drop a single one.

I file the information away for later.

"Thanks," I say begrudgingly as I start to head down the stairs.

By the time I make it over to the leasing office, the guy is already locking up the door, but thankfully he is willing to stop long enough to talk for a few seconds.

"What can I help you with?" he asks.

"Hey, Mark. I was just wondering if you had talked to Clara earlier today." I ask, trying to look calm.

"Hmmm, Clara, not today. I did talk to her on Saturday though, she confirmed that maintenance was going to be by on Thursday for your heating check. Is that time still going to work out for you guys?" he asks.

"Yeah, yeah, of course, works great." I pause. "So no Clara then?"

"Nope, not today."

"Does anyone else work in the office during the day?" I ask.

"That talks to residents? Nope, just me, short staffed, you know how it is," he explains. "Why do I get the feeling this isn't about maintenance?"

"It's not, I just, she's just gone radio silent and I'm just checking everywhere I can think of to see if anyone has talked to her since this morning."

"Ohhhh, I'm sure everything is fine, she probably just lost track of time at the lab, wouldn't be the first time, you know?"

"Yeah, hopefully, that's my next stop."

"Well, good luck," he says as he starts to head toward the parking lot.

"Thanks," I call out as I start moving toward my own car. Only one more option. School.

IT'S ALWAYS amusing to me that the labs are always bustling the later it gets in the day. Clara always jokes about how she goes first thing in the morning because everyone is still asleep and she has the whole place all to herself. At least this way I was able to ask basically everyone she has classes with if she was there today. Hell, I even managed to talk to the Google guy, who is still sticking around going over projects with students. He hadn't seen Clara either but told me he heard a lot of really good things and was looking forward to checking on her project later in the semester.

I can't believe she missed the Google guy. She was so stoked about him. I even asked a couple of the guys if she had asked them to take notes for her. The one time she had the flu and missed class, she called like four people to take notes so she would have backups of her backups so she didn't miss anything. Nothing though. No one had heard from her at all.

In any other situation, I would really believe that something happened to her, like she fell and had an accident or something. She does love running on the trails around campus. But they are well traveled and even if she fell and got hurt, it doesn't explain how basically every trace of her disappeared out of the apartment. That's the part that has left me a seed of doubt in my mind.

In the end, the only choice is to stop by the campus police office and see what they think. I'm pretty sure the answer to that question is they think I'm crazy.

"She's only been gone a few hours."

"People miss class all the time."

"Roommates don't always work out, we hear nightmare stories about roommates all the time."

And last, and my personal favorite. "We'll ask around and let you know." He actually said that as he was trying to usher me out of the office before he even managed to write down my phone number. Could it have been any more clear he wasn't going to take me seriously? Still, I wrote down my phone number and made sure to place it in his hand before I left to head back home.

The feeling of defeat washes over me as I walk back into the apartment. I must have looked rough because even Mr. Peterson turned and walked back inside his apartment when I was walking down the hall.

One thing is for sure, I certainly can't sit in my living room where every memory I have of Clara and I together is sitting on the surface of my mind. So I go for the only option left. My room.

Normally I love my room. I'm obsessive almost to the point of anal at keeping everything in its place. The soft twinkle lights on the ceiling and photo collage on my wall by my bed always makes me smile. My room has a strictly happy rule, only things that bring me joy (very Marie Kondo I know).

But there is no joy in this room right now. Sitting on my bed, I feel my body finally start to fold in on itself. The events of the day finally take their due. I can feel my eyes starting to well up with tears. I know I can't cry, though. I know if I start, I won't stop.

So instead, I wipe the one tear that made an escape off my cheek and look up at my nightstand.

That's when I notice something off. The lid to my jewelry box isn't closed, it's off center a little bit. My immediate reaction is just to readjust it closed, but something in me makes me lift the lid off the box.

It's the second time in one day that my world stopped turning.

Clara's locket is lying on top.

CHAPTER SEVEN

"ONE STEP CLOSER" BY LINKIN PARK

I t's funny how in life one thing can both make your entire world stop and in the next moment make everything start moving again. I had both those moments when I saw Clara's locket lying in my jewelry box. I don't want to believe what I am seeing with my own eyes. I can think of almost no situation where Clara would take that locket off. Two years ago we were worried she broke her foot on some ice and they wanted her to leave it with me while they took her for X-rays, she wouldn't. She would never take it off.

Her voice echoes through my head, "Trust, but verify."

I reach out to grab the locket out of the box, and I hesitate. I know I have to push through this feeling, but I don't want to. I want it to be yesterday. I want to talk about our plans for the week and hear Clara blather on about a new algorithm she is trying in her code. Anything but this.

The metal is cold in my hand, logically I know it must have been there for hours, but cool metal against my skin is a confirmation I never wanted.

I need a plan.

I've already been to the campus police, I should probably

wait until tomorrow to try and get more information. I know it hasn't been twenty-four hours yet, so I probably can't report her missing to Durham Police yet. I put the word out, everyone we know is aware they need to be on the lookout. Hell, I'm sure Mr. Peterson is even aware something is wrong.

Tomorrow is a new day, and I am going to find my answers, I don't care what it takes. Clara would never let me disappear without a trace, she would hunt me down to the ends of the earth. So why would I do anything less when it comes to her?

Tomorrow I'll go back to campus police. And if that doesn't work, Durham Police is next on my list. Technically I'm pretty sure she didn't disappear from campus so it should fall under them. Maybe I should go to them first. I can't help but find it unsettling that I'm not really sure what the steps should be in the event of an emergency.

After I put the locket carefully back into my jewelry box and replace the lid, I lie back on my bed, not even getting under the covers, to prepare for what is sure to be a night without any sleep.

BY THE TIME morning has come around, the weather has shifted. Normally I hate when it's gray outside and foggy, but today, it feels like a mirror of how I am doing. I think I was lucky enough to fall asleep a couple of times throughout the night. Not that it lasted for any kind of meaningful amount of time.

I call the campus police first thing and they actually let me make an appointment to come in and talk about Clara. So now the only thing left to do is pass the time between then and now. If you had asked me a few days ago what everyday life was like, I would have said something like, "nothing special." How wrong I would have been. It still hasn't been twenty-four hours and yet I know a piece of me is missing. Our lives together are far from "nothing special," we are family. The family we chose for ourselves after the world left us on our own. That kind of bond, there's nothing like it.

By the time I'm in my car headed to the police station, the butterflies in my stomach are overwhelming. And it's not the happy butterflies like when you are going on a first date, but rather the kind that are waiting for the other shoe to drop. I know I need help. I just have no idea if I am going to get it.

Standing in front of the station, I steel myself for whatever comes next. The sad thing is I actually take the time to remind myself to keep my emotions in check, because no one wants to be labeled a *hysterical woman*.

The morning dew is still on the handle of the door, so I take the time to wipe my hand on my jeans as I walk toward the front desk.

"Can I help you, hun?" The woman at the front desk looks like every stereotypical grandmother in a sitcom I have ever seen. She even kind of smells like cookies.

"Uh, yes, ma'am. I have an appointment at ten with Officer Kelly," I tell her.

A few typed words and an assurance that he'll be with me as soon as he can, and I'm back to waiting. They have those hard plastic obscenely orange chairs for you to wait in. Subtle it is not. Thankfully, the chair keeps you in such a state of uncomfortableness that my attention never wavers, so I see the officer start to walk toward me. I can't read him. He doesn't have a kind expression, but he's not hostile either. A practiced look of indifference.

"Miss Sharp?"

I nod.

"Follow me."

He leads me back into a bullpen of desks and cubicles,

before ultimately coming into a small meeting room and indicating for me to take a seat.

"So Miss Sharp, you're looking for your roommate," he says as a statement, not a question.

"Yes, I am."

"Have you tried reaching out to her, perhaps contacting some of her other friends or family?" he asks, poorly concealing a level of condescension that wasn't there a few moments ago.

"Of course, I talked to everyone we know, I even checked in with our neighbors and landlord. No one has seen or heard from her. I woke up yesterday morning and everything was fine and by the time I made it home in the afternoon, the apartment was cleared out of her stuff and she was just gone."

"Yes, I read that." He leans back into his chair and folds his hands up on top of his small beer belly. "Were you and Clara having any problems? Maybe fighting over a boy or maybe your personalities weren't meshing well as roommates? Happens all the time in college, you know," he says with a shrug.

"No. Nothing. There were no problems. Clara and I have been best friends for four years, we are family. And we certainly weren't fighting over a boy, neither of us are involved with anyone." I'm trying so hard not to get crazy irate. Seriously, this is his solution to why Clara went missing, we were fighting over a boy? How much more condescending can this guy get?

"Well, something must have happened for her to decide to move out."

Yep, turns out he could get more condescending.

"Look, officer, Clara is the most responsible person I have ever met in my life, and if you talk to anyone who knows her, they will say the same. Clara wouldn't move out without giving a thirty-day notice, and informing the landlord, and having a sit-down talk about it with me, complete with PowerPoint presentation about why she is moving out. There is no way she just randomly up and decided to pack up everything in the course of a few short hours without a peep to anyone." I can tell my voice is starting to get louder the longer this conversation goes on.

"Hey now, no need to get emotional," he says with an eyebrow raised. He even leans farther back into his chair, almost with an amused look on his face. How I managed not to say anything is beyond me. "I did make a couple of phone calls, and it seems like you didn't know your roommate as well as you thought you did, because it seems like up and leave is exactly what she did."

"What are you talking about? Did you talk to Clara? Is she okay?" I ask, with a tiny shred of hope in my heart. I can live with Clara leaving as long as she is okay.

"I didn't speak with Clara. But Clara did communicate with some people on campus and it seems as if she decided to leave the university."

"What are you talking about? She would never leave school, she loves her program, and she's even making plans for graduate school. There is absolutely no way," I declare.

"Well, I'm awfully sorry to tell you, Miss Sharp, but Clara emailed her adviser right around noon, thanking her for all her help and notifying her that she was planning on leaving the school. I went ahead and called the registrar's office, and they have on file her withdrawal forms, signed and everything. Her uncle went up there himself to drop them off in person. So maybe you didn't know your roommate as well as you think you did."

"Wait, what? Uncle? What uncle? Clara doesn't have an uncle," I say emphatically.

"Like I said, seems you didn't know your roommate all that well."

"Look, she might have been my roommate, but I have already told you she is my best friend. And I can tell you without a doubt, she does *not* have an uncle. Both her parents were only children, and both her parents have died. So if someone came to campus to withdraw her from school, then it definitely wasn't her *uncle*. Something I am sure you could verify super easily." I'm barely hanging on at this point, I want to crawl over this table and smack him in the face.

"Look, Miss Sharp, I don't know what to tell you. Your roommate clearly isn't interested in continuing her education, and she clearly didn't feel like telling you about her decision. Who knows, maybe she was embarrassed that she couldn't stick it out to finish. I see it every day. People just can't hack it here." He says like he is God's gift to humankind. I'm sure this asshole never finished college either, so why he is getting off on acting like Clara is just some girl who couldn't handle the academics is beyond me.

"Seeing as how Clara isn't here to defend herself, I'm only going to tell you once. I don't appreciate the way you are talking about her. If you actually took the time to ask questions about the person who is missing to people who knew her, you would know that she is doing incredibly well here. She's happy here. She just won one of the most prestigious internships offered in her department. She was more than just 'hacking' it. If you had done even the slightest amount of checking into Clara at all, you would find she has no living relatives. In fact, I'm listed as her emergency contact with both her doctor and with the school," I say with a huff.

"I don't know what to tell you, miss, but Clara has an uncle because he turned in her paperwork. There is no case. She is not missing. She left. I suggest you move on and look for a new roommate." He starts to stand like he's getting ready to leave.

"You have got to be kidding me. That's it? Case closed, she can't be missing. Guy says he is her uncle even though she doesn't have an uncle, and that's good enough for you? Kind of don't think Clara is the one who isn't *hacking* it, it's you. Because clearly you can't be bothered to do your job at all." I admit, at this point, I may have been shouting. Not quite yelling. But definitely what my dad used to refer to as "talking with purpose."

"Now you look here, missy, you don't get to come in here and start throwing around accusations—"

"Not really an accusation if it's true," I retort. "So just to be clear, you have no intention of looking for my missing friend. Right?"

"She's not missing," he snarls.

"So, not going to do your job, then?" I ask one last time.

"No, I'm not going to waste my time looking for someone who isn't missing, who isn't a student at this school anymore, just because her roommate is overly emotional and panics!"

"Fine, I'll do it my fucking self!" I yell at him. Yes, I yelled. I couldn't help it.

It's beyond clear that everyone in the station heard me scream at this guy, because they weren't exactly subtle with their stares. Some wore looks of shock, disbelief that I would have the audacity to yell at this guy. Some didn't look surprised. But the look that hit me the most was the sweet little old grandma receptionist.

She looks sad. She looks at me with pity in her eyes as I walk past her.

This won't be the last look of pity that I see.

FUMING WOULD BE AN UNDERSTATEMENT. I don't know why I was expecting anything other than this though. It's not like campus cops have a stellar reputation nationwide. And considering the crimes I have seen on the news that have actually been covered up to save face for the university, I shouldn't be surprised that they weren't going to investigate someone who is missing, especially when there isn't any actual evidence that the person in question is missing.

Maybe I was being naive, but I really thought I would get a lot further than I did. I can't help but hope that it is just this guy. That this guy is just a misogynistic jerk, the one bad apple in the bunch. The thought is actually kind of comforting.

Sitting in my car, I think about the experience I have had on this campus for the past four years. I think of the experience that Clara has had. Sure, we have had our share of boring teachers, or crappy graders. Every university is bound to have their own crowd of mean girls, but honestly here, it's not that bad (and I say that after being the target of Chanel for months). But at the end of the day, I love it here. I know Clara did too. The people here are great, and I can't believe that no one is going to help me find her. I have to believe that I just need to find the right people, and once I do, I can finally make some progress.

Driving home feels so surreal. The anger and rage that was flowing through my veins is slowly starting to dissipate with the reality that I am once again going home and when I get there, Clara won't be there.

Once everything slows down, I can't help but latch on to one thing. The uncle.

I know Clara has no uncle. There is no living relative on either side of her family. Which also means I am the only one who is going to push this. I'm her only option, her only hope, if she is really in trouble. And the fact that some random man calling himself her uncle dropped off withdrawal paperwork, well it just doesn't sit right with me.

By the time I make it to the front door of my apartment, I am already starting to plan out my next move. The Durham Police are my next stop. Clara didn't go missing on campus, and we don't live on campus, so I should be able to go to the

Durham Police and report her missing as soon as it has been twenty-four hours.

I put the key in the lock to my door when it hits me. Clara's keys are gone.

If I truly believe that Clara has gone missing due to some outside force, like, say, an uncle that doesn't exist; that means those keys to our apartment are probably in someone else's hands.

The realization hits me like a ton of bricks. I hesitate to go inside. Someone has access to my house. The more I think about it, someone went really out of their way to make it look like Clara left because she wanted to. She took everything she owned (minus the locket, of course), she emailed an adviser, and she even signed withdrawal paperwork. I'm certain someone else took those steps, but why didn't they leave the keys? People who move out, don't take their keys. They leave them on the counter, or drop them off with the landlord, they don't take the keys with them.

The chill that runs down my spine is enough for me to decide maybe going inside and waiting isn't the best plan I've ever had. Even if no one is in there now, they have access whenever they want. I have to fix this.

I lock the door and turn back around on a new mission. Buy a new lock and a dead bolt and then go to the police.

I'm not ashamed to admit to myself that I am truly terrified of what comes next. But having a plan, something to focus on, it's enough to get me through to the next part.

CHAPTER EIGHT

"FIGHT SONG" BY RACHEL PLATTEN

The process of filling out a missing person report is a much easier experience than I was expecting. That's probably because not a lot of people ask that many questions. It's just 'here, fill this out.' And of course, the form has limited space so condensing the last day into a manageable amount that fits in a tiny box was challenging to say the least. I gave them a recent picture of Clara, we took pictures before the night of the party last week. And then came the part that will stick with me for a long time after this. They asked me about scars and tattoos for easy identification. Or the question about if I have anything that might have her DNA on it. It's fucking creepy and not a place I am even remotely ready to go to.

In the end, it took a few hours to fill out everything and then to eventually talk to someone who was going to follow up on all the information. I have yet another business card to file away in my wallet for safekeeping.

By the time morning rolls around, I realize that once again I am not sleeping. I can probably do this for another day or two but at some point, I am going to run out of steam and crash. I've heard about this kind of thing before, where when someone you love is in danger or sick, your entire focus shifts and you forget to take care of yourself. That's where I am at. I can't remember the last time I ate, so I truly have no idea how my body is still moving forward at this point.

I grab a Diet Coke out of the fridge and stare over at Clara's coffee maker on the counter; the regret of not drinking coffee is strong. I could use the assist. I finally decide to just make myself a sandwich and sit down at our little kitchen table to eat. We almost never use this table, so it's probably the only place in the apartment that isn't attached with strong memories and an overwhelming sense of sadness.

I just took a bite when my phone finally rings. I chew as quickly as possible and then answer the phone, the phone that is now attached to me at all times.

"Hello." Please be Clara.

"Hello, is this MacKenzie Sharp?" the voice asks.

"Kenzie, but yes, this is her," I say.

"Yes, hello, Kenzie. My name is Sergeant Cooper, we spoke briefly yesterday when you reported your roommate missing."

"Of course, yes, thank you for calling." The hope starts to build up in my chest. This guy has a kind tone to his voice, so already this is going better than yesterday.

"Well, I went ahead and got a lot of phone calls checked off my list last night, but I also was able to make contact with everyone else I needed to speak to this morning," he explains.

"Do you have any news? Any idea what happened to Clara?"

"I'm sorry, Kenzie. I do not. I spoke with the officer assigned on campus, and I can see where your level of frustration came into play."

"Ah, so he was just as condescending to you I take it?" I asked, not at all surprised.

"Not the word I would use, but yes, he definitely had a bit of an issue. Unfortunately, from his perspective, he was correct, there isn't a lot left for him to do. As far as the university is concerned, Clara gave notice that she was leaving, turned in the appropriate forms, and has been formally withdrawn from the university."

"But there is no way she would have done any of those things! And I swear she doesn't have an uncle, and that's who they are saying dropped off her forms. No one actually saw Clara do anything related to leaving the university," I say, pleading for him to see what I'm saying.

"Yes, I agree, it does seem out of character for her. I spoke with a number of people whose numbers you provided, and the general consensus was that there was no way Clara would just leave the university. Everyone seems just as confused as to what is going on as you. I also ran her name through our system to see if Clara had any interaction with local police, and it came up empty."

"Thank you," I say to him.

"For what?" he asks.

"For calling the numbers I gave you, for taking this seriously, for actually seeming concerned."

There is a pause before he responds.

"If I were in your position, I would be just as worried. I completely agree the situation seems out of character for her. And there are definitely some lingering questions about why things played out the way they did. But I am sorry to tell you from a police perspective, there isn't really much to be done. It does appear that all the steps were taken to leave school, she didn't just up and leave and not complete those steps. It's clear she moved out of your apartment, taking all of her belongings, making it seem like she did, in fact, leave willingly. You stated there was no breaking and entering, so there is no reason to believe that Clara was not behind the removal of her things."

"But she doesn't have an uncle," I plead with him, the feeling of hope slowly draining from my body.

"I know, I looked into it. But to be fair, a lot of people are called uncle when they are just family friends. And I asked the registrar to fax me a copy of the withdrawal paperwork as well as something else with her signature on it, and from what I see, it looks like her signature. The writing looks like hers, it doesn't look rushed or like a copycat. I have no reason to believe that she wasn't the one who filled it out." He sighs. "I know this isn't what you wanted to hear, but right now, the police department doesn't find any foul play. Until we actually speak with Clara, the report will remain open, but it's being marked as low priority, as the conclusion is that she most likely left on her own."

I can't help it. Tears start to well up in my eyes. I can't stop the sniffle that follows.

"If you were me, what would you do?" I ask him, pleading with him for some kind of direction.

"So far, I would say you have done everything right. You've spoken to friends and teachers, you asked neighbors and the landlord, you have gone to every available police agency for help. If I were in your shoes, I would say keep doing what you are doing. Keep asking questions, write down every piece of information you have, keep documenting. We aren't closing her case, so hopefully we will hear something back. We even put in a request with the phone company that once her phone turns back on for it to ping a location and send it to us," he tells me.

"Really?"

"Yes, really. I completely understand your concern, unfortunately with missing persons, it's sometimes difficult because unless we get some kind of indication that foul play was involved, there often isn't a lot for us to do."

"I understand. I just, I feel like no one believes something is wrong," I tell him.

"I think you're wrong about that. I talked to a lot of people yesterday and today, and everyone agrees this is completely out of character and they are concerned for her. *I* don't believe you are overreacting, there just isn't anything for me to do at this time. But if anything changes, if you get new information, don't hesitate to call me, I will help whenever it's in my purview," he tells me.

"Thank you for that. I just don't know where to go from here."

"Keep talking to people, don't give up," he says.

"I won't," I vow to myself.

"You have my number if you need anything else," he says. "I'm sorry I wasn't able to give you more information."

It's funny how two conversations with basically the same end result can leave you with completely different feelings. The campus cop left me feeling enraged and like he didn't care what happened to Clara. Sgt Cooper, on the other hand, was completely understanding, spoke with kindness, and even though he couldn't do anything else, he left me feeling seen. I admit that the more time that passes, I am starting to feel like I am going crazy. Maybe this is all paranoia. But now, I feel less crazy and more validated.

Even with that, though, I still feel like I am left here doing nothing. I am just supposed to go on with my life like nothing ever happened. Go to classes every day, and just keep casually asking people, *Hey has anyone heard from Clara?* Because that seems like insanity, and I don't think I can do that. I'm not sure there are many other options though.

A FEW HOURS LATER, and one sad attempt to get some schoolwork done and distract myself from everything that has happened in the past day, I am left sitting on the couch in the living room staring off into space.

The one thing I can't seem to let go of is this man. This "uncle." Who is this guy? If you removed him from the equation, I might actually start to believe that Clara did this on her own. But that's the one piece of the puzzle that just doesn't fit in any way. In four years, I'm beyond certain that if Clara had some sort of family friend that she knew well enough to call an uncle, I'm sure I would have met him by now, or at the very least she would have mentioned him at least once. After her mom died, she finished high school living with the school guidance counselor because she had nowhere else to go. If she had an "uncle" why wouldn't she have lived with him? It just doesn't make any sense.

So he is where I have to start. I know it. If I can get more information about this guy, maybe it will actually give the police something to check out and we might actually have something to go off of and possibly find her.

What do I know about this mystery man? He went in person to the registrar's office to drop off the form. So he interacted with at least one person. Sgt Cooper said the form did look like Clara filled it out, so at least in that regard, it doesn't seem like this guy forged anything. He definitely, without a doubt, is not related to one of Clara's parents. I know they were only children. The fact that he had a form signed by Clara and presented himself as her uncle tells me he knew her or at least knew of her. This isn't like a grab and go off the street. If this is nefarious, he's clearly covering his tracks, and honestly, it's working.

My only option is to start poking holes in this theory that Clara woke up one morning and just decided it was time to leave. And I'm starting with the only outside player that literally no one knows anything about. The only thing I can think about is the only way I have any kind of chance of identifying this guy is to actually get a picture of him.

He went inside when he talked to the registrar, so with any luck there will be some kind of surveillance camera going on there, and he will have been caught on camera. If I could see him, maybe I would recognize him. Or at least have something to show other people.

It's not like I can just walk into the registrar's office though and be like, *Do you have cameras and if so, can I please look at them?* I need someone with authority to go and look at them. And as nice as Sgt Cooper was, he basically told me he doesn't really have any cause, so I doubt he is going to ask for camera footage. No, I need someone else to do it.

I know exactly what needs to be done, but I'm already regretting it.

Collin's dad is a police detective, and he knows me. He might actually be willing to go out on a limb for me and look more into this uncle guy. Unfortunately for me, when Collin and I broke up, I may have rage erased everything in my phone that pertained to him. So I don't have his parents' phone numbers in my phone anymore. Which leaves me with only one option. Collin. Luckily, I have his number memorized.

I'VE ALREADY CALLED ONCE with no answer. I call again with the same response. I don't really consider what I am going to do if he decides not to answer the phone when I call him. Given that Chanel seems permanently attached to his hip, there is a good chance that he might not ever answer when I call. That means my only option would be hunting him down, which honestly is not something I would be excited about. I'm sure that confrontation would only end in drama and most likely a lot of yelling.

Just as I'm about to call him again, the phone starts ringing in my hand. I take a deep breath to steel myself for this shit show this conversation is sure to be.

"Hello," I say, trying to sound confident.

"Kenz?" Collin asks. It's quiet in the background so I get the impression that he is alone, I could be wrong.

"Yeah, it's me."

"You shouldn't be calling," he says real quiet like. Almost like he doesn't mean it.

"Do you really think I would be calling you if it wasn't really important?" I ask.

"Don't be like that, Kenz."

"Be like what, Collin? Honest. After the past few months, can you blame me?"

There's an awkward pause that passes between us. It's weird to think that at one point we both thought we were going to spend the rest of our lives together, and now we are reduced to awkward pauses.

"No. I get it. I just wish it wasn't like this between us," he says quietly.

"I'm pretty sure that was a hundred percent your choice, Collin."

"I know. I just... What's going on? Everything okay?" he asks.

"I was hoping you had heard."

"Heard what?"

"Clara went missing," I tell him.

"What are you talking about? Clara's missing? Like *missing* missing? When did this happen?"

"Yes, really, missing. A little over twenty-four hours ago, she was supposed to meet me for lunch, she even left me a voice mail saying she couldn't make lunch but she wanted to talk that night. And then I get home and she's gone—"

"Define gone."

"Like everything she owns is gone. Like someone moved out everything that belonged to her in a few short hours."

"Was anything else missing?" he asks.

"Nope, just stuff that was Clara's, anything that was

communal was left. Well, except for her furniture, that was left too," I say. "And her locket."

"Wait, Clara left her locket behind? She never takes that thing off."

"I know."

"That's super weird."

"Yeah. I went to the police but they say that she actually withdrew from school and basically that adults are allowed to disappear if they want."

"Wow." Collin lets out a big sigh. "Okay, so why are you calling me then? I haven't heard anything."

"I was actually hoping you would be willing to do me a favor," I say, steeling myself for the possibility that I might have to persuade him.

"A favor? From me? I dunno, Kenz..."

"It's not a big deal, Collin, and honestly, after the way you have treated me and allowed your girlfriend to treat me, I think you kind of owe me the world's smallest favor," I snap at him.

"I, uh, I... okay, what kind of favor?"

"I was hoping you could put me in contact with your dad," I tell him.

"I dunno, Kenz. I don't think I can. Chanel really hates how much my family still talks about you, and if she finds out that I helped get you and my dad together, she will lose her mind," he says.

"Are you fucking kidding me? Clara is fucking missing, and you want me to be concerned with your little girlfriend's fragile ego? Are you serious right now?" I demand.

"Kenz, come on, seriously. You already said you talked to the police, what exactly do you expect my dad to do, I mean, really? I'm not going to put myself on the line for something that doesn't even mean anything," he explains, the defensiveness in his tone is enough to make me scream.

"Oh really, Collin?" I seethe. "Not going to *put yourself on the line*? You know Clara, you were friends with Clara. She's *missing*. And you can't be bothered to maybe upset your girlfriend. Seriously? How many favors did Clara do for you? How many times did she grab you a coffee or make you a lunch, or did you just forget that her tutoring is the only reason you made it through math class?"

"It's not that simple, Kenz. I have a reputation to protect now, and Chanel is important in that. If you really need to talk to my dad, I can't be a part of it. But honestly, I would kind of appreciate it if you left my dad out of it, I have enough problems of my own going on right now."

I'm seething. If this conversation were taking place in person, I think I would be well on my way to a night in jail. I can't believe this guy, this guy I thought I was going to *marry*.

"I don't even know you anymore, Collin. I've been telling myself for weeks that you're still you, the nice guy I met freshmen year, the good guy. That you just made some rough choices, but that you really didn't mean to hurt other people, that you didn't mean to hurt me. But I was so wrong. All you care about is yourself. I don't know what happened to you, or why you suddenly think that you're God's gift to the world, but I'm ashamed that I had anything to do with you."

"Hey, come on, that's not fair—"

"No, it's exactly fair. And just to be clear, you *are* going to get me in touch with your dad. Because if you don't, I have no problem sharing the emails you sent me for weeks after we were broken up and you were with Chanel. I wonder how much Chanel will enjoy seeing how you talked about her, and how you proclaimed over and over how much you still love me?" I threaten.

"You wouldn't." He sounds nervous. Good.

"Oh believe me, I would. There is nothing I won't do to get Clara back, and if you have to suffer a little bit to make that happen, then so be it."

I can hear him swallow hard on the other end of the line.

"I'll text you his number," he says. "I'll let him know you'll be in touch." He pauses. "For what it's worth, I am sorry. I didn't mean to hurt you."

"You didn't think about me at all, Collin. I was never even a part of the equation," I tell him before hanging up the phone.

Progress.

CHAPTER NINE

"DON'T GIVE UP ON ME" BY ANDY GRAMMER

After pacing my way through that phone call with Collin, and honestly trying not to scream at him, my whole body feels almost a sense of relief once it's over. My shoulders drop down, releasing the tension I've been holding, and I'm finally able to take in a deep breath. As the air flows through my nose, the thing I notice the most is the smell. Clara loves wallflowers, we have them all over the apartment, and the scents of Christmas and winter are still going strong throughout the living room.

A smile slowly forms on my face as I remember our many trips to the mall whenever there was a good sale for new scents. I plop down on the couch, letting my back just fall back against the cushions. This next part shouldn't be as hard. Collin and I clearly aren't in a good place, the animosity is palpable between us. But Collin's dad and I always got along great. Not getting to be a part of that family for the rest of my life is really true heartbreak that I still struggle with. I miss them.

It doesn't take long for Collin to follow through with his promise for his dad's phone number. I type out the message for Collin's dad, the whole time thinking about how it's possible he might not want to help me. Hell, he might not miss me. We weren't family, not yet. And yes, we got along great, but there's no telling how he is going to react to basically a cold call after a few months of radio silence.

~

KENZIE: Hi, Mr. Fitzpatrick, this is Kenzie. Collin was supposed to mention that I was going to get in touch.

Mr. Fitzpatrick: Kenzie! Collin said you are having some kind of problem

Kenzie: Yeah, it's kind of complicated... Clara is missing and I'm not really getting anywhere with the police, and I was just hoping that you would be able to help me.

Mr. Fitzpatrick: Can you meet tonight?

Kenzie: Yes, absolutely, any time.

Mr. Fitzpatrick: Great. There's a Starbucks right near the station, meet me there in 30?

Kenzie: See you there.

~

I NEED to leave as soon as possible if I am going to make it in time. Rushing to my room, I slip off my jeans and pull on some fleece-lined leggings. I love winter more than any other season, but the continuous shaking and goose bumps are getting old. I'm in the basic college girl studying outfit, leggings, some Uggs, and a hoodie. As long as I start getting somewhere with my mission, I don't care if I am dressed identical to Chanel.

~

THE COLD METAL against my skin stings as I pulled the door open to the Starbucks. Pausing in the entry so I can look around and see if Mr. Fitzpatrick is here yet, I am relieved to find that the place is mostly empty. I order my favorite salted caramel hot chocolate from the bored-looking barista at the front, then sit down in one of the booths to wait.

I can feel my stomach churning with nerves about how this meeting is going to go. I trust Mr. Fitzpatrick. He has always been so good to me. I have no reason to believe that is going to change just because things with me and his son didn't work out. Reality, of course, being that this is my last real shot. Every other person in power has turned me down. Reluctantly I have to admit to myself that I get it. There isn't much to go on. They have other real provable crimes to work on, and right now they have nothing actually saying Clara is missing. If I were them, would I be helping me? I don't know the answer to that question.

I hear the bell ding and before I even have a chance to look up, I hear the familiar footsteps of heavy boots with quick steps. Walking with purpose, he used to tell me. I stood up to greet him, feeling awkward and nervous, pulling on my fingers as I look up at him.

He was always kind of a bear of a man. Taller than me at six feet, with a stocky build that I wouldn't call athletic or fat. Perhaps the most identifiable feature he has is his hair, and it's almost comforting to see that it hasn't changed since the last time I saw him. Tonight he has his hair pulled back to the nape of his neck, normally he wears it slicked back, making the sandy blond start to appear more brown, but tonight it's clearly blond. He looks tired with shadows under his eyes, but the smile he has for me puts me at ease.

"Hi, Mr. Fitzpatrick." I feel my lips tilt upward in a small smile as I look up at him.

"Sweetheart," he says as he moves forward and wraps his arms around me. I breathe in deep and smell his familiar leather-scented cologne. It's comforting. "I think we can go with

Joe from now on, don't you?" He moves back and indicates for me to sit back down. Ever the gentleman waiting for me to sit before joining me in the booth.

"That's gonna take some getting used to," I tell him with a chuckle. I settle my hands around the cold plastic of my cup, not knowing really how to begin.

I feel the warmth of his hand on mine. "Tell me what happened."

I spent the next few minutes going over all the events from the beginning. I don't think I even paused to breathe. I just word vomited everything that happened starting from Sunday when we were talking about our plans for the week. Every mundane thing I could think of, I told him. The whole time he never broke eye contact with me, he kept his hand on mine, somehow keeping me grounded and focused. By the time I run out of steam, I feel exhausted, just emotionally wrung out.

"I'm sorry, Kenzie. I can't imagine what it has been like for you these past few days." Empathy radiated from him. I wonder how a man as kind as him could possibly have created someone who turned out to be so self-centered. Even so, I feel a 'but' coming, "Why don't you tell me what exactly you want from me?"

My first instinct is to say help. To find Clara. To actually do something when no one else would. But I knew that was asking for too much. It wasn't realistic. So I went for the one tangible thing I could think of.

"The uncle." I blurt it out and it feels so matter of fact as it leaves my mouth. "He's my proof. Clara doesn't have an uncle. Everyone is so willing to accept that this random older man, who no one has heard of or seen before, is the proof that Clara left on her own. No one saw her leave the apartment, *she* isn't the one who showed up on campus, anyone can write an email. The only thing that even remotely points to this being a planned move is this so-called uncle. And I don't buy it."

He sits back into the booth and just looks at me. I can tell he is sizing me up. Trying to make a decision about something. The silence is starting to get to me and I feel like squirming in my seat under his examination, but I hold still. Waiting.

He releases a big sigh before breaking his examination of me.

"Kenzie, you know I love you like a daughter, hell I thought you were going to be my daughter. I want to help you, and you have done everything right. I understand why you are suspicious. I've met Clara more than a few times over the years and I think this doesn't add up." He chuckles. "Hell, out of the three of you, Clara was always the most responsible, the most focused, the one with the most clarity about where she was going and why. I can't imagine her leaving the way you are describing. But from a police point of view, she took all the steps necessary to leave, to walk out of her life. Yeah, there are questions, and we have an alert out on her name, so maybe one day we will get the answers to those questions. But foul play doesn't really seem to be there in this case."

I can feel my body just sink down along with my heart. I've been holding myself up so tall for days now, letting my mission be the thing that keeps me upright and moving forward. With every blow I can feel myself sinking, not holding myself quite as straight, the defeat invading my shoulders until I'm in a slumped-over hunch.

"I had to ask." The words flowed out so quietly I was shocked that he actually heard them.

"This isn't my case, but my unit works on missing persons so I will do what I can, okay?"

My head snaps up so fast I'm shocked I don't get whiplash.

"Don't get too excited, even if I find something about this uncle guy, it doesn't mean it is going to change where we are now, with no proof anything happened."

I found my head nodding along with every word. "Of course, I just can't give up."

"I know. It's one of many things that I admire about you." He holds my hand again. "I'm sorry that I didn't reach out when things with you and Collin ended, but you need to know, just because you and Collin aren't together, doesn't mean that I can't be there for you. If you need anything, anything at all, call me anytime, day or night."

I couldn't stop the tears welling up in my eyes. This was what I had missed so much about my broken relationship. Family. A parent figure who would always show up. The relief in my heart at knowing I hadn't lost that was overwhelming.

"Thank you, thank you so much, Joe. I can't tell you how much it means to me."

"I've got night shift tonight, so I'll start digging in tonight and call you tomorrow with whatever information I find out."

As we get up to leave the store, I can't believe how much better I feel. Like I'm not alone in this. Sure, our friends all agree with me that something doesn't seem right, but I have a partner now. At least temporarily. Someone who is going to help carry the burden and get the information that I need so much.

I NEED something to pass the time while I wait to hear back from Joe, and frankly, being in that apartment is starting to feel like my own personal haunted house. Too many memories, too quiet, not enough music or scents of food cooking in the kitchen or takeout on the counter. So I do the only thing I can think of. I go to class.

Normally I love my classes. I don't always love every piece we read, but I love the conversations, the discourse, the comparing and contrasting from different time periods and geographics. But sitting here in class, none of it is holding my attention. I am like a zombie going through all the motions, giving clipped answers to thoughtful questions, sitting at a desk with my fingers hovering over my notes on my laptop but never making connection.

I can feel my professors' eyes passing over me with concern the longer classes go on. Even some of the students I normally interact the most with during class are starting to look at me. I've been avoiding looking in the mirror, but I'm sure that the lack of sleep I've been getting is showing up on my face. Besides, it's not like I am putting in any effort into my appearance. No makeup, day-old messy bun that has turned more rat's nest, and clothes that probably should have been reserved for sleeping only.

I don't care though. I just need to make it until my phone rings.

Just hold on until the phone rings.

It's like a slap in the face when maintenance shows up and apologizes for being late to replace the filters. They were only in the apartment for a matter of minutes, but it left me unsettled for hours. The last plans Clara and I made was to be home for the filter change. The most mundane of tasks. Something not to even think twice about. And now it's come and gone and she missed the whole thing.

The phone call comes long after my classes end and I am back on my couch, just waiting for answers to drop in my lap. The exhaustion has infiltrated my body so much that my head keeps slowly sinking backward before I jolt upright, right as I hit the edge of sleep. I'm not sure how much longer I can keep this up.

The ringing of my phone is enough to not just jolt me awake, but also give me a much-needed second wind.

"Hello." My excitement getting the better of me as the words almost come out at a shout volume.

"Hi, Kenzie. I got some information for you." His voice is like magic to my ears, it might have a natural rough, husky tone, and his New York City accent is stronger than normal, but it is the most comforting sound I've heard all week.

"Okay, I'm ready."

"I did a deep dive into Clara and her family. Girl's got a pretty slim family tree." There is a pause while I hear him sip what is sure to be a cup of black coffee. "I couldn't find anyone that was related to Clara or either of her parents that could possibly have fit what we have. If we opened things up a little further, I'm sure I could find second and third cousins, but based on what I found out about the family, it doesn't seem like they would have any contact with relatives that far out."

"So I was right then, no uncle?"

"Yep, no uncle."

While it is satisfying to know I am right, that this guy is an impostor, I'm not actually sure if that changes anything at all.

"So what's next?" I asked.

"Kenzie, I want to be very clear here; there isn't that much left for me to do. I did ask for the surveillance footage from the registrar's office, where we obviously know this guy was. He was literally the definition of unidentifiable. If I had to make a sketch of this guy, it would look like the Unabomber. He kept his head down and he was wearing a hat. I have nothing to go off of." His voice becomes more animated the more he explains, I can tell he is frustrated by the situation. "I'm sure that someone already mentioned to you that it's possible this guy is just a family friend, after all, Collin calls my best friend Uncle Jack. It's something people do. And without a name to really look up…"

"There's nothing you can do," I whisper, defeated. "Do you really believe that he's just a family friend?"

The silence on the other end starts to eat up the space.

"No. I don't."

"But that doesn't change anything, does it?" I ask, my voice taking on a begging tone.

"No, it doesn't. I've added a still shot of the guy to Clara's file. We have a flag on her. If anyone runs her name or stops her, we will be notified. I put a flag on her credit so as soon as she pops up anywhere, we will know."

"Are you allowed to do that?"

"She has a missing person report, and I ran it up the chain, so it's okay. I just don't think there is anything else I can do from my end. Not until either she flags in the system or some new evidence comes up for us to investigate."

"I can't just let this go," I implore him.

"I knew you were going to say that." His hearty chuckle vibrates through the phone.

"So what do I do?"

"I'm going to give you a name, a guy I know of in town. He used to be a cop, he works as a private investigator now. He's pretty well respected around here, and whenever he gets information that can help the cops, he always passes it along. He's a little rough around the edges, but I think he's the best shot you have."

"A PI? Really?"

"It's really your only option at this point. The police aren't going to be able to do much more than we have already done, and as much as it pains me to admit it, until something changes, the investigation is going to remain pretty passive. At least with a PI, you will have someone in your corner looking out for your interests, and you decide when it's time to stop. He can put in the manpower to really talk to people and run a real investigation."

I think about it. He is right, of course, we both know the police aren't going to do any more than they already have. And I think what Joe has been too kind to say out loud is that I have no experience on how to find someone and I'm probably not going to get anywhere besides just spinning my wheels on my search for Clara.

"Okay, can you text me his information?" I ask.

"Of course, I just texted it to you." I feel the phone vibrate in my hand, signaling that the information is waiting for me. "If you need anything, anything at all, I'm here, okay?"

"Thanks so much, Joe. I can't tell you how much this all means to me."

"Anytime, don't be a stranger, okay?"

"I won't. Promise."

I pull up the text message as soon as we get off the phone. William Anderson of Anderson and Associates. Talk about generic sounding. I call the number that Joe sent, but no one answers. I leave a brief message with just my name and phone number and sit back down on the couch to wait.

What are the chances that he is going to call me back tonight? I don't have time to wait. I know right now, at this moment, that this is going to be my last chance, and if crime TV has taught me anything, time is the thing you have the least of when it comes to a missing person.

My legs eat up the space in my living room in mere seconds as I reach my computer and sit down to pull up Google. In just a few short seconds, I have his address pulled up. A quick photo snapped with my phone of the address, and I am out the door, determination flowing through my veins.

CHAPTER TEN

"AIN'T NO SUNSHINE" BY BILL WITHERS

The sun has already set, even though it's still early evening by the time I make it to the address on my GPS. I love winter but I hate that it's dark outside so early. The building stands on its own, not attached to anything else, and it seems like it's the only business in the building. I look around what I generously refer to as a parking lot to see if there is some kind of sign marking it as a business. The short answer is no. It's not until I take a closer look at the building itself that I see a small white sheet of paper with the words "Anderson and Associates" typed on it and taped onto the window of the entrance.

The building itself looks like it's in pretty good shape, made of what looks like red brick, but it might be more orange in the daylight. It is literally the definition of nondescript. You could easily mistake this building for a small house if you weren't paying close attention, and even then, it's really only because of the four defined parking spaces that make it look like a business. Without any signage or really anything to grab attention, it would have been so easy for me to just drive by this place without a second thought. Thank God for my GPS.

Rain starts to hit the windshield as I'm grabbing my bag from the passenger seat. The cold bites at my skin as I exit my car, causing my entire body to do a quick shiver. The droplets of rain hitting the skin on my face and hands add a stinging sensation as it sporadically falls on me. At least the cold is good for one thing, keeping me alert. The last couple of days are starting to really wear on my body, the exhaustion filling, making my muscles feel like weights. The crunch of the gravel stops being noticeable when the sound coming from the office hits my ears. It takes me a second to place the slow rhythm, but once I figure it out, I know that any time I hear this song again, I am going to think of this moment.

I can see through the front office window as I listen to Bill Withers lament about the lack of sunshine. I can see a pair of feet propped up on a desk, clad in black leather motorcycle boots, kind of tapping to the beat of the music.

I don't know what to make of this. This man is obviously still at work after hours, so at the very least I know he must care about his work enough to not run off as soon as quitting time comes about. Definitely not opposed to his choice in music, a nice solid, classic choice. As I move closer to the front door, I can see more of him. He's got papers in hand so I can't see his face, but I can clearly see his other hand. The other hand that is holding a very generous serving of brown liquid. Generous might be an understatement. So basically this guy is getting drunk at his office, great. Classic.

"He's your only option," I remind myself.

The rain starts coming down a little harder and the cold finally pushes me into making the decision. Going inside.

The smell is the first thing I notice. I remember it from when I was a little girl, my dad and his friends used to hang out in the backyard smoking cigars and drinking beers while cracking jokes. For just a split second in time, I am back in those memories. My eyes scan the room until I find the source of the smell. A cigar propped up in an ashtray, the trail of smoke wafting up toward the ceiling.

"You lost?" His husky voice startles me. My eyes rapidly find the source of the voice. He is still leaning back in his chair with his feet up on his desk, but the papers in his hand have been lowered down to the desk. They aren't papers, they are photos. Who still prints photos?

"Not lost," I tell him. "A friend of mine gave me your information and said maybe you could help me."

"That right?" He reaches behind him to turn off the music, which I then realize is coming from a record player. He moves to put his feet on the floor and then gives me a slow once-over. I try my hardest not to shrink under the examination. Something about this guy makes me want to take a step back. He feels almost larger than life, even though he is still sitting down behind a desk. It's not scary though, he doesn't make me feel afraid, rather he makes me feel like I'm an open book. It's a little unsettling.

While he takes his time sizing me up, I take my time to do the same thing. I can't tell how tall he is since he is still sitting down, but based on his build, there is no way he is under six feet tall. He has wide shoulders, that I can tell are well-muscled because he's wearing one of those compression shirts people work out in. He's got at least a couple days of beard growth going on, but it's not super well kept, making me think it's more a lack of caring than an aesthetic choice. The lighting in the office isn't exactly bright, but even with the lack of light, he has a kind of golden appearance. His hair is clearly a golden brown, which goes along with his light-brown complexion. I wonder briefly if it's a tan or natural.

"You sure you're not lost?" he asks one more time with his eyebrow raised up, reminding me slightly of the Rock.

"Yeah, I'm sure. Hard to get lost with GPS." My voice was laced with sarcasm.

"She's got teeth. Interesting," he says, crossing his arms over his chest. I was right about the well-muscled thing.

"You're not a people person, are you?" I ask.

"What would make you say that? I was employee of the month last month," he says with a smirk.

I do a quick survey of the office. "You're the only employee, aren't you?"

"And smart too." He stands up and moves out from behind the desk before sitting on the edge of the desk. Definitely over six feet. "So who do I owe a thank you to for sending my way?"

"Detective Fitzpatrick."

He loses the smirk on his face. The switch from low-grade amusement to serious takes place in milliseconds.

"Fitz works homicide, last I checked."

"Yeah, that's the one."

"He sent you to me?" There is definite doubt in his voice.

Not wanting to get bogged down on how I ended up here in the rain after business hours, I decide the best option is just to prove it to him. I pull my cell phone out of my back pocket and pull up the text message from Joe before handing over my phone.

He stares at it briefly before finally reaching out and taking the phone from me. It only takes a few moments before he is handing me back my phone.

"Alright, Fitz sent you," he states.

"I've already been to the police and I've gotten as far as I am going to get, so he sent me to you, hoping you could help."

"I'm not really taking on any cases right now."

"You're not taking on cases? Isn't that like the whole point of the business?"

"Fine. What I should have said is I'm not interested."

"Not interested?" I can feel my blood pressure rising with every one of his responses.

"Yep." He popped the *p* at the end for emphasis.

"You don't even know anything about the case."

"I know enough."

"Are you kidding me right now?" Getting angrier by the second, I'm not sure how I manage to keep myself together.

"Dead serious. I'm not interested. Thanks for stopping by." He kind of motions half-heartedly toward the door and then starts back around his desk.

"I'm not leaving. I don't know what your problem is, but I am not going anywhere. You are literally the last option I have right now, and there is no way that Joe would have given me your information if he didn't truly think you were good at your job and a good guy. So, like it or not, you and I are going to have to work something out." My breath is coming out faster and faster and I hope he can't see through my bravado.

"Joe, huh? Not Detective Fitzpatrick, but *Joe*?" he asks.

I shift nervously back and forth on my feet.

"Yeah, what about it?"

"So you know *Joe*, this is a personal favor." He states it matter-of-factly, not at all a question.

"That a problem for you?" I retort.

"How do you know *Joe*?"

"Could you stop saying it like that?"

"Like what?"

"Don't fuck around, you know what I'm talking about," I say, exasperated.

He laughs. He really laughs. Like a belly laugh from deep in his stomach.

"I was wondering how long it would take for you to break." The last bits of his laugh still present in his statement.

My heart pounds in my chest and I can feel myself getting warm, and without a doubt, my skin is starting to get flushed. This guy was really starting to piss me off.

"Are you kidding me, is this a joke to you?" The volume of

my voice getting increasingly louder the longer this bullshit continues.

"Not a joke, just... amusing." He pauses to take a sip of his liquor before plopping back down in his chair and putting his feet back up on his desk. "How do you know Fitz?"

"Is that really important?" I ask, feeling myself start to deflate now that this guy has made himself comfortable in his chair.

"It is if you want this conversation to continue."

"I've known him for years."

The silence that follows is deafening. He looks like he is frozen, like someone just pushed pause, as he stares me down, waiting for me to elaborate. I can't help but squirm under the pressure.

"I used to date his son," I finally tell him.

"Ah." He takes another sip of his liquor. He's quiet for a while after that, like he's working through what he wants to do next. The adrenaline from our banter starts to wind down and suddenly I'm feeling every bit of the exhaustion of the last few days all at once. I take a chance that this is going to move forward and I sit down in the leather chair in front of his desk. "Alright then," he says.

"Alright?" I ask with closely guarded hope laced in my voice.

"Alright, tell me why you are here, but maybe start with who you are first," he says.

"Right, okay, I'm MacKenzie Sharpe, but everyone calls me Kenzie," I tell him as I lean forward with my hand extending toward him.

This time, he doesn't hesitate. He reaches out and takes my hand in his. I can feel the calluses on his fingers and his hand is a lot warmer than mine, but it's a gentle handshake, something I wasn't expecting. I expected it to be like everything else about him: abrasive and quick.

"Will Anderson," he tells me, even though I have already figured that much out. "So what brings you here to my office after hours? Nothing good, I take it."

"No. Not exactly. I need your help finding my best friend."

He leans back in his chair again.

"She went missing a few days ago, I've talked to everyone I can think of, I've been to the police on campus and the police in town and I'm out of options."

"Nothing like being a last resort," he jokes, breaking a little bit of the tension between us. "Alright, start from the beginning," he says as he once again props his feet up on his desk.

So I take him through the entire story, how everything was normal, and then poof she vanished like she was never there at all. I tell him all about the locket, how this mysterious uncle showed up out of nowhere to withdraw her from school and why the whole thing rings false. I leave nothing out. And even though he is sipping on liquor and leaning back with his feet up, he is fully engaged in listening to my story. Asking questions when he wants more details, confirming key facts; basically he's doing everything I wanted him to do since the moment I walked through the door.

When I finally finish my story, I feel like I just went five rounds in a prizefight. I've told this story what feels like a million times by now, but no matter how many times I tell it, it never seems like I get anywhere with it.

Time feels like it slows down, and I can hear the sounds of the heater kicking on in the office while I wait for Will to say anything about what he just heard. The fear of being told once more that there is nothing anyone can do for me is suffocating. He just sits there looking at me while he swirls the remaining half an inch of liquid in his glass.

I break when I can't stand waiting any longer and ask, "So what do you think, can you help?"

"I don't really do these kinds of cases anymore."

"But you did before?" I ask.

He looks away before answering, "Yeah."

"Okay... look, I'll do whatever I need to do to get you to sign on for this. I know this probably doesn't mean anything to you, but this case, Clara, she means everything to me. I would never be able to live with myself if I didn't see this through. I know everyone just thinks that she just left, but I know her, I know her better than I know myself some days, and there is no way she would just leave."

Will raises his eyebrow at my declaration.

"And even if she did leave on her own, and everyone is right, I have to at least know that wherever she is, she is okay. She would do it for me."

"Well, I can see where the police had their issues, and frankly, I'm surprised Joe went as far as he did, flagging every-thing the way he did. There really just isn't enough manpower these days to really work missing persons cases when there are so many other immediate crimes that need to be dealt with. You're lucky that he got involved enough to go that far," he tells me. I know what he's saying is right.

"But you're not the police."

"Not anymore." He sighs, long and hard. "Look, I agree, something smells fishy. And assuming everything you told me is correct and your friends and her teacher back up everything you told me tonight, then yeah, I can understand why you are coming to me. Can't say I would do anything different in your place."

"But..." I say, waiting for the other shoe to drop, this is where everyone else has said no in the past.

"But nothing, but you need to be prepared. These kinds of cases often don't come with anything but disappointment. Best-case scenario your best friend ghosted you and doesn't want you in her life and you're out cash, time, and heartache. Worst case, well, worst case can look pretty bad. You need to start preparing yourself for a scenario that is going to be painful, time consuming, and depending on how long this takes could end up costing you a whole lot of money."

"How much money are we talking about?" I ask.

"Simple searches like running background only cost a couple hundred, but what you are talking about borders on a police investigation. For this kind of thing, I charge a three-thousand-dollar retainer fee before I even get started working the case, and from there it's an hourly rate."

"Three grand? Three grand and you'll be on the case?"

"Yeah." He leans forward in his chair, puts his feet on the ground, and looks me dead in the eye. "I need you to really understand. I said I don't do these kinds of cases anymore for a reason. You seem like a nice girl, and I understand why you are doing this, but you *really* need to start preparing yourself. In my experience, there is not going to be a happy ending, no pot of gold at the end of the rainbow."

In all this time, no one has really put it like this before. No one has been this blunt. And if I am being honest with myself, I haven't really thought this through. Every time I walk back into the apartment, I expect to see her in the kitchen cooking or sitting at her desk working on some math problem I would never understand. I've been on this mission for the past couple days, and I never even considered what it would look like when it was over. Did I really just think everything was going to be hearts and flowers? That she was going to pop up and tell me everything was a misunderstanding but she was home now? The whole uncle thing had hit me as sinister from the second I heard about him. It left a pit of dread in my stomach. But I never let myself think about what sinister meant. Where she is now. If she is even alive. What she is going through or went through.

Reality hits me like a ton of bricks. My vision starts to lose focus, and it's not until I feel the stinging in my eyes that I realize my eyes are starting to build up with unshed tears. As I blink rapidly to try and clear my vision, I see Will just looking at me. Patiently waiting for my reply, letting me process without any judgment or rush.

I'm afraid. The truth I am so desperate to find is scary. But I have to know, and I think I really need someone like Will who will tell me how it really is without trying to spare my feelings. He's the first one to make me truly confront what everyone was probably thinking but not saying.

"I have to know. Whatever it ends up being, I have to know. If there is a chance she needs me, then I want to be there, and right now I'm the only one who even cares, so yeah, I'm sure."

"Alright then. I take cash or check, but won't start work until the check clears. Either one works for me."

"I won't be able to do anything until tomorrow, but I can get it to you as soon as possible. It may take some time," I admit to him.

He reaches across his desk and grabs a piece of paper and a pen before jotting down some information for me.

"Here's my cell phone number, text or call first, I'm not always in the office. Tomorrow morning I'll touch base with Detective Fitzpatrick and see if he can send over whatever information he has, that way I don't need to waste time repeating any steps they have already done for us."

"Okay." I nod almost absentmindedly, feeling like I am in some kind of daze with the realizations of this night.

"Until then, keep your eyes peeled. Keep talking to people, you never know what you are going to stumble on. Unfortunately, I get the feeling that your instincts aren't wrong, so keep following them, they have gotten you this far. Sometimes following your gut is all you have," he tells me, bringing me an odd sense of reassurance.

CHAPTER ELEVEN

"LULLABY" BY SHAWN MULLINS

The morning brings a new goal. Cash. Cold hard cash. Last night when he said it was going to cost three grand to start the process of looking for Clara, I didn't bat an eyelash. No amount of money would be too much to get Clara back. Or at least that's what my heart was telling me.

My wallet, on the other hand, was singing a different tune. The song of a scholarship student without a part-time job. I have enough money in my bank account from this semester's disbursement to cover my rent and a couple of meals beyond what I was getting for free off my meal plan, but disposable income was really as mythical as a unicorn. Where did I really think I was going to be able to come up with that kind of cash?

If I took the rest of the rent money for this semester, I would have almost two thousand. Granted, that could mean I end up homeless next month, but that's tomorrow's problem. How does a person just come up with a thousand bucks? I don't exactly have family I can turn to for money, my mom is too busy numbing her pain with pills and my dad is following right behind with alcohol. There is no way they have disposable income for me to borrow.

It's Friday morning and instead of getting ready to go to my last classes of the week, I am sitting here, coming to the realization that it's been an entire school week since I saw Clara. It's about to be my first weekend without her. I start thinking about all the ways people get money. Getting a job and waiting for a paycheck is going to take way too long. Selling plasma is only going to get me a fraction of what I need to get Will to take the case. I need something bigger, something that is actually going to bring me a decent amount of cash in a short amount of time, preferably in just a few hours. I'm pretty sure, barring committing some kind of felony, there is no way I am going to make a thousand dollars appear as if from nowhere.

My exhaustion finally caught up to me last night, and I finally got a few hours of sleep. It's probably the only reason why I am even mildly thinking clearly enough to realize I have no way of getting cash. Even still, my mind is running through not just the money problem but also the events of the past week. With a clearer head, maybe I will notice something I didn't before.

"Fuck it," I say out loud. I jump out of bed and head into the living room, finally having a plan. My feet eat up the distance between my room and the printer we keep in the living room. I grab a stack of computer paper out of the printer and head to the wall with the least amount of decorations on it. It takes only moments for me to empty the wall of photographs before I start tacking up the paper to the wall.

"That's right, Kenz, you're going full crazy, like every deranged character in a crime movie," I tell myself.

And with that, I start building my timeline. I start it on Sunday, our last meal out of the apartment. I write out the time, location, and all the bullet points of the conversation. I include notes on what our moods were like and our encounter with Chanel, I don't want to leave anything out. I repeat this process for Monday, which has a lot more information and a lot more questions. I put up the email with a note to get a hold of it. What time was it sent? Did it sound like Clara? I'm sure I would recognize her speech patterns in an email, so maybe it's a forgery. I put notes up about the voice mail and everything else I remember about that day, including the time I found the locket in my room.

I step back and look at my progress. Should I put the information I found out from the police on the timeline when I found it out or when it happened? Should I put information about the "uncle" under the conversation with campus police, or when campus police reported that he was actually on campus? Ultimately, I decide to do a combination of both. All information gets listed under when it actually happened, as well as when the information was provided to me and by who. Or at least that's the plan I make in my head.

By the time I lay everything out on my walls and stand back to observe my work, I can't help but realize I was right earlier. I've lost my fucking mind. If someone were to walk into the apartment right now, they would think I was batshit crazy. This is movie-level insanity. But it's not like I have any other options right now. As of right now, my brain is completely fried. I have nothing left. As much as I want to keep going, as much as I want to keep pushing myself, I know the only way I am going to be able to do that is to start taking care of myself.

It's time to start looking at this like a marathon and not a sprint. I need food and a shower, I need to feel like a human being again and not a zombie. I let my head drop in front of me, letting the feelings of defeat wash over me for just a few minutes before I get to work at taking care of myself.

MY WET HAIR is still dripping on my shoulders, leaving wet spots on my T-shirt as I sit on the couch munching on my sandwich and bag of chips. Not exactly the most nutritious meal I've ever eaten in my life, but at this point, food is food.

I threw caution to the wind and moved our couch to face the wall of clues as I've started to call it in my head. So now I'm sitting here eating my sandwich and staring at this insane wall, trying to figure out what I am going to do next. The words up on the wall are all starting to blend together I have been staring at it so long.

A lot of the questions I have are going to need the help of other people. I could talk to the person at the registrar's office. I could try and get my hands on the camera footage, but Will's got a better chance at that than I do. I could listen to my voice mail for the hundredth time, but I can't imagine what that is going to give me that I don't already have up on the Wall of Crazy.

"There has to be something," I murmur to myself as I shovel more chips in my mouth. My eyes finally find purchase on the email. Maybe there is something I can do with it. Obviously according to the school, Clara sent a message announcing her departure, not just sending some random guy to turn in her forms. I really want to see what it says. I can't even begin to count the number of emails I have received from Clara over the last four years. There is no way someone would be able to fake one from her without me knowing.

I hope.

Who knows when I am going to get the money to pay Will, so right now the only person moving things along is me. I can only rely on myself. So if I want Clara's email, I'm going to have to get it myself. I wipe the Cheeto dust off my fingers and then grab my laptop and start to get to work.

I've heard a million girls talk about how they "hacked" into their boyfriends' social media, when really they just guessed the passwords. I'm beyond confident that I can do the same thing with Clara's passwords. I pull up the university mail site and log out of my account, type in Clara's information, and think long and hard about what she would make her password.

It's probably complex.

She's a computer science major, for crying out loud, she probably follows all the rules. There are probably special characters and numbers, and chances are she changes the password every couple of weeks just to be on the safe side. So maybe guessing it isn't going to be the right track to go on.

I slide my finger over the trackpad, moving the cursor to the button labeled *"forgot your password."* This is where I hit pay dirt. It's challenge questions.

I was made for this. I feel like Ken Jennings going into a round of Jeopardy. Confident.

Question One: What is your paternal grandmother's first name?

"Yes, I know this one!" I shout. I type out *Alice* into the box and click the submit button. The half a second for the screen to reload feels like it goes on forever.

The second question appears on the screen in front of me.

"Yes!" I pump my fist in the air.

Question Two: Name of the street you lived on in fourth grade?

"Easy peasy lemon squeezy," I mutter under my breath as I type out *Cloverfield Dr*. I hesitate for just a second. I know I have the street name right, but would she have used the abbreviation or would she have written the whole thing out. I use the abbreviation, but I'm lazy, Clara has always been super precise. She would probably write the whole thing out. So I use my delete key and change the answer to *Cloverfield Drive*.

I hold my breath as I hover the little arrow over the submit button before clicking it.

Once more, the next question pops up.

"Yes! Thank you, thank you, thank you!" I chant while I wiggle around on the couch in a makeshift victory dance.

"One more time for question three," I tell myself, this is the last thing I need to do.

Question Three: What is the name of your childhood stuffed animal?

As soon as I finish reading the last question, my feet start stomping on the floor. I have it. No chance of failure now, I'm going to have access in a matter of seconds.

"Miss Piggy," I say out loud as I type it out. I'm completely confident about this because I have a stuffed animal that I brought with me to college and showed Clara and she told me all about hers that she lost in the house fire, and how much she wished she had been able to bring Miss Piggy with her to college. I told her that day that I would share mine with her whenever she needed it.

I'm then prompted to change the password, and I change it over to the password that I use for my email so it's easy for me to remember. In a matter of seconds, I am looking at her inbox.

The first thing I notice is that all of her emails are unread. Clara is one of those people who checks it several times a day. She reads them, replies, and then either stores them in specific folders or deletes them. There is never any buildup, so this is not an encouraging sign. Wherever Clara is, she isn't checking her email.

There are more than a couple messages from our friends trying to check in with her and make sure she is doing okay. The earliest ones don't seem all that worried about her, but as the hours turn into days, the tone of the messages start to take a turn into more worried territory.

I also see an email from the police department, and without a second thought, I click on it.

∼

To: Clara Tomas
   From: Durham PD
   Subject: Contact

Ms. Tomas,

This is Sergeant Edward Cooper from the Durham Police Department. There has been some concern about your well-being and whereabouts and a missing person report has been opened for you. If you could please contact me at your earliest convenience, we could clear this matter up quickly. My cell phone number is 919-555-0125.

Hope to speak with you soon,
Sgt Cooper

I FIND it somewhat reassuring that Sgt Cooper tried everything he could think of trying to get ahold of Clara, even though he had to know the chances that Clara was going to reply were slim. After exiting out of the message, I make sure to mark it unread just in case one day Clara does check her email, this one will catch her attention. There is nothing else really remarkable about her inbox, just a couple of emails that go out to everyone in a class with reminders of important dates or opportunities for lab time; basically all the mundane things you would expect to see.

Time to check out the sent folder so I can actually see what this email that explained how she was thinking about leaving school actually looks like. I notice something is off within seconds. As soon as I get to the sent folder, there is only one in the sent pile. I'm pretty sure the sent folder doesn't self-delete things, and I know Clara wouldn't have deleted them either, so why in the world would it be empty except for one?

Even though my mind is racing with the possibility that someone has already been in the email account, I move forward with checking out the message from Clara.

To: Margret Kwan
 From: Clara Tomas
 Subject: Enrolled Status
 Hello Mrs. Kwan,
 I hope this email finds you well. I wanted to check in with you to let you know I am considering withdrawing from the computer science program. The pace of this semester's coursework has been more intensive than I had been anticipating and it's becoming incompatible with my other responsibilities. Please be on the lookout for forthcoming paperwork concerning my enrollment status.
 Thank you for your time,
 Clara Tomas

WHAT THE FUCK did I just read? That was not Clara. Never in my entire life have I ever heard Clara talk like that, or have I ever read anything she has written that sounded like that. And I read every draft with cover letter for her internship application, and it was nothing like this. This reads like someone trying to sound smarter than they are and professional, but it's coming off as stiff and weird. One thing is for sure, either Clara didn't write this, or someone dictated it to her, because this is crazy.

Even though I am still dumbfounded by what is going on and wondering who the hell wrote this email, I know the most important thing to do right now is to save it. So I save a copy of it to my computer, and then print it out for my Wall of Crazy. Before I go to tack it up on the wall, I decide to keep looking around in Clara's account. Who knows, maybe there is something else to be found.

After a while, I realize it's the lack of something I should be worried about. Just like the sent folder, the entire rest of the email account has been emptied out. All of the folders are still there. One for each of her classes, one for past classes, a folder for friends, one for business contacts, all kinds of organizing folders, and still nothing inside any of them. Who would erase everything but leave the folders? It makes no sense. Either way, this whole thing feels like a clue.

Since I'm the only one in possession of the password for the email account, I decide to go ahead just to make sure no one else who shouldn't be on here can be. I try to pick questions that don't apply to Clara so she will know it is me, like what is your brother's middle name (she's an only child) and what's the name of your middle school (she was homeschooled in middle school). Either way, at the end of this, I feel pretty confident that the account is secure and I have more to go on now than when the day began.

I'm about to log out and settle back into the couch to keep brainstorming ideas for quick cash when a memory hits me like a freight train: *"Hold on, I need to save all this stuff to my cloud."* Clara saved everything to the cloud, she was obsessive about it. Every single time we left the house she always had to make sure she saved everything to the cloud, she talked about it all the time. Every student at the university gets a cloud, and it uses the same login and password as your email. So off I go to the login for the cloud server and the next thing I know, the welcome screen is up.

And that's when I know for sure I am missing something. The welcome screen lists right on the front when the last login was. It was months ago, back before Halloween. Clearly, nothing that she had been saving to the cloud was this cloud. So where was it? I don't even want to think about how many different cloud servers there are out there, and which one she was choosing to use.

I do briefly roam around what is there, and it's all copies of old papers, just a bunch of boring math stuff. Nothing that has anything to do with her going missing.

Nothing like the feeling of a dead-end road. Joe was right. I do need help. I have no idea where to go from here. Sure, I have new information, and I have a lot more new suspicions, but at the end of the day what I really have is a pile of new questions that need to be answered and no clue how to find the answers to these questions.

CHAPTER TWELVE
"SOUND OF SILENCE" BY DISTURBED

It takes a few moments before consciousness really sets in. The crick in my neck is clearly coming from the unnatural angle of my head, which I apparently decided was a good way to fall asleep. There's not even a pillow underneath my head.

Wiping the sleep out of my eyes, I slowly start to sit up and take in my surroundings. I must have polished off that bag of Cheetos, and if not, then they've been reduced to dust because the crinkling sound coming from under my ass clearly indicates I slept on the bag.

It takes a minute to clear the cobwebs from my brain, and I take that time to gather all my hair up and throw it back in a messy bun. I'm sure it looks more bird's nest than Instagram messy bun.

Sleep actually paid a visit to me last night, maybe it was the exhaustion catching up to me from a week of minimal sleeping, or maybe I just tired myself out last night making my giant Wall of Crazy, but I actually feel kind of human right now. Sleep is good. Sleep is necessary.

Thinking back on last night, I can't help but feel a little bit proud of myself. Everyone has been shutting me down at every opportunity, I don't have access to the kind of information that the police have, but yet I still got somewhere last night. I have a direction I need to go.

I need to find that cloud.

The thing is, if I had given up, or left it to the professionals, no one would even know this is important. Even if the police had believed me right from the beginning and a full-fledged investigation was ongoing, would it have ever occurred to them to look beyond the university-provided cloud? Would I? Probably not. I would have just assumed they were looking at it and nothing in it helped them, I certainly wouldn't have broken into it to find the answers for myself.

The police may have the skills, hell, Will probably has the skills to do the real investigative work, but I'm the one with the context. I'm the one that knew Clara best. I have all the nuances and daily routine, the mundane, the stuff that no one may think is important, but might actually be. I have all that. It's a big responsibility knowing that it's my job now, to sort through every interaction, every rogue comment, to see if it might have anything to do with what is happening right now.

The hard part for me now is going to be accepting that while I might know what questions to ask, and where to look next, I have no idea how to get those answers.

I feel it in my bones that finding this cloud server is going to provide us with at least some answers, maybe a direction to go in, or maybe even a real clue, but I don't know how to find it. My Google search from last night left me with a list as long as my arm showing how many different server options there are available out there. I don't have her computer, so it's not like I can go see what websites she visited, so I need help.

Which means I need Will.

Three thousand dollars Will.

Three thousand dollars I don't have.

I've never been a person who begs, I've always been someone who gets it done no matter what, but I'm starting to have to accept there just might be some begging in my future.

THE STACK of books on my kitchen table is getting taller and taller as I riffle through the apartment, trying to find every text-book I have that might be worth anything. I finally have a plan. I'm going to get as much money as I possibly can together and then beg in person. With cash. There is no way I'm getting to three thousand, at least not for a few days, but maybe I can convince Will to start now if I bring him as much as I can pull together. Which brings us to my plan, which starts with carrying this stack of textbooks out of my car.

By the time I make my last trip out to my car, I feel like I have run a mile. No, a mile is too easy, more like a marathon. Okay, a half marathon. My chest is heaving, my lungs burn from the cold air that stings when you try and gulp it down. My body that clearly was not made to sleep on a couch with no pillow is feeling all kinds of sore.

But none of that matters because I have a plan to put into action. Step one, the bank.

I'm normally the kind of girl who blares music super loud when she drives. I've been known to dance around in the driver's seat at stoplights while jamming out to classic rock. The minute I got my driver's license back in high school, I was on the open road. Anytime things got too suffocating at home, I would just hit the road. Turn on my music and let all of my worries and stress go. Sure, when I got home nothing would have changed, everything was always still waiting for me just where I left it, but there is something about the open road. It was like freedom. It still is. A respite from reality for as long as the car is moving in any direction.

So it's especially odd that today my car is silent. There are no '80s hair bands, or upbeat Pharrell talking about being happy, nothing but the sounds of traffic filling up the empty space. All I know is that I for sure don't want music playing right now. I don't want the respite. God only knows where Clara is.

As much as I want to believe the happy picture people are trying to paint me, can I really buy into the idea that Clara is just off somewhere living her best life? That college was just too much for her and she bailed, and now she's what? Hanging out on a beach somewhere where some hot guy brings her margaritas? I just don't buy it.

So why should I get to have a respite when Clara could be anywhere? Maybe she's scared, or nervous, or terrified. With all the stuff on the news and the things they talk about on my favorite podcast, *Crime Junkies*, the nightmares in my head tell me she could be in serious trouble. I can't let my mind go there just yet, but at the same time, I also can't seem to allow myself a break from it all either. And right now, in this moment, sitting alone on a quiet car ride with only my thoughts to keep me company feels like a dangerous proposition.

I've never been more grateful for the prospect of standing in line at a bank, but by the time I pull into the busy parking lot of my local bank branch, I'm more than ready to get the fuck out of my car.

It's a busy Saturday morning, and it seems like all the little old ladies in town have decided to do their banking right now. I've never been someone that I consider to be impatient but as I make my way into the bank and take my place in a line that is twenty-five people deep, I can feel the impatience start to take hold. The nervous energy running through my veins with nowhere to go. My foot finding a tapping beat just trying to relieve my need to keep moving. The longer I've been awake, the more amped I get about putting my plan into action. About making it through all the steps before I can go to Will and get the ball rolling. And now I'm stuck behind a bunch of blue-haired little old ladies, who want to do everything at the speed of a snail.

It takes forty-five minutes, but I finally make it to a teller. I haven't been in a bank in person for years, probably when I first moved to Durham and opened this bank account. The teller in front of me looks like she is straight out of a movie, the drab neutral-colored professional wear that doesn't seem to give her body any kind of shape at all. Her hair pulled back into one of those '90s oversized scrunchies that used to be considered professional but now is more like something you use to keep your hair out of the way while you wash your face before bed. And worst of all, she is wafting everyone's favorite overly floral Clinique Happy. I really thought I had smelled the last of that in middle school. Clearly, I was wrong.

"Hello, and what can I help you with today," she says almost on a sneer. I don't know what this lady's problem is with me, but if I had to guess, she probably isn't a big fan of my workout gear as clothing, or maybe it's the bird's nest on top of my head. The thought also crosses my mind that I have some remnants of last night's Cheetos marring my skin somewhere, but I quickly decide I don't care if I do.

"I need to make a withdrawal. And a cash advance," I state my business, hoping there isn't going to be a lot of questions or hoops for me to jump through.

"Hmmm, a cash advance, I assume you have a line of credit with us to be able to do that."

I nod.

"You are aware that cash advances aren't recommended, yes? The interest rate is quite high," she says it somehow managing to look down her nose at me even though we are relatively the same height.

"I'm aware, I'd like to take out the maximum, please." I'm

not engaging in more back and forth with people, I have enough drama on my own to deal with.

"Fill this out, please." She slides me a couple of slips, one for the cash advance and one for my withdrawal.

Thankfully, from then on, we don't seem to have any more problems, just silent judgment.

"Alright, two thousand five hundred dollars," she says as she starts counting out the twenty one-hundred-dollar bills, four twenties, and one ten.

"You have a nice day," I tell her, my voice filled with sarcasm.

As I'm leaving the bank, I can't help but feel accomplished and defeated at the same time. On the one hand, I almost have all the money that I am going to need to pay Will, on the other hand, rent is going to start becoming an issue and my emergency credit card is super close to being maxed out. The more I think about rent being an issue and I have to face the reality that I might not be able to afford my apartment for much longer, the more panicked I can feel myself getting. I don't know why I never thought about it before, but I'm pretty sure I am about to be responsible for one hundred percent of the rent now that Clara isn't there.

I'm going to need a roommate. I can't get a roommate, it's Clara's room. A job seems like the more likely solution, but I don't have the time to even consider what that is going to look like, and right now, in this moment my life is full of a lot more important things than pounding the pavement looking for a job.

～

AFTER THE BANK, it's time to head over to the bookstore that Clara and I have been to a million times to buy our books from. The place with the cheapest books and the best resale value.

No surprise that it's not the bookstore on campus. I'm fully aware I am going to have the same experience that basically every college student has; spending hundreds of dollars on textbooks only to be given a buyback number that if you are lucky, barely even hits twenty percent of the original price. Since I'm on scholarship, I'm not paying for my own books, but still, the whole textbook thing is a racket.

Lifting the stack of books out of my car takes more effort than I was ready for, and I sway backward before I have a chance to get my balance back. It takes a few minutes to make it to the back of the store and the buyback counter, but by that time, I'm crossing my fingers that this is going to come as close to five hundred dollars as possible. The closer I get to five hundred, the more likely Will is going to agree to give me more time to figure out the rest while he gets to work.

"Withdrawing?" the customer service guy asks while he scans each one of my books.

"I'm sorry?"

"You withdrawing?" he asks again.

"Uh, no, just um, cash poor." I shrug my shoulders.

"Ah yeah, bummer, I know the feeling."

Then it hits me. "You get a lot of withdrawals?"

"Yeah, normally about a month after semester starts, and then again right before finals. People either realize they hate college, or withdraw before they fail a class," he explains. "Basically everyone who withdraws comes through here, the last stop being movin' on. Trying to get every last penny back before movin' on to what's next." He pops his gum and then reaches over to the printer and hands me a sheet of paper.

The paper has every book listed, followed by how much it's worth and how much the condition of my books is going to net me.

"If you are okay with all the prices, just sign at the bottom and then I'll cash you out," he explains.

I look at the bottom total: $232.74. Not even close to what I was hoping for, but at this point, I'll take it. I scribble my signature as quickly as possible and then slide it over the counter.

"Are you the only one who works the buyback counter?" I ask, hoping he stays forthcoming. If almost every withdrawing student comes through here, maybe Clara did too. If she did, as much as it would hurt that she up and left without telling me, at least it would mean she was probably okay wherever she is.

"Yep, just me. Well, me and the manager. I'm the only full-timer and he's not exactly trusting when it comes to large sums of cash."

"Of course." I laugh a little. "A friend of mine was going to return some books a few days ago, you might have run into her, her name's Clara."

"Clara? Huh, let me think. There was a girl who came in earlier this week, but I'm terrible with names, not sure if it was your friend," he says and he starts ringing everything up in the computer.

"Are you good with faces, 'cause I'm sure I have a picture in my phone," I say with a smile.

"I never forget a face." His flirty smile tells me this is going to be a lot easier than I thought it was going to be.

"Oh yeah?" A little harmless flirting never hurt anybody. It only takes a second to grab my phone out of my back pocket before opening the Photos app. A few simple swipes later and I'm staring at a picture of Clara and me. It's a selfie we took in our living room on the couch. Right after the breakup with Collin. Clara was on a mission to distract me and we had so many ice cream sundae movie nights that we each gained five pounds. She has her arms wrapped around my shoulders as I take the picture, and it's a moment in time that I would give anything to go back to.

The ache in my chest gets stronger, and it takes a moment

before I'm ready to show Clara to the guy, but I pull it together and turn the phone toward him. "This is her," I tell him.

"Well, I certainly recognize one of these faces," he says with a wink. "But I don't recognize the other girl. Haven't seen her in here before, or at least not any time recently."

My heart sinks. I want so bad at this point for her to just have ghosted me. I take a deep breath and try to act as normal as I can. "That's alright, I figured I would ask."

"Well, here's your cash back, you have forty-eight hours to change your mind and buy back the books at the same price you got cash back for, if not, price goes back up to list. Make sure you have your receipt or the owner won't let us honor the policy, even if I do recognize your face." He gives me a friendly smile, that thankfully isn't creepy. I don't have it in me to deal with creepy right now.

"Thanks a lot."

Well, I guess it's a good thing I now have most of the money I need to pay for Will's services, I'm even more convinced that Clara didn't take off on her own now.

BACK AT ANDERSON AND ASSOCIATES, even though there are no *associates*, I get ready to make my case to Will. A quick glance around the parking lot and I see the same truck in the parking lot that was there the last time I came to pay him a visit. It's light outside this time though so I can make it out better. Of course he drives a truck, and basically the most common one on the road, a Ford F-150. He seems like the kind of guy who would prefer a truck. It's something that probably suits him in town as well as out in the country, and I'm sure it fits in in most neighborhoods.

I don't know a lot about being a private investigator but I'm assuming he probably needs a vehicle he can sit in for long periods and be comfortable while also not alerting neighbors that some random guy is outside watching.

I look a little closer at it when I get out of the car. I realize then that it's one of the nicer models of F-150, not that I really know the difference, but I can tell that this one looks like it has all the bells and whistles. The thing I find the most amusing, though, is that the truck is pristine. It's probably the nicest looking trust I've seen outside of a car dealership. I bet he washes and waxes the truck on the weekends. And when I peer inside the window, I can tell there isn't one speck of trash inside and the leather on the interior is gleaming. I bet it smells like new car too.

When I was in his office, it was anything but pristine. There were papers scattered all over the place, his computer looked like it had seen better days, and he had stacks of boxes piled up in corners all over the place. I can't really reconcile a guy who keeps his office looking like an episode of hoarders and a guy who clearly spends way more time than is necessary taking care of his truck. Oh god, I hope he's not one of those guys that is obsessed with his truck.

"You're back." I hear called out to me as I have my face pressed against the window. I can feel my cheeks start to heat up and I know when I turn around to look at him, there is no way I am going to be able to hide the blush from him. I don't even bother trying.

"Yep, I'm back." I spin to face him straight on. He looks the same as the last time. Same boots, same dark-fade jeans, even the same black compression workout T-shirt. I wonder if he's cold. I would be freezing if I was outside in a T-shirt right now.

"You pull the money together that quick?" he says with an air of surprise in his tone.

"Yeah, about that..." I start.

"Hmph, yeah, that's what I thought." He turns around and walks back into his office.

"Hey, wait," I call after him, rushing to follow him. I'm just about to start explaining everything when I trip over one of the boxes right by the front door. "Fuck!" I mutter as I lurch forward, knowing full well I'm about to become good friends with the floor.

Before I have a chance to fall on my face, I see black boots enter my vision and feel hands wrap around my arms, stopping my descent. My eyes travel from his sleek black leather boots up to his face.

I didn't get a good look at him last time, or at least not up close like this. He has light-brown eyes, like a smooth caramel color. He shaved since last time and given that he smells like leather and not cigar smoke, he's clearly changed since then too. He must just have a standard uniform, or severely limited wardrobe options.

"Thanks," I whisper, still looking up at him.

It takes a few seconds before he lets go of my arms, like he was making sure I was steady on my feet before he released me.

"You should really pay more attention," he scolds.

"Seriously? Have you looked around this place? It will be a miracle if all your clients don't start a visit with a trip to the ER," I snap back. Crap, I'm supposed to be sweetening him up, not pissing him off. I rib him a little with my elbow so hopefully he will think I'm just teasing.

"What can I say, organizing isn't my strong suit." He moves toward his desk. "So if you don't have the money, what brings you here today?"

"I have most of the money."

He scoffs as soon as the words leave my mouth.

"I'm serious. Two thousand seven hundred and thirty-four dollars. And some change if you are interested."

His eyebrow raises, and he gets an amused expression on his face.

"I was hoping maybe we could make an arrangement or something."

"The only arrangement I'm interested in is cash. Cold hard cash," he tells me as he crosses one leg over the other and leans back against the front of his desk.

"I know. I know. It's just time sensitive, you know? I can sell some other stuff, and get you the money as soon as I can, I just thought maybe if I gave you most of it, you would be willing to start work a little early."

Will stands up and looks me over. "You sold stuff?"

"Yeah, my textbooks." I try to make it sound like it's no big deal, I need him to agree to this plan, not harp over the details.

"Your textbooks. I thought you were in your senior year, aren't you going to need those?" he asks, an element of concern creeping into his tone.

"This is more important. Besides, you can find a lot of stuff on the internet these days, so I can probably do without them. It's fine. Anyway, I was hoping we could figure something out in the meantime. I was going over everything last night and I think I found something, but I need help with it." I can tell I sound like I'm rambling.

"Why don't you sit down and tell me what you found out and then we can figure out the whole money thing in a minute?" He moves to sit in one of the chairs in front of his desk, and after a couple of passing seconds, I take the chair next to him.

It only takes a few minutes to explain about the email and hand him the copy that I was carrying in my messenger bag. Then I tell him all about how Clara was obsessive about the cloud but how she hadn't signed into the university cloud in months.

"So, what do you think? The cloud's important, right? It has to be." If he thinks the cloud is important, then we might finally have an avenue of investigation to go down.

"It might not be, but yeah, it's something I would want to check out, especially if she is as obsessive as she is about saving to it." There's a pause before he continues. "Have you been to class this week?" he asks.

"What does that have to do with anything?"

"Answer the question."

"It's not important to me right now, *this* is what is important. Will you help? I know I don't have the full amount right now, but I thought maybe you could start looking into the cloud thing and I could take that time to come up with the extra money. I have no idea how to even start with finding out where she stores her information, so I figured you might be able to—"

"Hey," he interrupts. "Slow down. School is important, you've gotten this far, do you really think that Clara would want you just to throw everything away?"

I get to my feet in two seconds flat. "Of course she would! She would do the same thing for me! What, you want me just to sit in class and talk about Macbeth and pretend I don't go home to an empty apartment every night? Well, that's not going to happen. So either you help me, or I do it on my own, but either way, class is the last thing on my mind." I run out of steam toward the end and slowly collapse back into the chair and hang my head. Some of the strands from my hair have come out from my messy bun and are now hanging in front of my eyes. Slowly I lift my head back up and look over at Will. "I'm sorry, I just—"

"I know. It's okay." Will reaches over to me and slowly moves the hair out of my face and tucks it behind my ear. "I get it."

I release the breath I didn't know I was holding.

"Do you think we can figure something out about the money? Maybe I could help out around here until then." I gesture around the office. "I swear I'm really good at organizing, and I could really help out with getting everything organized around here. And then I could even be around if you had any questions about Clara. You never know what might end up being helpful, right?" I can't keep the hope out of my voice.

Will just sits there in his chair, looking at me. Like he's trying to size me up and make a decision about what he's going to do.

Finally, he nods at me. "I know someone who can help with the cloud thing. I'm okay at the tech thing but nowhere near an expert. I can make a call."

My heart skips a beat in my chest. "Is that a yes? That's a yes, right?"

"We'll see how it goes. But yeah, it's a yes."

I can't contain the excitement coursing through me in that moment, I dart forward and wrap my arms around Will even though the arm of my chair is pushing painfully into my stomach. The discomfort is totally worth it. Will, ever so awkwardly, pats my arms a few times.

"Thank you. Thank you so much. You will never know how much this means to me," I murmur in his ear and I keep hugging him.

When I finally release him, he looks me dead in the eye and with a haunted look on his face says, "Yes, I do, I know exactly how much it means."

CHAPTER THIRTEEN

"THE DISTRICT SLEEPS ALONE TONIGHT" BY POSTAL SERVICE

*K*nock knock knock knock

I startled awake, not having realized that I had actually fallen asleep on the couch. My fingers went to wipe my eyes to clear away the sleep fog that had me feeling dazed and confused. Clearly, I had fallen into a deep sleep because my eyes were so full of sleep that they felt plastered shut. My legs were propped up on the armrest of the sofa. Great, I fell asleep on the couch again. More abuse and cricks my body didn't need. I'm going to be just a ball of sore muscles if this continues much longer.

Knock knock knock knock

This time, I recognize what is happening. Four rapid knocks delivered one right after the other. Looking over to the cable box under the television, I see that it is after midnight. Who the hell is at my apartment after midnight? Even Collin never showed up this late when we were together, and Clara never had guests over this late.

"Clara," I whispered.

My body filled with excitement, maybe it's her! Reality set in after I got off the couch, but before I made it to the door. It wouldn't be Clara, she would be yelling at me through the door, telling me to open up already. Nervous apprehension fills my body as I start to approach the door. I know I am looking at the door like it is a monster that is going to jump out at me at any second.

I take a deep breath to steel myself before finally calling out, "Who is it?"

One word follows. "King."

King? I racked my brain. Do I know a King? No, I don't think so. I've met and talked to so many people in the past week but I couldn't remember a single one of them introducing themselves as King.

"Do you know what time it is?" I call out, still not comfortable opening the door.

"William sent me," the voice replies.

William.

Oh. Will.

Will sent someone?

It takes only a second for me to unlock the door and swing it open. I don't know what I am expecting to find on the other side, but whatever I'm expecting is not what I find.

She is tiny, like one of those elfin pixies described in fantasy novels. She looks like she is maybe five foot two, and if she is more than a hundred pounds soaking wet, I would be shocked. The most striking thing about her, though, is her hair. Bright blue. Like neon blue. I didn't know you could get hair that neon color. I've seen tons of girls on campus with blue hair, it's one of our university colors, so of course people dye their hair blue, but not this. I am pretty sure that if I dig up a black light, her hair would glow under it.

Despite it being the middle of winter, and I'm sure cold as shit outside in the middle of the night, she is dressed in a black miniskirt and a pair of tights with some sort of skull design all over them. I have no idea how her legs haven't turned into icicles by now. At least she is wearing a long-sleeve shirt, but it isn't heavyweight, just one of those long-sleeve red plaid shirts that you see in pictures from the '90s. Where in the world would Will even meet someone like this?

"Will sent you?" Skepticism filled my voice.

"Yeah. You going to let me in?" She kind of shoos me out of the way, I have no idea why I move, but I do, and she moves through the door and into the apartment without a single step of hesitation.

"Uh, can I help you with something?" I don't know if I am still just too tired to function or what, but this tiny little pixie woman is commandeering my apartment without so much as a fight from me.

"You got any grape soda?" Her voice isn't soft and tiny like she is, it's more firm and matter of fact. I'm just standing by the door watching as she sets a bag on the couch in the living room and pulls out a laptop before moving over to where the television is located.

"Grape soda?"

"Yeah."

"Nope, sorry, don't keep any grape soda in the house."

She shrugs, and then completely ignores my presence as she starts pulling my router out and inspecting it.

"So, you're the computer expert?" I ask slowly, still watching her as she pulls her laptop toward her and sits cross-legged on the floor before resting her laptop on her knees.

"You could call me that."

"Ooookay."

I slowly creep into my living room, like I'm trying not to spook the girl, who's now furiously typing on her laptop. I move to sit on the couch.

It takes a while before it dawns on me that this is my house. I'm actually paying Will, so doesn't that, by proxy, mean that she's like a subcontractor? I should be able to ask some questions, right?

"So, can you tell me what exactly you are doing?" I finally find my voice and ask.

"What you asked." Her voice betrays no emotion, just the same tone throughout, short and sweet, no room to argue.

"What I asked?"

A heavy sigh escapes her, and I finally hear some kind of emotion coming from her, annoyance. "The cloud."

"Okay." That makes sense, of course, man, I must still be exhausted. "So you can do that with the router?"

"Yeah." She goes back to ignoring me.

"How?" I ask, still prodding for more information.

"History."

Oh my god, does this girl not know how to have a conversation? Or at least talk in full and complete sentences?

"Like web history?"

Her nod is almost indistinguishable.

"I didn't know you could pull web history from a router."

She turns her head slowly and looks at me like I have two heads. "Seriously?"

"Yeah," I say slowly.

She raises her eyebrows and mouths *wow*.

"I thought you needed someone's computer to look at the history," I explain to her, trying to sound like I'm not a moron, which clearly, she thinks I am.

"Nope." She pops the *p* at the end.

I let my body kind of fall to the side slowly so I can try and see what is happening on the laptop screen. I can't tell much about what is going on, I especially can't read what is on the screen, but what I can tell is that she is scrolling through what looks like a list of something. This goes on for a few minutes, but every once in a while, she highlights something before moving down the list again.

The silence is really starting to get to me. It's the middle of the night, some random girl is sitting on my living room floor, and answers might be right around the corner. I start wringing my hands together to try and avoid bothering her, she really doesn't seem to enjoy my questions.

"I'm Kenzie, by the way," hoping she will give me a little more information than she had.

"I know."

"And you are?"

"King."

"King? Your name is King?" For whatever reason, I have my doubts that her parents named her King.

Another deep sigh and then finally, "Blake King, my name is Blake King."

"And you do computer forensics?" The pitch of my voice gets higher and squeakier at the end, like I'm nervous or something.

She scoffs. "*This* is not computer forensics. Joe Blow from Geek Squad could figure this out."

"Oh." Well, now I feel like a moron. I was so proud of myself earlier, telling Will all about how I managed to get into her email account, and now suddenly I'm back to being a computer moron who has no idea how any of this works.

Finally, after a few more minutes, Blake sits back, rests her back against the couch and looks up.

"Well, that's not creepy at all." That's when I realize this is the first time she's really looking at my timeline I built on the wall. She's not wrong, it is kinda creepy, if I was in some stranger's apartment and saw this on the wall, I would find a reason to leave.

"Uh, yeah, sorry, I just, I'm better with, you know, visuals," I scramble, trying to sound reasonable.

Blake sets her laptop on the coffee table in front of the sofa before pushing it toward me. "Recognize this?"

I look at the screen and find the highlighted line on a list of web addresses. It's something called Blue Sky Cloud. She did it. She really did it.

"No, I've never heard of it." I turn to look at her. "This is it, though, right? This is her cloud?" I ask.

She shrugs her shoulders and pulls her laptop back toward her. "Probably."

"So now what?"

"Now you wait."

"Wait?"

"It's gonna take a second for me to open everything up."

"You're going to get into it now?"

The look she gives me once again just reinforces that she thinks I'm a moron.

"Well yeah, that's what you wanted, right?" She's taken to speaking slower, as if it will help me follow what she is saying.

"Yeah. Yes. Of course. Yes."

Blake rolls her eyes at me, but she goes back to work. I'm not even going to pretend that I have any idea what Blake ends up doing. But at least this time I can see the screen on the laptop as she is working.

She keeps moving things around on the screen, flipping between tabs, opening different programs, so fast that I have no idea how she is following any of this. Then after a little while, she stops. I take this opportunity to really study what is on the screen. I recognize it from so many movies and television shows, a black dialogue box on part of the screen with this white text in it. She's really going to break into Clara's cloud, we are actually going to get somewhere.

"How long do you think it will take?" I whisper.

"This program is a beast. But not long." Turning, she looks at me once more and studies my face before saying, "You sure you don't have any grape soda?"

I can't stop the giggle that escapes me. "I'm sure. I have a Diet Coke if you're interested though."

I can't help but laugh at the look on her face, she looks like I just offered her the most disgusting drink on the planet.

"No. Just no." She shudders.

We both wait, patiently staring at the screen of the laptop, waiting for the answers I'm praying it will bring. The silence in the room is stifling, the only sound I can hear coming from the apartment is the sound of my own breathing and the gentle whisper of the heater running.

"Got it," she announces. There was no sound. I don't know why, but I was really expecting that it would make like a ding or something to indicate it was done. But there was nothing. Just silence.

I hold my breath while Blake sits there and does some more work on the laptop, this is the moment. This is what it all comes down to. If there isn't anything in here, I have to figure something else out and I don't know if I have any ideas to work with right now.

The login screen pops up, and she fills in the fields and next thing you know, there it is. A screen full of files. Little blue folders of data. Data that could answer so many questions.

"Looks like there's art," Blake mutters and starts opening up files.

All at once, the breath is stolen right out of my chest and I gasp. Right there in front of my face is Clara. With Collin. She looks like she is out of breath, her mouth slightly open as she stares right at Collin's face. It seems like whoever snapped this photo caught them right in the middle of some kind of intimate moment between the two of them. It's clear based on how close their heads are to each other that they have to be standing only mere inches apart from each other or with no space at all.

My mind races at the possibilities. For a split second, I seriously think that she and Collin were involved with each other.

It certainly looks like they are involved. Anyone looking at this photo would think so. Why would she do that, though? It doesn't make sense. She was so angry when she found out about Collin and Chanel. Was she mad because she was mad for me, like any best friend would be? Or was she mad for another reason? Was she mad because he was cheating on her too? How can this possibly be happening? I'm nothing but frozen as these thoughts run through my mind at breakneck speed.

"It's cropped." Blake's voice breaks me out of my downward spiral.

"What?" I say.

"The picture. It's cropped."

I look at the picture, closer this time. She's right. It is cropped. Now that I look at it, it's not the standard size of a photo, the dimensions are wrong. It's too wide and too short for it to be a standard photo.

"There's no background," Blake continues. "They cropped out the body position and the background."

She's right. I can tell they are outside because I can see the blue sky above them, but that's it. I can't even tell the time of year it is because there is nothing other than a small amount of sky showing. No trees, no buildings, no leaves on the ground, no ground at all.

"That's weird," I murmur and Blake nods.

She opens a few more files and they are all pictures of the same event. At first, I thought it was the same exact photo but then I realize it's not.

"It's rapid fire," I say to Blake. "All taken one right after the other."

"The crops are different too, like they are moving so the crop has to be changed." Blake starts humming to herself then pulling up some other information and screens I don't get.

"What are you doing?"

"Metadata," she replies.

"Metadata." Blake nods, never missing a step. "Like location and stuff?"

"Should be. There isn't. Someone removed the metadata."

"You can do that?"

"You can do anything if you know what you're doing," she explains.

"Cause that's not scary," I retort.

She snorts but keeps going.

"That it is. Everything is data these days, it's freaky to know a few keystrokes can change the trajectory of your life."

"Don't worry, I only use my powers for good. Not evil." She actually winks at me when she says it. Well, at least the girl has some kind of sense of humor. Suddenly she stops typing, and I can see the lines around her eyes crinkle. "That's odd," she mutters almost so softly I didn't hear it.

"What's odd?"

"I can't open this folder."

"What do you mean?"

"I can't open this folder."

"Yeah, that explains everything."

She sighs. "Okay fine. I can open it. But it's encrypted, so it's basically unusable. I'm running my normal decryption programs but—"

"But what?"

"Who is this girl?"

"What do you mean?"

"Why would she have encrypted files?"

"I don't know. She's missing. I'm looking for clues, so I'm basically the definition of clueless."

"Okay, but who is she?"

"What. Do. You. Mean."

"Like is she a girl who found an encryption program on the internet and ran it with no effort, or is it something else?"

"Oh. Yeah, she's like a math and computer übernerd. She works on machine learning or something like that. And some kind of math that makes no sense to me." I shrug my shoulders. "She's tried to explain it, but I don't get it."

The more I talk, the more Blake's shoulders sink down.

"So she could have encrypted this herself?" she asks.

"I'm not really sure I know what encrypting is, but yeah, probably."

"There is no way I can open this tonight."

"Wait, what?"

"This is custom work. She locked this up tight. My standard programs won't work. They are designed for the weekend warrior computer guy, not someone who can write encryption on their own. Will didn't say anything about this," she starts, shaking her head.

"I don't think Will really knew. I told him we were in college, but we didn't really get into likes and interests. I'm just trying to find her. It's hard to know what's important," I try explaining because honestly, it's the truth. It's so hard to figure out what is important and what isn't. It would take me weeks to tell someone everything there is to know about Clara's and my life over the last four years. How do you boil it down to what's *important*? What has been going on for a long time, and something Clara said to me in passing like a month ago, is important? How am I supposed to remember this?

"This is going to take work."

"I'm sorry." I start to freak out that maybe she isn't going to want to keep going or maybe she is going to want more money because this isn't an easy case or something. "Do you need something more from me, because whatever you need, I'll get it."

"I like a challenge." She smiles at me as she starts packing everything back up in her bag and getting ready to leave.

"So that's it."

"Yep. This is not plug and play," she tells me. "But at least now you have some stuff you can add to your creepy wall." She gestures over to my timeline.

"I've been calling it my Wall of Crazy." I laugh.

"That works." She looks around the room one last time. "You start adding to the Crazy and I'll get to work on opening these files."

"Do you think it will take long?" I ask, knowing time is of the essence.

"Depends. If she is really trying to keep people out, then yes, if not, then it will go a lot faster." She starts walking through the living room and to the front door, I follow close behind.

Right before she opens the front door, she turns to me, I'm sure she is going to say something well-meaning just like everyone else, or maybe something awkward because no one knows what to say to me anymore to make me feel better, but instead she says, "Next time, have grape soda."

Stunned would be an understatement. But not stunned enough not to agree.

CHAPTER FOURTEEN

"DON'T FORGET ME" BY WAY OUT WEST

Kenzie: We need to talk
            Collin: I already hooked u & my dad up wut
else do u want
Kenzie: It's about Clara, it's important
Collin: So talk
Kenzie: In person
Collin: Come on u know I can't
Kenzie: I found some information and you're in it
Collin: Wut r u talking about
Kenzie: You know I'm looking into Clara being missing. So imagine my surprise when I find a stash of photos and you're all over them
Collin: Ur full of it
Kenzie: Okay, I'll just turn this stuff over to your dad then.
Collin: wait
Kenzie: You'll meet me?
Collin: Just tell me wut u want
Kenzie: To meet in person. ASAP.
Kenzie: I'm not fucking around, Collin, I only care about

Clara, and if you end up collateral damage, well, let's just say I can live with that.

Collin: Fine deets?

Kenzie: Coffee shop by my apartment 30 minutes

Collin: no way

Collin: someone might see us

Kenzie: OMFG Collin, pick a place and I'll be there

Collin: the track

Kenzie: It's raining

Collin: even better no one will be out

Kenzie: Fine. Half hour or I send this stuff to your dad.

Collin: u wasn't this bitchy when we were 2gether

Kenzie: Don't push me.

I THROW the phone onto the coffee table. I have a few minutes to kill before I need to leave for the track. He's right, no one is going to be out there in the rain, the school has an indoor track that works just as well and you wouldn't have to get wet or freeze your ass off.

Staring at my wall, I think about all the things that I have been running through my head. Mostly about the pictures. The more I think about it, the more confused I get. Someone had to take them. It certainly wasn't Clara or Collin. And there is no way either one of them would have arranged for them to be taken. Clara would never do anything to hurt me, of that I am sure. And Collin has way too much to lose with his crazy girlfriend, pictures of him and Clara together like that would only cause problems for him. And if the pictures were from before Chanel and Collin were together then there would be no reason there either.

Like with everything, as soon as I get some answers, I also get a million more questions. The difference is this time someone else might have some answers. Blake had emailed me the photos after she left, although how she got my email, I have no idea, and frankly, that is not a question I want answered. I printed them out for dramatic reveal purposes, and to see how Collin reacts to them when I show him.

Up until now, Clara has been the only one who possibly has the answers I am looking for, well maybe the uncle guy too, but basically everyone who has answers is out of reach. But now I finally have someone I can confront. And if I get to freak out my douchebag of a cheating ex in the process, well, all the better.

THE RAIN HITS my windshield as I wait in the parking lot by the track. It's actually not raining too hard, more like a light drizzle, but with the cold, there is no way I am going to stand outside in the parking lot waiting for my ex to show. And of course he hasn't yet.

Looking down at my phone, I see that Collin is already five minutes late. Not surprising. Jerk was always late, even when we were together. Nice to see some things don't change.

The windows are starting to fog over from the heater running in my car and the cold air up against the glass. So, of course, it's no surprise when the sudden knocking on my passenger side window has me about jumping out of my skin.

Not really being able to see out the window, I roll it down instead.

"It's cold. Can we do this in here?" Collin asks as he sticks his head in my car.

A quick touch of a button and my car doors unlock. A few short seconds later, Collin is sitting in my car blowing into his hands, trying to warm up.

"So what's so important?" he asks in between blowing on his hands.

"I told you, I found some stuff about Clara going missing and you're all over it."

Collin spins in the seat and looks at me. Hard. "You can't seriously think I had anything to do with Clara going missing?" he demands.

I just raise an eyebrow. Of course, I don't think he had anything to do with it, but I want to see how he reacts if I keep poking the bear.

"Oh, come on, Kenz, why would I ever have anything to do with Clara going missing? I mean really, think about it. Besides, I'm always around people these days, how exactly was I supposed to pull it off?" he demands.

I let him squirm a little bit longer before finally letting him off the hook. "No, I don't think you had anything to do with her going missing. But I do think you know more than you think you do, and I need answers. Real answers. Not some bullshit you are going to try and sell me on."

"Ugh, fine. What did you find?"

"Pictures. Of you and Clara. Together. Very close together." Technically, I'm not lying, but he doesn't need to know that yet.

"WHAT?"

I just stare at him dead in the eyes, no emotion, no nothing.

"Kenz, I swear, that never happened. Look, I know it's hard to believe me, I know I fucked up, I get it. But honestly, I have never been up close with Clara. Seriously, you have to believe me."

"I have the pictures, Collin." This is getting fun.

"You can't, I'm serious, it never happened. There is no way." His neck starts to flush red and I can tell by the pulsing in his neck his heartbeat is skyrocketing. Man, he is squirming, and honestly, it's kind of believable. "Seriously, let me see the pictures because they have to be fake. They have to be."

After letting him squirm for a few more seconds, I finally

reach into my car door and pull out the photos I printed a few hours ago and hand them over.

I see the shift in Collin almost immediately. As soon as they are in his hands he deflates, "Oh," he murmurs and starts flipping through the stack. "Wait, what is this?"

"Pictures of you and Clara." Sarcasm lacing my voice.

"Yeah, I get that, but how in the hell did you get these? Someone was taking pictures of this?"

"Like I said, I've been looking into her disappearance and we found these."

"Yeah but why? Why would anyone take pictures of this?"

"I don't even know what *this* is."

"It was here."

"What do you mean here?"

"It was after we broke up, like right after we broke up. You weren't answering my texts or responding to my emails, and I tried talking to our friends, but no one would talk to me about you."

"Gee, I wonder why," I say, eyebrow raised.

"Yeah, I know. I'm a shitbag. Got it. But seriously, I was trying to get someone to talk to me, tell me how you were doing, so I decided my best shot was Clara." He exhales heavily. "You know, sometimes we used to run together, when I would stay overnight at the apartment." He shrugs before continuing to flip through the pictures some more. "We would come out to the track since it's right by your place and we would run together. We never really talked or anything, but you know Clara, she had a routine, she did it every morning, so sometimes I just went with her. It wasn't a big deal."

"So this is that, you guys running together?"

"Well, no. Obviously after things ended with me and you, we didn't run together anymore. Hell, she used to throw power bars at me whenever I showed up anywhere she was. Same flavor every time, that shitty caramel she knows I hate."

The imagery is perfect, and I can totally see Clara throwing food at him. "Yeah, that sounds right."

"Yeah, well, one morning she wasn't paying attention, and I saw her out on the track running. It was later than she normally was out so I wasn't expecting to see her, so I decided to take a chance. I waited for her over there by the benches." He points over to where the benches are that people use to store their stuff while they run. "I figured she would run past and yell at me or something, but it's like she didn't even see me. She was almost right on top of me when I said her name. She basically tripped over her own two feet. Reminded me of you for a split second, always falling over your own feet." The look of nostalgia on his face makes my chest ache. I really did used to love him.

"Then what?"

"I caught her, just like I used to catch you." He brings the photos up closer to his face and then reaches up to turn on the overhead light. "Yeah, this is that day, I'm sure of it."

"How?"

"I remember the little purple mark she had on her jawline. You can barely see it here, but in person, I was like an inch from her face, I noticed." He shrugs again.

I reach over and snatch the photo out of his hands.

He's right.

There is a small little purple mark on the side of her jaw.

Super easy to miss if you aren't looking for it.

Is it a bruise? How did she get a bruise? I would have noticed a bruise on her face, wouldn't I? What kind of person lives with another person and doesn't notice a bruise on their *face*?

"Then what happened?" I demand.

"That's it. I caught her. End of story." The confused look on his face tells me he isn't trying to be a pain in the ass.

"You just caught her and walked off?" Skepticism runs deep in my voice.

"Well, no. I asked if she was okay, I think. She didn't really say much. I remember it was weird, at this point she had made throwing food at me a life goal, so her not yelling at me was unexpected."

"And then what?"

"I dunno, I asked her about you?"

"About me?"

"Yeah." His face flushes again, and he looks out the window.

"What about me?"

"Geez, why does it matter? Can you just let it go, Kenz?"

"No. I can't. She's missing, Collin. Missing. As in, God only knows what is happening to her right now. I have no idea what is important and no idea what isn't. So no. I can't let it go." My voice starts to resemble a shrieking harpy and Collin's eyes have gotten exponentially bigger.

"Okay, okay. I asked how you were. I asked if you were okay. I dunno, I just wanted to know how you were doing with every-thing, you know?"

"Oh, then you cared," I retort.

"I always cared, Kenz. I just, I dunno, made bad choices?"

"Are you asking me?"

"No. No. Of course not. I just, god, I dunno." He throws his hands up in defeat. "She wouldn't tell me anything anyway, she just told me to get lost. I went to leave, she sat on the benches for a while, and then I left and I don't know what happened."

"That's it?"

"Yeah, that's it."

"Okay." As much as it pains me to say so, I follow it with, "Thanks, Collin."

"No problem." He's got his hand wrapped around the door handle before he turns back and says, "You can tell my dad, you know, maybe it's important?"

"I will."

"For what it's worth, I hope you figure it out. I hope you find her." He pauses and sighs. "I still miss you guys, we have a lot of good memories hanging out."

"Yeah. We did."

"See you around, Kenz."

And with that, Collin once more walks out of my life.

I SIT in my car for a while after that. Not really ready to go back to the apartment, but also not really having anywhere to go yet. I should probably tell Will about everything, give him more to work with. Collin's story makes sense to me. And Clara never mentioning it makes sense too. She never wanted to bring up Collin unless she absolutely had to. She was fierce when it came to protecting me and my feelings, especially back then, when everything was still so fresh.

The bruise is really what's bothering me. I can't believe I wouldn't have noticed it. It's like running a movie in reverse, trying to find the moment where I wasn't paying attention to my best friend, to my only family. I have to be honest with myself, if this was right after everything with Collin, would I have noticed? At the very least, it certainly would have been a lot easier for Clara to hide it.

And if she was hiding it, why would she be hiding it? If she had just fallen or something, there would be no reason to. We would have had a good laugh about how she was starting to take after me with my level of klutzy. But if she got it from a person, it wouldn't have been a laugh. I would have raised hell about it. Maybe that's why she hid it.

Finally, I give in and decide it's time to call Will and tell him everything.

It takes a couple of seconds, but before long, I hear Will's steady voice piping through my car speakers. "Will Anderson."

"Hey, it's Kenzie."

"I hear you met King."

"Yeah. Thanks for the heads-up."

"It's best if people go in cold when it comes to meeting King."

"Better for you maybe, so you can have a good laugh at everyone else's expense."

He chuckles in response. "Touché."

"I take it she filled you in on everything."

"Yep, complete with illustrations."

"You've seen the pictures, then?"

"Yep. Pretty sure I recognized the little snot-nosed kid too. Kid's got a carbon copy of Fitz's eyes."

"Yep, that's Collin."

"Your ex, right?"

"Yeah."

"Hmmm, well, that's interesting." He pauses. "You already talked to him, didn't you?"

"Of course I did."

"Couldn't have waited for me? Would have been nice to get a read on him."

"Sorry, I honestly didn't even think about it."

"Amateur," he says it like a joke though so I'm not offended.

I take this opportunity to run him through everything that had happened in the last hour, and everything Collin said. When I was done, there was just silence on the other end.

"Will?"

"Clara have a boyfriend?"

"Uh, no. No one. Not in the four years I've known her, and she didn't have any boyfriends in high school either," I explain.

"I would have remembered reading something about a boyfriend in the paperwork," he says kind of distractedly.

"You got the reports?" I ask.

"I've had the reports. There's nothing useful in any of them, but I have them."

"Oh." I was really hoping there was something in them that the cops hadn't told me.

"So far, you're the only one who has come up with anything to go off of."

And suddenly I feel a lot better. Will, the professional, thinks I'm coming up with better information than the cops did. I can put the feather in my cap and keep trucking along.

"So you believe him?" Will asks.

"Yeah."

"No doubts. None? Not even a little. No little niggle in the back of your brain telling you to keep pushing him?"

I think about it for a second. "Honestly, no. I wouldn't say I trust Collin, but there is no way anything was going on with him and Clara, no matter what those photos were trying to show. Absolutely no way. There is absolutely no way that the first guy Clara decided to get involved with in college would be my ex."

"Had to be asked."

"I know."

"So, what now?"

"You aren't going to like this, but we wait. We wait for King."

"You're right, I'm not going to like that."

"Encrypted files are a good sign. People don't encrypt things without a reason. There is going to be information in those files. Once we have it, we'll have a better idea of what comes next."

"Alright."

"You should get some rest. Take care of yourself. There's a good chance this is going to be a marathon and not a sprint."

I exhale hard. "I know. I'm going to walk around here for a bit, see if anything jogs a memory or something," I tell Will.

"Alright, let me know if you find anything."

"You too."

After I hang up, I shove my phone back into my pocket and brace myself for the cold morning and drizzle that's still falling.

I've always liked watching my breath leave my body as I exhale when it's cold outside. Such a cool phenomenon. I wish you could blow it into shapes like you can with smoke.

If I hadn't been distracted thinking about my breath, I would have noticed when I got closer to the benches that there were flyers taped on them. The rain had already started to do a number on them, with the ink becoming harder to read, and paper starting to tear off around where it was taped to the bench.

A quick look around and I see a girl over toward the athletic building not far off from the track. From the short distance, I can tell she's the one handing out the flyers. A quick glance at the quickly disintegrating flyer shows me that there is a picture of a person on it. Figuring I have nothing to lose, I head over to check it out.

As I get closer to the building, I can hear her as she shoves flyers at the people trying to walk past her into the gym.

"Have you seen her?"

Wait. What?

My steps quicken as I eat up the ground between me and her. As soon as I am within arm's reach, she's shoving a flyer at me and repeating herself, "Have you seen her?"

My hands are shaking as I take the flyer and look down at it. Right on top, it reads *"Have you seen me?"* and underneath is a picture of a girl who is easily my age. Underneath the photo are the words, *"Missing since Thursday"* and a number to call.

Clara isn't the only one missing.

CHAPTER FIFTEEN

"DON'T FORGET ME" BY WAY OUT WEST

"Your friend is missing?" I ask the girl passing out flyers.

"Have you seen her?" Looking at her is painful, she reminds me of me. She looks so worried, but at the same time, determined. For a brief second, I wonder if I should be passing out flyers of Clara, but then I remember that as far as everyone else is concerned, Clara took off and dropped out of school.

"I'm sorry, I don't think so." I stare down at the picture on the flyer just to double-check. She's pretty though. I find myself looking for similarities between her and Clara. Outside of the same almond-shaped eyes, they don't much look alike.

"Oh, well thanks for looking." She moves to keep passing out her flyers.

"My friend is missing too. Since Monday," I rush to tell her.

She stops dead in her tracks. After a slow turn, she looks me up and down, like she's trying to size me up. "Really?"

"Really. I reported her missing, but the police don't really think she is missing. I had to hire a PI," I explain.

"Wow. I'm sorry." She shifts her weight. "The police are

looking for Jenny, a bunch of people reported her missing, so at least they are taking it seriously, so far it doesn't seem to have made much of a difference. She's still not here." I can see her eyes filling up with tears.

It breaks my heart, and if she is anything like me, she's feeling pretty lonely and up against the weight of the world. I try and comfort her with a hand on her arm and a reassuring smile, but I'm pretty sure it didn't make much of a difference.

"Would it be okay if I took a few of your flyers? I want to show my PI, two missing girls on campus in a week, makes me nervous."

"Yeah, of course, if you think it will help." She peels off a couple of flyers before handing them over. "I hope you find your friend."

"You too."

NEXT THING I KNOW, I'm flying down the highway, jamming out to my music, on a mission. Two missing women. One week. That can't be normal. Especially on one campus. Will has to know about this. Maybe there are similarities between the two of them, maybe there aren't, but Will will know what to do.

After whipping into the parking spot I am beginning to think of as mine, I do a quick scan and find Will's truck parked in its normal spot as well. Careful not to crunch the flyers, I grab them and head inside.

I'm not even a foot inside the door before I'm already talking. "There's another one, Will."

"Pretty sure I told you to go home and get some rest." I hear Will's voice say, but he's not at his desk like he normally is. Looking toward the direction of his voice, I find Will over on the left side of the office at what apparently is a mini coffee bar.

"You're right, you did. But this is way more important than a couple of hours of restless sleep. There's another girl missing," I explain.

"There's always another girl missing," he says before taking a sip of his black coffee. "How do you know this has anything to do with Clara?"

"I don't, but it feels wrong. She went missing on Thursday. Clara went missing on Monday. Doesn't that seem like a lot of missing girls for only one week?"

Will starts back toward his desk with his coffee, before finally admitting, "Yeah, that's a little something. You're sure about this?"

Thrusting the flyers at him, I explain, "I met her friend this morning, she was passing out flyers. I told you I was going to walk around for a bit and see if I found anything. Well, I found something. Someone just like me, doing anything and everything she can think of to find her friend." I collapse into a chair in front of Will's desk. "I know it's a long shot, but just something in my gut tells me this isn't a coincidence."

I can tell by the look on Will's face that he's gearing up to disappoint me. "Look, Kenzie, you're right, it's strange. But it doesn't mean the two things are connected. Believe me when I tell you that people go missing all the time. Most of the time, one has nothing to do with the other. I'm not saying it's not nefarious, because God knows I have seen my fair share of evil out there, but we don't even have all the details worked out for Clara's disappearance, let alone if there are any similarities between the two of them."

I know he's right, of course he is. Doesn't mean that the reality check was any less hard to hear. I want to see a lead on every corner. I want a clue to appear every time I talk to someone new. Rationally I know clinging to something that I'm not even sure is real yet is both not helpful and just wearing me down.

"Look, I'm not saying you're wrong. But what I am saying is

let me look into it. The flyer clearly lists the police as the point of contact, so I'm assuming they are already looking into this?"

"That's what the friend said. Something about a couple different people reporting her missing. She made it sound like there was an open case," I tell him.

"Alright, I'll call my contacts and get whatever information they have on this girl—"

"Jenny. Her name is Jenny." I need to keep in mind that these are real people and not just people on paper. Real life. Real people. Real consequences.

"Of course. Jenny. I'll get the file." Will looks at me like he is starting to get a little bit worried, but he also seems like the kind of man who isn't going to say anything.

"I know you said go home and rest, but honestly, that's not going to happen, so maybe I could stick around and start working on the office?"

"Suit yourself, but do me a favor, okay?"

I nod in agreement without even hearing it because, frankly, this guy has done nothing but help me out so far.

"Don't try and get everything done in one day, this mess is going to take weeks to figure out, and you really do need rest."

Laughing, I say, "Hasn't anyone ever told you that repeatedly mentioning to a woman how tired she is is not really conducive to long-term survival?"

"True enough." He smiles at me and we both go our separate ways in the office.

THE SWEAT IS BEADING up on my temples, making the hair that has escaped my messy bun stick to my forehead like glue. It's winter. And I'm sweating. If it didn't make me sound crazy, I would ask if we could turn on the air conditioning.

This place is a mess. There is no rhyme or reason for

anything. I've taken over a corner of the office and quickly gave up trying to sit next to a table to start going through things. No, now I'm on the floor. Sorting boxes of paperwork into piles. It seems like his only sorting system for all the paper he has in this place is where the nearest pile is when he sets something down. There are huge date jumps from sheet to sheet, cases that aren't related to each other are sometimes paper clipped together, pages and pages of notes with no kind of identifying information, so I have no idea what these notes are actually about. I've taken to making piles of receipts, client information, copies of documents, and the rest by periods of time.

Will was right. This is going to take forever. And honestly, if this is going to be this much work, I might as well digitize everything so we can get rid of the paper forever.

Swiping the sweat off my brow, I finally give in and ask, "Seriously, Will, how do you work like this? How do you find anything?"

"I don't." He shrugs without looking up.

"Wait, what?"

"I keep the important stuff on the desk until it isn't important anymore, then it goes to a pile. If I end up needing something that made it to a pile, I normally just try and acquire it again."

"You don't even look?"

"Nah, too much effort, got better things to do."

"Then why don't you just throw all this stuff out?" I'm beyond confused, this whole place is basically a hot mess for no reason at all.

"It's work product. You can't throw out work product. What if I have to testify or something? Plus, receipts are in here, and you never know when you are going to get audited. Better keep it to be safe."

"What good is any of this stuff going to do you if you can't find anything?"

"Eventually I was going to get around to hiring someone to work the office." He paused before turning to look over at me on the floor. "I'm sure eventually you will find the ad I was going to place looking for an employee."

"Will, that's ins—"

The door to the office slams open and in stomps the tiny elfin pixie who looks like she's been painted black. Literally. I think she painted her clothes black. You can see swatches of the original color peeking through. Not even going to try and figure out what the point of that is.

"You're going to want to see this. Now." She stomps through the office before rounding the desk and moving all of the stuff Will was working on out of the way before placing her laptop down in front of him.

"I was working on that," Will protests.

"Not anymore," Blake informs him.

"Did you get everything unencrypted?" I ask from behind them.

Blake jumps up at least six inches, I guess she didn't see me on the floor when she barged in. "Goddess, you scared me!" She glares at me accusingly. "And it's decrypted. The word is decryption." She starts muttering under her breath, but I can still make it out. "Unencrypt, who says unencrypt?"

Will barely manages to suppress a chuckle but still looks my way and smirks at me.

"So, did you *decrypt* it, then?" I ask, standing up to see what she brought for us.

"Mostly."

"Mostly? I'm guessing you found something interesting?" I prod.

"Would I be here if I didn't?"

Man, it's like pulling teeth.

A few more keystrokes and she steps away, leaving the screen open for Will and me to look at.

The screen has several documents open on it, placed far enough apart that you can see them all at once. It's clearly some kind of report, but multiple variations of it. There are three in total and it takes a second before I realize what they are. Campus security reports.

I can't stop the gasp from escaping when I realize these are all reports of stalking. I keep reading, only to find out a detailed history from these girls about how someone had been sending them what they thought were harmless messages for weeks. Until they took a turn. Soon it became apparent that someone was following them, messages about how the stalker didn't like what they were doing, and eventually photos of them started to be emailed.

"The photos," I whisper to myself.

"That's what I thought," Blake affirms before moving to sit in front of Will's desk, letting us continue going through everything.

"We should talk to them." Will grabs a Post-it Note off the corner of his desk and starts writing down the girls' names on it.

"Can't." Blake crossed her arms and stares right at us.

"Why not?" I ask, terrified of the answer.

"Look at the other documents," she explains.

I can't bring myself to look, instead I'm frozen just looking at Blake. She has this look of pity in her eyes, like she knows things that are going to break me.

"Jesus," mutters Will. "You sure about all this, King?"

"Positive."

My head bounces back and forth between Will and Blake. "What? Positive about what?"

"Each girl withdrew from school. Blake tried to track them down and couldn't find them," Will explains.

"Maybe they're hiding, they had stalkers. People with

stalkers sometimes hide to get away," I try to bargain with Blake.

"True. But they aren't good at it. Almost no one is good at disappearing, the electronic trail is too much to overcome."

"But maybe—"

"I would have found something. There isn't anything. They were there, and then" —she snaps her fingers— "and then they weren't."

"Will—" The panic closed my throat. Next thing I know, Will has his arms around me and is guiding me to the chair next to Blake.

Crouched down in front of me, his words are clearly trying to give comfort, but his eyes don't believe it. "It might be nothing. We don't know it has anything to do with Clara—"

"Yes. We do," Blake says softly.

Will turns and looks at her. "Lay it out for me."

Blake's eyes dart my direction as if asking if she should in front of me.

Will's warm hand surrounds mine as he takes my hand in his before he nods at Blake.

"Okay." And then Blake turns my world upside down. "Clara wasn't the first. The folder is full of copies of emails from whoever was watching her. They start out like nothing, just annoying flirting type behavior, like from someone who doesn't know how to tell a girl he likes her. She ignored it. As it escalated, Clara started tracking him. Trying to figure out who he was. She did everything I would have done. His tracks were covered. So she started looking in the real world. If I had to guess, she figured a cyber stalker that good didn't just wake up one day and become a cyber stalker, he must have done it before."

"Good thought," Will mutters. His thumb's steady strokes against my thumb is the only reason I'm not hyperventilating at this point.

"She found these reports, which I assume she hacked." Blake looks at me for confirmation.

"Yeah, she could have hacked it, she went to Nullcon last year to try out some new programs and when she came home, she was really excited. She said they performed better than she expected."

"I need to meet this girl," Blake says with a smile. "Anyway, she found four people—"

"There were only three reports," Will interrupts.

"No. I only put three up on the screen," she says with a stern look. "There was a fourth girl, a girl Clara made contact with, they were planning on meeting up, but Clara went missing before that ever happened. I checked campus security this morning. The fourth report isn't there anymore. It's been wiped from the system."

"We need to talk to this girl." My heart rate starts increasing and I look at Will with what I am sure are panicked eyes.

"Kenzie, I don't think that's going to happen," he tells me while wrapping both of my hands in his.

"What do you mean? She was planning on meeting Clara, she has to know something!" My voice is starting to turn into a screech, but Will's eyes never falter from mine. His hands stay steady around mine. A rock against whatever is coming next.

"Because I think Blake is about to tell us that the fourth girl is missing too." He looks over to her for confirmation and out of the corner of my eye, I see her nod. Will squeezes my hands in his and then turns to look at Blake. "The girl, her name is Jenny, isn't it?"

"Yes."

I check out after that. I can hear Blake and Will talking to each other, but it's like my brain won't process the sound. I can still feel Will's hands around mine, but what felt like a warm comfort on my skin a few moments ago now feels like dull numbness.

The reality that this is bigger than I could have ever imagined is just too much for me to take. Four other girls. Four. And Clara knew this whole time. She never said anything. She never told me. I would have helped her. I would have done anything for her, didn't she know that?

THE LIGHTS in the office aren't really enough to combat the darkness that has set in outside. I've made myself a nice little corner in the back of the office on the floor. I printed everything. Nothing escaped my reach. From every mundane email that only said something innocuous like, "I liked your answer in class today" or "did you do well on the pop quiz yesterday" to the escalating "I love you in that purple shirt" and the talk about how Clara always orders peanut butter raspberry smoothies on Tuesdays. I print all of it.

I keep trying to understand why Clara didn't say anything to me, and honestly, after a while, I kind of get it. She would have seen this as a challenge. Something fun to do with her spare time, trying to track down a secret admirer. She probably figured it was someone in her program, an awkward guy with skills to match hers. She was always looking for a challenge and ways to improve her skills. This wouldn't have fazed her at all.

But then I get to the parts where it becomes clear this isn't a guy with a crush. This is a guy with a problem. There are the emails with the photos of her and Collin. I think at this point he must have really been watching her, because his messages start talking about Clara needing to stop or how it might not be Clara who reaps the *consequences*. He never comes right out and says it, but it's clear he's referring to me in the later emails.

At least now I have some kind of answer as to why Clara decided to go at it alone and not involve me. Besides, it's not like I've been in a good place lately, she probably didn't want to stress me out any more than I already was. I wish I could go back in time and tell her how much I wish she would have stressed me out. How it wouldn't have been stress if it meant keeping the two of us safe.

After looking through the emails, it's the last couple that really leads me to believe I know why Clara disappeared. She was getting too close. She reached out to Jenny, made a fake email and everything. The two of them were going to compare notes but didn't want to do it online, Clara clearly thought a guy with these skills was probably watching electronically.

She was probably right.

Clara never made the meeting and a few days later Jenny was gone.

The girls before them also went missing, but none of them were reported missing like Clara and Jenny were. As far as Blake could tell, they all withdrew from school and then no one ever heard from them again. I asked her to get me information about the girls, and honestly, they remind me a lot of Clara and me. No one on paper to report them missing. One girl grew up in foster care and aged out, another girl was raised by her elderly grandmother who died the year before, another had a detailed online history talking about her estrangement from her family. The outlier here is Jenny. Jenny had family, and they reported her missing. The police took the report seriously and are actively looking for her.

I just don't understand how this could be going on for three years without anyone noticing. Okay, I *do* get it. It was spread out, no family, they formally withdrew after clearly having a hard time on campus, so it made sense they would leave. And as much as universities love to deny it, women on campus are targets for all kinds of things, this probably didn't even raise any alarms until Jenny.

As much as I want to be in denial about this whole thing, that maybe all these women aren't connected to Clara, Clara has made sure that that isn't even an option. She connected the dots. She moved the needle. And she made sure the information was protected so if she couldn't finish it, someone else could.

Clara may have started this, but I know I'm going to finish it.

CHAPTER SIXTEEN

"AN EVENING I WILL NOT FORGET" BY DERMOT KENNEDY

There's a warmth on my face that feels so comforting, I just want to crawl inside that warmth and not come out. I'm not ready to face reality yet, so I keep my eyelids closed while I lay motionless. I feel the gentle brush of my hair being moved across my cheek before being softly tucked behind my ear. I'm not sure exactly what is going on in this moment, but I know I like it, and that I want to stay in this moment for as long as I can.

"Kenzie." I hear whispered toward me, the warmth of someone's breath gently moves over my face. There's a faint smell of scotch in the air, but almost undetectable. "Kenz, come on, sweetheart, let me take you home," the voice whispers.

The fog of sleep is still clouding my mind, but one thing I know for sure is for the first time in a long time, I feel safe, and I would do just about anything to not give up that feeling.

Unfortunately the voice has other ideas.

I feel a hand softly grasp on to my shoulder and start to gently but firmly rub my arm before the voice starts up again. "Come on, sweetheart, this can't be comfortable."

Eventually I give in and my eyes slowly start to open. The

fuzzy outline of a person crouched in front of me takes a moment to come into focus. It's Will. It takes a minute to realize the reason why he's crouched is because I apparently passed out on the floor going over everything. As I'm shifting my body on the floor, I hear the crinkles of the papers I fell asleep on. Hell, I even have one stuck to my cheek. Will chuckles as he peels it off the side of my face.

"Come on, I'll take you home," Will says again.

"No, it's okay, I'm awake," I protest as I try and fail to smoothly sit up, Will has to steady me more than once as I finally get back into a sitting position on the floor.

"You're exhausted," he says it like it's the most obvious thing in the world and that I'm being completely unreasonable.

Maybe I am being unreasonable, but I don't care. "No really, I'm fine, just give me a few minutes to fully wake up and I'll be fine," I tell him as I yawn, earning me a glare. "Just tell me what happened while I was sleeping. Did you get anywhere with Blake?"

Come to think of it, where is Blake? I look around the office to see if anyone else is in the building, but as far as I can tell, it's just me and Will left in the building. It's still dark outside so at least I know it's not Monday yet. Well, not Monday morning yet, it's probably technically Monday.

"Blake did her best to track the emails but didn't have a lot of luck. Or at least not a lot of luck that's going to give us a quick answer," he explains.

"Public place?" I manage to ask between yawns.

"Yeah, library. No requirement to register users in order to use. We've got time stamps and I'm sure the police can pull surveillance, but it's going to take time, and Blake is pretty confident with this guy's skills that we won't find anything." Will gives up on the crouch and moves to sit next to me up against the wall. The sigh he lets out feels bone deep. Like this is really affecting him, not just some paid case he took on.

"You okay?"

"Course. I was just really hoping you were wrong. Now we have five missing young women and there is no telling if that's all of it." He shakes his head before looking at me straight on. "I'm meeting with the police in the morning. I need to lay out everything we found, they need to know what they are up against."

"I know."

"I figured you would want to come with me."

My head snaps to look at him dead on. I almost can't believe it. "Yeah?"

"Yeah. Without you, who knows how long it would have taken for them to make a connection between Jenny and Clara and the rest of the women."

I watch his face while he's speaking. His eyes look like they are getting circles underneath them. He looks a little bit beaten down and weary. I think he's living with this case as much as I am. It's both comforting and not at all at the same time.

I reach out for Will's hand, it feels a little different this time. He's always been the one to initiate touching, and normally we are not sitting leg to leg against a wall on the floor, but I'm worried. "You sure you're okay?"

There's a small squeeze on my hand before he sighs and answers, "Yeah. I'm good. Promise."

"What aren't you saying?" I push.

"I've done this before. Missing women. It used to be my job."

I raise my eyebrows but never look away from his eyes.

"Back when I was a cop." He shakes his head like he's trying to clear away bad memories. "I went in so naive, the belief I could stop bad things from happening to good people. It's not how it works. Not really. You clean up the mess. If you're lucky, you find the bad guy. But nothing is ever the same again."

"And now?" I ask.

"Now I find people who can't keep it in their pants or employees who can't keep their hand out of the cookie jar. I avoid the life and death stuff."

"But you were good at it, right?"

"I did okay."

I get the feeling he's being modest.

"Then why not use your skills?"

"Because by the time things actually get to you, the clock has already been running. Truth is when it comes to crime, it's a short window. You get a finite amount of time to actually save someone, and most of the time you don't even get that. Most of the time, it's all over before you even get the call. Even when you win, you lose."

I squeeze his hand because I don't know what to say. His words ring true, they bounce around in my head for a while. They are the words I knew in my heart but haven't been ready to hear yet. Tingling hits my eyes and I know tears are trying to escape. I lean my head down to Will's shoulder, trying not to put more of a burden on Will but not willing to give up this moment.

We sit there in silence for a while, side by side, hand in hand, my head on his shoulder. The amount of time I've known this man is next to nothing, but it feels like we are in it together, and his strength is the only thing keeping me together right now.

After some time passes Will finally breaks the silence. "Come on, it's after one and we're supposed to meet the police early tomorrow, let me take you home."

"I don't want to," I whisper.

He pauses and lets it sit in the air for a while. "Because she's not there?" he asks softly.

I can't bring myself to answer, just sniffle as the tears finally start to break free. My hand tightens around his, trying to steal his strength.

"It's okay," he assures me as he reaches his other hand over to hold my small hand in both of his.

"I can just stay here, if it's okay?" I look up to ask.

He reaches up to wipe the tears from my cheek. "I can't let you sleep on the floor here, there isn't a pillow or blanket to speak of. But I do have a guest room if you want?"

Shock rushes over me. He'd let me stay at his house? "Really?"

He nods.

"I don't want to impose, I can just go back to my place if you would rather, it's okay really," I stammer.

"Kenz. Really, it's fine. We have to get up in a few hours anyway, this way we can just go to the meeting together."

"Okay, yeah."

Will keeps looking at me a little while longer before finally letting go of my hand and starting to stand up. "Stay here, let me get everything all ready to go."

I nod and spend the next couple of minutes watching him move around the office. First to turn off the coffee maker. Next, to put all the glasses into the small dishwasher in the kitchenette before turning it on to run.

He methodically goes throughout the office and puts things back where they belong, navigating around the clutter without so much as a second thought. It's like he's memorized the maze and doesn't even have to look down to make sure he isn't going to trip over something.

He also seems to have a security routine he runs through as well. Checking each of the windows to make sure they are locked and bolting the back door. By the time everything is done and secure, I can feel my eyes starting to get heavy again, even though I'm sure it's only been a few minutes since he got up. Pains me to admit it, but I get why he kept offering to drive me home. At this rate, I'm sure to become a statistic about people getting into accidents after falling asleep at the wheel.

It's not until I hear Will clear his throat that I realize my eyes have closed and I've started to drift off. When I open my eyes, I see his hand close by, offering to help me up.

Within a minute or two, we are out the door and Will is setting the alarm system for the office, before taking my arm and helping lead me over to his truck.

"Do you need anything from your car?" he asks as we arrive at his truck. He opens the passenger side door for me before helping me up into the seat.

"My gym bag has an extra set of clothes and supplies," I mumble.

"Pass me your keys."

Next thing I know, I feel the truck jolt as Will closes the door after he has retrieved my bag and is already in the cab. The heater is already on and the warmth is filling the cab nicely.

Will reaches back behind the passenger seat and produces a scruffy-looking blanket that looks like it's well used, before spreading it out over me. "I'll wake you up when we get there," he assures me.

It doesn't take long after that for my eyes to start to close and the gentle rumble of the truck to lull me back to sleep.

MY NAP on the way to Will's house is enough to make sure that I'm fully conscious when I get out of the truck and approach the house. I'm not sure what I was expecting. Maybe an apartment with a lot of amenities so he could just do everything at his building. No, that's not him, too many people.

Will strikes me as more of the loner type.

Maybe I was expecting more of a bachelor pad. Something small and just kept up enough to be considered respectable, but not much beyond that.

The state of his truck should have been my first indication that I should have had higher expectations.

It's late so I can't make out everything in the darkness, but from what I can tell, his place is beautiful. There are huge swaths of pine trees on either side of a well-kept front lawn. Complete with nicely landscaped bushes and flower beds. He also has some really nice outdoor house lighting, because even though it's pitch black outside, the lighting makes sure that no matter where you are near the house, your path is fully illuminated.

I have a brief moment where I consider if he bought the place like this before I quickly discount it, he seems like the kind of control freak who would have done all this himself on his days off.

The house itself is typical of North Carolina, built with a substantial amount of brick with siding mixed in, the front littered with plenty of windows for an abundance of natural lighting. I can tell just from looking at the outline of the front of the house that this place is packing a fair amount of square footage.

Definitely not a bachelor's pad.

No, this is much more a family home.

But even with as little as I've gotten to know him over the past couple of days, I have no doubt that he lives in this house all by himself. The consummate loner.

"You coming?" Will calls out from near the front door, my gym bag slung over his shoulder.

"Sorry, I was just—"

"Surprised?" he says with a laugh.

"Impressed," I admit. "It's beautiful. Really."

"Thanks," he mumbles. "Come inside." He motions for me to follow him inside before he goes through the front door.

From everything I can see in the night light, the house is impeccable. Someone took a lot of time picking out everything and making sure it was installed just right. The whole thing does not seem to jibe with the way his office looks. One is a complete mess in a building that's in good working order but nothing to write home about. Whereas the house is probably one of the best-kept houses on the block if not the neighborhood. Kind of like how his house is so nice, so is his truck.

Will is kind of a dichotomy I haven't yet figured out.

As soon as I walk through the front door, I can tell the inside matches the outside. Everything is well kept and nice looking, albeit a bit on the minimal side.

"Come on, I'll show you the guest room."

I follow him up the stairs and to the right before he stops in the doorway of a nice-sized bedroom. It's full of simple furniture and a nicely made bed with a gray comforter on it, but nothing in the way of decor.

"Bathroom is across the way, I'm sure there are some spare supplies in there if you need some toothpaste or anything," he tells me while gesturing to the door across the way from the bedroom. Pointing to the end of the hall, he tells me, "I'm over that way. If you need anything, just give me a knock. You're welcome to anything in the fridge if you get hungry."

"Thanks, Will. Really, thanks for everything." I quickly wrap my arms around his waist and press my head up against his chest. It only takes half a second before he wraps his arms around my shoulders and gives me a gentle squeeze.

"You're welcome. I don't want to tell you that everything is going to be okay, but I will tell you that I'm in this with you. We'll figure this out, I promise."

I look up at his kind eyes, still wrapped around him before weakly smiling at him. "Thank you for not sugarcoating everything for me." I slowly release him and then start walking toward my bed for the night.

"Night, Kenz."

"Night, Will."

AFTER AN UNSETTLING DREAM when I could see Clara but yet couldn't get to her, I knew there was no way I was ever going to get back to sleep. The sun hadn't come out yet, it was still probably a half hour away before it was due to start coming up for sunrise.

I didn't bother changing out of my clothes from the night before, so I don't really worry about rolling out of the bed and heading downstairs to the kitchen.

The kitchen is just as minimal as the rest of the interior of the house is, and after checking out the fridge the one thing I am sure of is that he is definitely a bachelor. He has beer, pickles, ketchup, and some orange Gatorade. Clearly this man eats all of his meals out.

After digging around for a glass and getting myself some water, I find myself sitting at the kitchen table staring out into the blackness.

I'm nervous about meeting with the police. So far, I haven't had a lot of luck at getting them to listen to me. My head knows this is not how it's going to play out this time though, we have too much evidence to just ignore. There are too many dots that are connected and too many people that just left town only to never be heard of again.

I should be excited about the progress. But it's hard to be excited about something that almost definitely means that Clara is off somewhere in a sinister situation and not out sipping martinis. I wish she had just told me what was going on. Even if there was no way to prevent what happened, at least I would have already had an idea of what was going on, I would have been five, maybe ten, steps ahead and we wouldn't have wasted all this time trying to find the pieces and put them together. I want to be so mad at her, hell, I *am* mad at her. But at the same time, how can I be? Who knows where she is right now, and she was clearly trying to do the right thing by these women. She's not the bad guy here so I can't justify being this mad at her.

So instead of focusing on it, I just sit at this kitchen table feeling the coolness of the glass in my hand and wait for the sunrise. Wait for a new day to bring new challenges and new facts that are sure to break my heart even more than it already is.

Instead, I think about the people who have come together to help me in this. How good it was to see Joe again, and how much I missed being a part of his family. How he helped me when it would have been the easier thing to just not get involved. How because of him, I was able to connect with Will.

How wrong I was about Will. That first meeting he just came off as a short, abrupt, kind of jerk who wasn't really interested in doing any work. The more I think about it, I can't actually say I've seen him do much work. But he knows every detail of this case. He got Blake invested, and without her, we never would have made the connections that we have so far.

These people are good at what they do and in only a few short days, they have shown how invested they are in this. It feels like a team. A team where I'm on equal footing. I might not have their skill sets, but they have trusted me at every turn to point them in the right direction.

Blake might come off a little abrasive, but she's a powerhouse. I think she and Clara are going to get along great when they meet.

And Will. I was so wrong. I thought he was going to be an epic jerk who I had to push every step of the way. Instead he holds my hand and worries about how much sleep I'm getting. He delivers the bad news but has this way about him that has me believing that he'll catch me if I fall. Will makes me feel so safe without even trying. I don't remember the last time a man made me feel that way.

I'm just comfortable with him. When he's in my personal space, it doesn't bother me. When he reaches out to hold my hand, it feels natural. When his fingers brush my cheek to wipe away my tears or to tuck hair behind my ear, it just feels like something he's been doing forever. And it's only been a couple of days.

I honestly shouldn't be thinking about things like this. My best friend is missing and we seem to have stumbled onto some sort of serial case, and here I am thinking about a man. The truth is I'm lonely. I probably have been for some time now. With Clara gone, it's just become more obvious.

It's the wrong time to be attracted to a man. My head knows that. But the rest of me? The rest of me wants to be comforted. Wants to go home to an apartment that isn't just four empty walls. I want the security of not being on my own when the bogeyman comes to call.

But it's more than that. It's someone to share meals with, to talk through the random things that run through my head. Especially now. I have all these random thoughts about what is going on, and sure, most of them are probably nuts and aren't going to be helpful. But I want someone to work through them with. I want someone to hold my hand when the floor drops out on me, which seems to be happening every couple of hours.

When I first met Will, he came across as so abrasive, I thought he was going to be the biggest jerk on the planet, but his actions say something entirely different. Maybe he's just a good guy who feels sorry for me. Maybe he has a soft spot for me because of Clara. Is it even possible that it's something more? Could he be attracted to me too? I have no idea.

The real question is, am I willing to put everything on the line and risk getting closer to him when I still need his help with Clara?

CHAPTER SEVENTEEN
"BROKEN" BY LOVELYTHEBAND

"Y ou ready for this?" Will asks as he turns the key in the ignition, starting up his truck.

"Yep," I say with a shiver as I reach over to the knob that controls the heater before turning it all the way up.

"Do we need to talk about how the meeting is going to go?" he asks as he starts reversing the truck out of the drive and begins our journey.

"I figured we were just going to lay everything out for Joe. You know, tell them everything we've learned," I say, confused.

"So you're okay with telling them everything?"

"I honestly never even considered not telling them everything. I need everyone looking, which means ringing as many alarm bells as I can."

"Okay, good."

"Did you think I wanted to hold something back?" I ask, confusion still lacing through my voice.

"Not all my clients are comfortable being so forthcoming with the police," he explains. I turn in my seat to face him, hoping the look on my face conveys my disbelief, or rather non-disbelief, that there are people out there who don't want to share information with the police. Clearly, he gets the message when a deep chuckle comes out of him. "To clarify, I don't hide important information from the police, no matter what my clients want."

"Do your clients know this?"

"They would if they read the details in the contract I have them sign," he says with a shrug. Oh yes, the terms and conditions, like anyone reads those. Wait a second.

"I didn't sign a contract."

"I know."

"Why didn't I sign a contract?"

"Does it matter?"

"Yes."

"Why?"

"It just does," I sigh with exasperation.

"Well, you didn't."

"I know, but why?"

"It didn't seem necessary."

"Not to sound like a broken record, but why?" I ask one final time.

He pauses before answering. "Because when I finally decided to help you, I knew I was going to see it through, no matter what a contract said."

My eyes blink slowly as I focus more on Will's face. My body deflating into the seat as the rapid-fire back-and-forth from just a few moments ago turns into something else. Is he trying to say he would have helped me without the money, or if I give up, is he going to keep going? Why would he do that?

"What do you mean?" The words leave my mouth slowly.

"Just what I said, I'm going to see it through." The determination in his voice is more than a little surprising. He never wavers, though, just keeps looking forward through the windshield at the morning traffic in front of us as we head into Durham.

"So if I run out of money or get hit by a—"

"I'm seeing it through, MacKenzie. No matter what." I've never heard him call me MacKenzie before. I kinda like it. Especially when he says it while declaring he's going to see this through to the end. Not gonna lie, it was more than a little hot.

But hot or not, I still couldn't figure out why.

"Why would you do that?"

I can tell by the large sigh that escapes him that he really doesn't want to continue this line of questioning.

"Can't we just leave it at I'm on the case?" His thumbs start tapping against the steering wheel in a steady rhythm. A nervous tic, maybe? My curiosity is piqued.

"Sure we can. But if you want to tell me, I would really like to know." He sighs again. "Look, I'm not trying to look a gift horse in the mouth, but I know why I am in this. I know her, I love her, she's my family. And there is no doubt about it that I'm ecstatic that you are in this for the duration. I'm more grateful than you will ever know. But it doesn't mean I'm not curious. You know so much about what's going on in my life right now, and I know so little about you. What can I say? Inquiring minds want to know, I guess," I say with a shrug before turning to look out the window. Hopefully, not staring at him directly would feel less like an inquisition, and he might actually open up to me.

The cab of the truck fills with a heavy silence. Both of us kind of waiting each other out. After a decade of grief in a house where no one spoke to each other, I was beyond comfortable sitting in uncomfortable silences. If it was an Olympic sport, I would win gold every single time.

Thankfully, he doesn't make me wait that long.

"I was a cop," he says simply.

"I know."

More silence. More waiting him out. I don't think he realizes yet he's not even close to having a fighting chance at waiting me out. I just keep staring out the passenger side window, watching the pine trees fly by as we speed down the highway.

"Clara's case. The reason I didn't want to take it at first, well, it's, it hit a little close to something."

"You used to work missing persons cases?" I guess out loud.

"Not often, but sometimes one would come my way. They were never the ones with happy endings."

"Oh," I whisper. "Does that mean you don't think Clara—"

"No, I'm not saying that. I'm not saying that at all." He slows the truck as we start to hit traffic coming off the highway. Out of my peripheral, I see him turn to look at me before I follow suit. "Look, by the time I got missing persons cases, there wasn't a chance. The crime was normally committed before anyone ever was reported missing. Hell, sometimes weeks went by after the crime before anyone was reported missing. But my last case. My last case was... different."

The questions start racing through my mind at warp speed. I want so badly to just blurt them out at him in rapid-fire succession, to get all the answers as quick as I can. But I can tell this hurts him. So I try to give him the space he needs to tell me in his own time. And while I wait, I pull Will's go-to comfort move with me. I reach out and rest my hand on top of his, if only for just a few moments, hoping beyond hope it helps him the way it does me.

The small smile he gives me lets me believe it did help.

"The girl that was missing, someone saw her get taken. So we knew she was alive, and we knew most likely we were up against a clock." His thumb starts up the earlier rhythm against the steering wheel.

"You don't have to, Will, it's okay," I tell him. I thought about all the times in the past couple of days I had to lay out everything for people, over and over again, and how each time it felt like ripping a piece of myself out. It was painful. It felt like it was going to leave a scar. And by the way Will was speaking just now, whatever happened, I think it left a pretty big scar.

"No, you should know. You didn't just hire me, you're working in the office for now, you should know. And if at the end you don't think you want to work with me, that's okay, I'm still going to see this through, okay? No matter what." Our eyes meet across the cab and he looks nervous. Nervous, but serious.

"Okay," I tell him, but the word drags out slowly.

"The case. The girl..." He turns to look back out toward traffic. "It didn't end well for her. I tried. I tried everything. Hell, I almost lost my job. But in the end, I was still the one standing over her broken body, I was still the one listening to the screams of her mother that I still hear all the time." His shaky intake of breath lets me know that scar might be an understatement. He was still living it. Trapped in that moment in a way. I recognized it. I've lived with people trapped in time before. It's painful to watch.

"Will—"

"No, just let me finish. We knew who it was. We knew quickly who it was. We just couldn't prove it. I knew she was out there; I knew she was running out of time, but when we picked him up, he wouldn't talk." He paused. "I've never crossed a line before, not once. When I swore in to be a soldier, when I swore in to be a cop, I believed. I was a believer of the words I was saying, of the code we had to live by. But this guy. He had a record, he had done this kind of thing before, but always managed to get out of it, not enough evidence, technicalities, he was never going to stop. So I pushed. I crossed a line. I came clean on my own, got a slap on the wrist, and as much as I want to regret it, I don't. I got what we needed, but it wasn't quick enough.

"These cases, they haunt you. You live and breathe them

day in and day out. And the bottom line is after we found her, there was always going to be another case right around the corner. So I left. I didn't want to ever not get there in time again."

I can't find words to say to him. You watch these procedurals on television, and everything is nice and neat and wrapped up in sixty minutes. But I know from experience, real life is messy. I can't imagine what it was like for him. I'm not sure I want to even try. I know I want to say the right thing though, I want to comfort him. To let him know that I don't hold him responsible for her death, that no one in their right mind would.

"I'm so sorry, Will."

His head whips around to face me, the look of disbelief mixed with confusion speaks volumes.

"I can't imagine what that must have been like for you," I say as I reach over and take hold of his warm hand in mine. Will stares at me for a few seconds longer before turning to look at our joined hands. "I wish I could say I'm sorry for bringing you into this case, but I can't. Without you, I don't think we would be as far as we are. So I'm sorry that this is probably bringing back a lot of bad memories for you, but I am so grateful that you are here with me. And I know if Clara were here right now, she would say thank you too."

"It doesn't bother you?" I'm sure my face must display my confusion because he follows up with, "I crossed a line, you wouldn't be the first who didn't want to work with me because of it."

"The thing is, if it meant even a chance of getting Clara back, I'm not sure there is a lot I wouldn't do. I would break laws for her. I wouldn't care if I ended up in jail, if the payoff was her being alive. I can't exactly judge you for doing whatever you thought you needed to, to find that girl. I get that."

After a pause, he finally just nods his head in finality. The air is heavy with the weight of our conversation, but I can tell he doesn't want to go further than what has already been said. And that is fine with me.

WE PULL up to a cute little mom-and-pop diner, Alice's Diner. It doesn't seem to have a lot of business, judging by the number of cars in the parking lot. Rush hour is winding down, so maybe their morning crowd tends to be the much earlier crowd.

Whatever the reason for the lack of customers, I was grateful, the subject matter we were supposed to be discussing wasn't anything anyone eating breakfast would want to hear about anyway.

Pushing open the heavy door to Will's truck so I can hop down, I brace myself for the cold that is sure to be startling. I don't wait for Will, instead I just start moving toward the door. I am on a mission. I need the short walk to shore up my nerves anyway.

Right as I go to reach for the door, Will reaches out and turns me toward him.

"It's going to be okay. Whatever happens in there, it's going to be okay." We look at each other, my eyes searching his, hoping to take some of the faith that he has that this is all going to be okay from him.

"Okay." I nod.

The rush of warm air that hits me as soon as I step into the diner causes my skin to pebble up with goose bumps. A quick stomp of my feet on the welcome mat to make sure I'm not bringing in mud gives me some time to scan the diner. Back in the corner, I see Joe. He is sitting in a back booth, no one sitting at any other tables around him.

He looks tired. Worn down. I can see the darkness underneath his eyes, even from across the room. He doesn't have any food in front of him, instead he seems to be nursing what has to be a cup of black coffee, the way you would nurse a glass of bourbon.

My feet carry me to him quickly, as my worry for his well-being mounts. He sees me halfway to him and slides out of the booth. There is the beginning of an awkward pause when we just stand in front of each other, unsure of how to greet each other now that the dynamics of our relationship are so different.

"Fuck it," I declare as I throw my arms around his neck and hold tight. There is no hesitation as his arms wrap around my torso and hold me tight. I pull back slightly to get a better look at his face before being as honest as always. "You've looked better."

"That's my girl," he says, following a big belly laugh. "Nothing a good night's sleep won't fix," he assures me.

"If you say so." I let go of Joe and move to slide into the booth across from where he has been sitting. Will slides into the booth next to me.

Not going to lie, I am definitely enjoying the smaller booth and how it leaves his left side pushed up against my right, our thighs with no space between them. But despite the little butterflies trying to take hold in my stomach, I know we are there with a job to do. So, I try to push them aside and get down to business. Will beat me to it.

"Thanks for meeting with us." Will nods toward Joe in that manly way only guys can pull off.

"You said you had some new information about Clara, something time sensitive."

Will looks over at me, and a silent conversation passes between us, with him letting me take the lead.

"It's not just about Clara, we found a lot of information Clara was compiling on her own before she disappeared, all about girls who also went missing."

Slowly Joe set his coffee on the table and just stared at me, his worried expression amplifying. "Tell me exactly what you mean by *missing*."

"Well, you know Clara is missing." He raises an eyebrow but nods at the same time, almost an acknowledgment that even though she wasn't technically missing, we both agree she is. "And Clara had files on three other girls who seemingly left school like she did, never to be heard from again."

"Define never heard from again."

"I ran them all, none of them ever used credit again, signed a lease, utility, not even so much as an inquiry on their credit. They left campus and school but after that, nothing," Will fills in the blanks.

"Well, that's disconcerting," Joe replies.

"Yeah, but there was someone Clara was talking to right before she went missing, someone she had planned on meeting up with. Before they could meet, Clara went missing and by Thursday she was missing too," I explain further.

Shock fills Joe's face. Ever so slowly, he sets his cup of coffee on the table. "Tell me her name isn't Jenny."

I know he already knows the answer, so instead I just look at him and nod.

"You're certain about this?" Joe asks, making direct eye contact with both Will and me.

We both nod, and then Will pulls a file out from his left side and slides it across the table, "We made copies of everything."

Joe doesn't touch the file, instead just asks, "What's the connection, why was Clara in contact with Jenny?"

"Everyone on the list had filed reports with campus security about stalking, or more specifically, cyber stalking, that was clearly being done by someone who was on campus," I tell him.

"I checked with campus security myself. I had them pull everything with Clara's name and Jenny's. Clara's name only brought up the report from you, and Jenny's name was only mentioned briefly as a witness to a car accident that she saw happen in a parking lot. There was *nothing* about stalking in any of the files."

Will and I look at each other once more before he goes on to explain, "I know, I had a friend of mine check their system. None of the reports from any of the girls are on campus security's mainframe anymore. But we have all the copies off of Clara's files, and I put each of them in the file. Clara also saved every email she ever received from the stalker, so you can see how he escalates slowly. She also saved all the correspondence with Jenny. Everything is in there."

We all sit in silence as Joe reaches for the file and starts to work his way through it. I hate watching him because I can see on his face how serious things are. I watch as his jaw tightens with every passing email, how his eyes focus intently on the security reports, the sighs that escape him when he goes over the names of the other women and their lack of activity after they left school. I can see him making all the same connections that we did. It's so hard to be excited about progress when it means talking about someone who is skilled enough to be responsible for what could be five women going missing and never being heard from again. Someone skilled enough to cover their tracks, even as far as to remove vague reports of him that had no shot of being traced back to him.

When he finishes, he closes the file gently before looking directly at me. "I'm sorry, Kenzie. You never should have had to be the one to find all of this stuff out."

"But there's a connection. A big one," I reply.

"Yeah. I've got to get all this stuff back to the office, and we will run some of our own checks, but right now, yes. I would say we are looking for a serial offender."

"So what happens now?" I ask.

"It may take a few hours on the other girls, but I can add Clara to all the alerts with Jenny. I'm sure we will be alerting the media to try and get some outside help. Basically, the calvary."

"Really?" I ask.

"Really. Kenzie, if you had listened to everyone and stopped looking, it might have taken months to start making these connections, hell, we may have never made some of them. You did good, kid, really good," he tells me with his New York accent growing stronger.

I might be homeless in a few weeks, and I don't have any books to use for my classes, but right now, in this moment, it's all worth it.

AFTER PARTING ways with Joe so he could head back to the police station to get to work on everything we had just given him, Will and I also start making our way back to the truck. As soon as we cross the threshold, I can't help myself, I jump up and down, bouncing with the excitement coursing through my veins.

"We did it!" I exclaim to Will.

"Yes, we did," Will says with a smile that probably matches mine, wide and full of teeth.

"I can't believe it, I can't believe we did it, I can't believe any of it."

"Of course we did it, you were never going to give up," Will tells me.

"I know, but still..." I stop bouncing and take a good look at Will. Honestly, without him, I'm not sure I would have gotten this far, and certainly not this fast. I love the happy expression on his face, that he's just as invested in this as I am. I feel like I have a partner. Someone to lean on, someone I can depend on, someone who is going to fight this battle with me. I reach out and take both of his biceps in my hands.

I can feel the muscles tighten underneath my hands. The strength he has in those arms becoming more obvious as I feel them flex beneath me. I look up at him, he still has the smile on his face as he raises his hands up to take hold of my elbows. His fingers wrap so gently around me, somehow delicate and supportive at the same time.

"I never would have come this far, this fast without you, Will. Thank you so much for doing this with me."

"Of course." One of his hands squeezes my elbow gently. "We still have a lot of work left to do," he tells me with a smile.

It feels like time is slowing down in this moment. I can feel my heart beating in my chest, the butterflies in my stomach taking hold. I feel like I'm on top of the world. Like in this moment, after everything that we have been through the last couple of days, that I could do anything. Not giving myself the time to really think about it, I just go for it.

I feel my weight shift as I start to lift up on my tippy-toes, moving toward Will. I feel Will's hands take a firmer grip on my elbows, but not to hold me in place or move me away. I hear the exhalation of breath before I feel it gently against my skin as it leaves Will's body.

My lips are only a fraction of an inch away from his when everything shifts. Instead of meeting my lips with his, he shifts his head ever so slightly to the right. When my lips make contact with him, it's at the spot right next to the corner of his mouth. Will's hands are still holding me tight. Our bodies are still connected, even though a mountain of space has started to form between us.

My heart sinks in my chest. Embarrassment floods my cheeks as they begin to flush pink. What are the chances that Will thinks the flush on my face is from the cold weather? Slim, I'd guess. Panic starts to flood my bloodstream alongside my embarrassment. I want out of this situation. And fast.

Quickly I let go of Will's arms and release the tension in my feet, allowing my whole body to rapidly fall back down to the ground with the help of gravity and take a few steps backward from Will.

We both stand there for several seconds, I can tell Will is trying to make eye contact with me, to figure out what to do next, but I can't bring myself to do it. I can't bring myself to look at him.

"Kenzie," Will eventually starts to speak.

All I know is I don't want to hear anything that is going to come out of his mouth. Whatever platitude or gentle dismissal, nope, it's not for me.

"So I guess we should get back to it, right?" Not giving him a chance to respond, I turn and walk toward the truck.

There's a couple of seconds before I hear Will's sigh and then the sounds of gravel crunching under his weight.

I waste no time getting in the truck the second I hear the car alert that the doors are unlocked.

Just keep looking ahead, I tell myself as I pray Will won't push this. Clearly it was a mistake. No need to talk about it, right?

The entire drive back to the office is full of tension. Tension that continues to build with every passing mile. Thankfully, the drive is short and traffic is light, because before I know it, I can see my own car in the parking lot of the office. It's my salvation. My way out.

As soon as I hear Will shift the truck into park, I start to make my exit.

"I'm gonna get some rest before going over all the stuff King got. I'll um, I'll call you or uh, see you back here if I find something." *Great, that was smooth.* I had envisioned that going much smoother in my head.

"Kenzie, wait," I hear Will say as I slide out of the truck before closing the door a little harder than necessary.

I start "walking with purpose" as Joe would have said before throwing up a hand before getting into my car. Will is still standing next to his truck as I pull out of the parking lot with a look on his face that I have no hope of deciphering.

Reliving the first and only time I've ever been dodged like that, I can feel my cheeks flush even harder, the warmth leading me to believe I was now more red than pink. How in the world was I ever going to face him again?

CHAPTER EIGHTEEN
"SOMEONE TO YOU" BY BANNERS

I wake up a few hours later in my own bed, how I managed any bit of sleep is beyond me. It must have been the embarrassment, even my brain didn't want to remember the rejection, so instead it finally let me get some quality unconscious time. Whatever the reason, it was much-needed sleep.

I lie there on top of my bed, staring up at the ceiling in my room. I can see the little yellow specks on my ceiling, the ones that glow in the dark. I smile at the memory of how they got there.

Clara and I were talking about the moments in our childhood that made us smile. She told me about how her and her mom used to camp out in the backyard. How it was this huge adventure every time. Her mom would tell her scary stories, they would make s'mores and grill hot dogs over a fire, how they got so good at building the tent in the backyard that they used to try and race against their best times. It sounded magical. The kind of magic you can only really find when you are a child and the real world hasn't tainted your worldview yet.

When she asked me, "What about you?" I didn't know what

to say. So much of my childhood is full of me being the adult. My dad off on another deployment. My eight-year-old self trying to keep my mom alive with my rudimentary cooking skills. How I spent the week before school started learning how to walk the route to school because I was too close for the bus but my mom barely got out of bed so I had to walk it. Using the ATM to get cash out so I could buy groceries on my way home from school. If it wasn't for my dad paying the bills even on deployment, I don't think we would have had power and running water. As an adult, I can look back and realize someone should have called CPS.

But I was able to come up with some memories. My favorite was when I was five. I had accidentally seen a scary movie and suddenly was afraid of the dark, I was always trying to sleep with the lights on, and my older brother used to tease me about it. It wasn't until he realized I was really afraid that he came up with a plan. He came home one day from school and told me all about how we were going to solve this "afraid of the dark" business. He was so much bigger than me, being seven years older, that he could actually reach the ceiling whereas I couldn't. So, he told me to lie on my bed and direct him about where I wanted my stars to go. He made me laugh the whole time.

When it was done and my ceiling full of scattered stars was complete, he told me the next part was the most important. He was going to spend the night with me that night, because the magic of the stars only worked if they were charged. And he was going to charge them. He was going to put all of his "big-brother magic" into the stars, and from then on, they would protect me from anything. No reason to be afraid of the dark if I was lying under stars full of big-brother magic.

Years later, I know it's the kind of thing only little kids would believe in, but it's the only thing I miss about that house. And how I sometimes still miss waking up and seeing the stars that my brother put up for me. Like it's the smallest piece of him I still had. After she died, I never wanted to leave my room, because it was the only place where I still had him.

I cried when I told Clara the story, and so did she. The next day she had gone out and bought stars, and she told me how we weren't going to replace the old ones but rather put new ones up to honor him. So every morning I will know my brother was still watching over me while I slept.

Just another of a million different reasons why Clara is my best friend. I can't help but believe that she and my brother would have gotten along.

Without any warning, I start to feel guilty. Sitting here thinking about Clara, I realize I'm not doing anything to help move this investigation forward. Clara is out there with God only knows who and here I am, trying to avoid going back to the office because I'm embarrassed about some guy. Some guy who I have no business catching feelings for right now. Clara should be my only priority. She's what is important right now.

Even though I am berating myself about this while I roll out of bed and start getting ready to get back to work, I can't help but hear Clara's voice in the back of my head. I know she would be cheering it on, telling me to go for it. We were always each other's biggest cheerleaders, and I know she would have been thrilled that I finally found a guy that I was crushing on besides the giant dumbass Collin. Hell, she probably would have thrown a party that I was moving on. The thought makes me smile, and as I walk into the living room, I can just imagine her coming home with a giant bag of every flavor of Ben and Jerry's she could find at the store. Ice cream parties are always a huge hit at our apartment. The two of us watching early 2000s rom-coms eating out of ten different pints of ice cream, who could want anything more?

Now when I look around my living room, her absence is overwhelming but her presence remains strong thanks to my lovely Wall of Crazy. No more putting things off, time to figure things out.

Obviously, there is a big bad guy behind this whole thing. But *who* is the million-dollar question. Every crime show I've ever seen flashes through my brain, especially *Criminal Minds*; it would be great if Reid were here to lend a hand. What was it they were always saying in every episode with a stalker? Most stalkers have some kind of interaction with their obsession, even if the target doesn't realize it. Clara was kind of the definition of not social. She loved hanging out at our apartment, homework was actually enjoyable, and she always wanted to spend time at the computer labs on campus. The girl invested in the highest quality noise-canceling headphones she could find just so she wouldn't have to hear other people talking around her. There were no sororities or social clubs, no boyfriends or regular parties. She barely hung out with the people who I knew, the closest thing you could say she had to friends were the people in the same program with her at school.

Sure, she was a creature of habit, she went to the same places for food on the same days, so maybe she ran into someone there. Either way, I need to make some kind of weekly timeline of what each week looked like for her: classes, food, home, lab time, all of it might be important.

While I am making a detailed timeline, I am trying to run through any possible options for the perpetrator, or *unknown subject* as Reid would say. I snort as I envision myself in a conference room trying to lay out all my theories. I roll my eyes at myself, how ridiculous I have become.

Okay, suspects. I need a list of suspects.

First up, Collin. Not likely. He's in the pictures that were kind of used as blackmail for Clara. Sure, he could have arranged for someone to take those pictures, but that would mean involving someone else in his scheme, and this guy seems to cover his tracks. Plus, Collin wouldn't know what to do with a computer if it hit him in the face.

Moving on.

Like a light bulb, I realize, of course, someone with computer skills. Someone on Clara's level or King's level. Clara took precautions. She put everything on a cloud server that wasn't traced back to anything having to do with her school stuff because she must have thought someone was watching. She encrypted the files. King said it was strong encryption, not just stuff you get off a website.

Plus, the reports from campus security weren't on their server anymore. So unless we are talking about an actual campus security officer who could have removed the reports off the server manually, it's probably someone who removed them remotely.

But still, it could be a campus security guard.

I write *campus security* down underneath Collin's name, which is scratched out. Quickly I scribble out a note about how the reports are missing, but I am still not super convinced it was a campus security guard.

Moving on, back to computer geniuses. Clara came in contact with a ton of those types. And not just the people in her classes. She had professors and TAs, guest speakers, she's even interviewed at more than a couple of the big tech firms here looking for an internship. The list would probably be extensive. And honestly, I wouldn't even know how to begin cataloging each person's area of specialty.

That was one thing Clara made perfectly clear to me. Most people have a specialty. King would qualify as security, I know that much. Some people are programmers, and not everyone uses the same language. Some people deal with hardware. Or software. Some people are more mathematicians than others.

I start trying to run through every memory of Clara talking about all the people she came in contact with the last couple of years. If there is one thing every girl on a college campus has a list of, it's douchey guys who think they know so much more than some girl. And oh, how Clara used to encounter that.

Clara was always at the top of the class, she set the curve. And there were more than a few guys who didn't always appreciate that a quiet bookworm girl was showing them up at every turn. There was, of course, the one guy she talked about who was going to be super pissed about Clara getting the internship.

God, what was his name? It's one of those snobby sounding names, and I remember his first and last name started with the same letter. P I think it was. I snap my fingers as soon as his name enters my brain.

"Preston Pierce." I exclaim.

He even talked to her more than once about how she should move on since there was no way she was ever going to get it, that he was a shoo-in. Clearly that guy has some level of computer skills, plus it wouldn't be that hard for him to figure out Clara's schedule since at their level, the group of students like them is small. But how would all the other girls have met him?

Timeline wise it works out. The missing girls start back three years, this guy is a senior like Clara, so he would have been in school at the same time as when the girls started to go missing. Maybe in the first two years, there was some overlap with core classes? But the latter two girls, where would they have crossed paths? Jenny wasn't a computer science major, and it seems like he was stalking both Clara and Jenny at the same time, that had to be time consuming, so where's the crossover?

Either way, she makes number three.

I keep thinking about what all three of these women must have had in common. Clara makes things difficult because I know how little she put herself out there.

In the end, I have my list:

1. ~~Collin:~~ unlikely-in photos & didn't cover tracks

2. Campus security: nonspecific b/c of missing reports but do they have computer skills, and if they did would they really be working a campus security job?

3. Preston Pierce: Super douche. On campus the right amount of time. Probably skilled enough to do the computer stuff. Need connection to other girls.

So who else would make the list? It was like running the last few years in reverse like a movie, trying to pick up on every person who ever warranted a mention, basically impossible. There's the creepy neighbor across the hall, but no way he knows the other girls, and I seriously doubt he has any level of computer skills. Seriously doubt.

Every student on campus has a teacher they feel are out for them, I have more than one. Clara only had one though, and it was early on, like second semester freshman year. He was a jerk. A super jerk. And I remember her telling me that he gave off that creepy vibe, one of those men who stand just a little too close or touch your shoulder under the guise of a kind gesture but really, it's just creepy. She told me the girls never went to office hours without someone with them, no one trusted this guy. A professor teaching an intro class like that has tons of opportunity to meet students from any major. And he was definitely here for all the disappearances. I have no idea how I am even going to go about checking if he has any computer skills. But I do know how to find him.

Rate Your Profs, one of my favorite sites. Check reviews from other students about the professors. Clara and I used it a million times to decide on what teacher to take for classes. And at the end of every semester, Clara wrote a review for each of her professors, good or bad. With only a few keystrokes, I have Clara's profile pulled up and all of her reviews. A few clicks later, I have his name. Professor Conner Lanier.

I'm pretty sure this guy is going to make number four on the list, but honestly looking over the reviews on this guy, he gives off such creeper vibes I don't think he would be any good at covering his tracks. Plus, the more I think about it, the more I wonder why he would wait more than two years to start harassing Clara. She was in his class freshman year, we were about to graduate, why the delay? The more I think about it, the less I think he is a contender. I am missing that feeling in my gut telling me I am on to something.

That being said, I do think I am on to something about someone in a teaching position. Maybe not a professor though, someone like a TA. They would fit in on campus, could be in any number of student groups, no one would think twice about a TA being around other students. It would fit for Clara. The douche guy used to call Clara a teacher's pet, and honestly, I get why he would call her that. She took school so seriously right from the beginning. She loves learning more than anything in the world, so she would introduce herself to every professor and TA, she would go to every extra study session, even if she didn't need to, if there was an extra credit assignment, she would do it. I used to say she was crazy, I mean, why put in all this extra effort when you are already getting an A in the class? She used to laugh and smile and say, *"for the experience,"* like it was the most obvious thing in the world. By junior year, I stopped asking, she loved it, why bug her about something she clearly loves?

With her habits, a TA fits the bill. But there's no Rate my Prof for TAs, they aren't listed on transcripts or schedules. The bigger the class, the more of a chance it would have more than one TA. Four years of TAs feels like an impossible task. I can't help but think it would have to be someone from last year or this year, but that's all I got.

Ultimately, I only have three more to add to the list, and I'm only even mildly confident about one:

4. ~~Creepy neighbor~~ No access to the other missing & doubtful he owns a computer

5. ~~Handsy professor~~- Widely known creepy - not the kind of guy who covers up after himself

6. Teaching Assistant- Fits the best. But who? There have been so many. Good access, could be skilled, blends in

I'm out of ideas.

CHAPTER NINETEEN

"YOU ARE THE REASON" BY CALUM SCOTT

I t feels like a waiting game. We've turned over all the information that we have to the police, and now I just have to hope the ball is moving, and quickly.

I want to call Will, if only to see if he has gotten information from anyone about how things are progressing. Are the cases officially linked yet? Do they have any links between them? Any suspects to speak of?

But I can't call Will.

My body starts to heat up as the memory of my embarrassment floods my system. I can't believe I tried to kiss him. What was I thinking?

Oh yeah, that he's hot. And he makes me feel safe. He's helping me when he doesn't have to. Hell, he comes off as the world's biggest closed book, but instead he opened up to me about his past.

Of course, I want to kiss him. The loneliness has grabbed hold, and this guy is literally everything I didn't know I want right now.

Plus, he has all the ins with the police department, so if there is any movement, he would probably know about it.

Nope, can't do it. Can't call him.

But he's not the only one with an in at the police depart-ment, after all my in is how I found Will in the first place. A nice text to Detective Fitzpatrick sounds like the solution to all my problems right now.

⟿

ME: **Hey, I just wanted to check in and see how things were going, any news?**

Joe: **You were actually on my list of phone calls to make today. We are bringing in anyone who might have informa-tion to the police station for formal interviews, do you have time to come in today?**

Me: **Of course**

Joe: **Great, can you be here around 1?**

Me: **Yep. I take it this means all the cases are linked now?**

Joe: **We are still waiting on some information to make it official for everyone, but unofficially, yes.**

You did good, kid.

Me: **Just did what she would do for me. See you soon.**

⟿

I KNOW I don't need the validation, but it's nice to have. Now I just need to find something to do until it's time to get grilled by the police.

⟿

THE WOMAN who leads me into the interview room doesn't say much on the way through the bullpen. Honestly, I don't think she said a single word, more like she spoke in grunts and head motions. Not exactly oozing friendly vibes, that's for sure. She's already hightailing away from me the second I crossed the threshold to the interview room.

Interview room might be a little generous. It's clearly one of those interrogation rooms you see on crime shows. No windows. Metal table with some kind of loop attached, which I assume is so they can chain people to the table. Hell, there is even a mirror on one wall. Standing there staring at the mirror, I keep trying to remember that TikTok video about how to tell if a mirror is a two-way mirror or not with your finger. I don't get a chance to test it out before I feel someone touch the back of my arm.

"Please, have a seat," the man says. It's not Joe. Clearly, he's a cop, he just gives off that vibe, I hope he doesn't spend a lot of time doing undercover work, because there is no way in hell a criminal on the streets is not going to peg him for a cop. He's got that high and tight haircut that's popular in the military, but being this close to Fort Bragg, it wouldn't surprise me if he was ex-military. I can't really tell what shade of brown his hair is, the haircut makes it too difficult to really tell, but it's definitely brown. Rigid posture accompanies him into the room as he gestures me farther in.

Without any other options, I walk farther into the room over to the chair he is still gesturing at. Thankfully, he leaves the door open, so it doesn't exactly feel like an interrogation, but I don't think there is anything they could do to this room to make it feel friendly. It takes a couple seconds for me to talk myself into sitting in the chair, but once I finally do, I cringe a little internally. Something about this place gives me the creeps.

This stuck-up guy is definitely watching me be creeped out. He still hasn't said anything, he's just standing next to the table watching me. After a while, he finally takes one of the other two chairs across the table from me. I will say one thing about this guy, he's got the stare down, down pat.

I take the opportunity to do the same. I'm not about to

engage in conversation while he is trying to make some kind of power play. I hate guys like this.

He's wearing a button-down, standard business wear, so basically like all the other detectives. But he's clearly trying to stand out among the crowd because he is wearing a leather jacket. Clearly, he wants to be the badass cool guy. I can't help but to roll my eyes, everyone knows when it's cold out a leather jacket is only going to help with the wind, it's definitely not going to help you with the cold unless it's lined, and this one isn't. It's all for show. The kind you could wear in the middle of summer while riding a motorcycle to avoid getting road rash if you lay down the bike.

I can see the face of his watch sticking out from underneath the jacket. It's one of those oversized watches that look fancy, but somehow, I doubt this thing is worth more than a hundred bucks. I'm a little surprised he's not wearing an Apple Watch, if only for the workout apps. There's no way this guy doesn't have a PT routine he does every morning.

And that's when I hear it. Tapping. Rhythmic tapping. Great. My biggest pet peeve on the planet and this guy, of course, has to be a tapper. I lean back in my chair, cross my arms, and raise an eyebrow in his direction.

He smirks back. Great, he knows he is annoying me.

"I knew I shouldn't leave the two of you alone," I hear from the doorway. My head snaps quickly toward the familiar voice.

"Hey, Joe." I smile at him.

"Hey, kid, good to see you. Thanks so much for coming in," he replies as douche canoe next to him huffs while Joe takes a seat in the chair next to him. "You got something to say, Jones?"

"Nope." He pops the *p*.

"She's not a suspect, Jones, we've been over this." Joe looks exasperated as he stares down Jones.

"I never said she was, just that it was awfully curious how

she has all this information at her fingertips, like maybe it's a little suspicious. That's all."

"Seriously?" I exclaim. He can't be serious. He can't seriously think that I am involved in all of this. What kind of moron would I be to be involved and yet at the same time bring a stack of information connecting all the crimes together, giving the police way more information than they had to begin with? "Please don't tell me this guy is serious?" I implore Joe.

"He is. He means well, I promise. It's fine. Swear," Joe tries to reassure me. It's not exactly working.

"If you say so," I reply with a huff and lean back in my chair.

"Okay, so how about we get this started? Kenzie, meet my partner, Detective Matt Jones, Jones, this is Kenzie." Joe waves his hand back and forth, gesturing to both of us. Jones and I make no move to do anything other than continue staring each other down.

Joe chuckles a little with an eye roll before continuing on.

"We've had people in all morning who had connections to the women in the files you gave me. We've been looking for any sort of similarities between them, and connections they might have to each other or a specific place or person. Anything anyone remembers about when they left school, that kind of thing."

I finally break eye contact with Jones and nod my head at Joe.

"So, I know we have a lot of information from you already, but I was hoping you would run both of us through the sequence of events from when Clara went missing, how you came across your information, up until through now," Joe says.

"Without leaving anything out," Jones adds.

"Of course, sure. Anything you need," I tell them both, but focus my attention on Joe. This Jones guy is going to annoy me to death, I can already tell.

For what feels like the millionth time, I go over all the information again. This time Joe is here to ask questions along the way, occasionally sliding over a piece of paper with corresponding information on it that backs up what I am saying. By the time I'm done running through it all, I feel like I'm out of breath and exhausted. I look down at my watch and I realize I've been sitting in this room going over all this information for almost an hour and a half. It's like a time vortex in here.

"Anything else you want to add, Miss Sharp?" Jones asks. He honestly seems a little less suspicious after all this time, maybe he's finally on board with me.

"Actually, yes. I've been thinking a lot about it and I have a couple of people I wanted to mention," I tell the two of them.

Jones actually flips open his notepad like he's going to take notes. Well, color me surprised.

"Let's have it," Jones says.

"So I've been racking my brain about all the people Clara could have come in contact with, and honestly, it's not that many people. She's basically the opposite of social. So unless we are talking about some random guy in a coffee shop she bumps into that she has no real connection to, there aren't going to be a lot of suspects in her personal life."

"She didn't go out much?" Jones asks.

"I've met Clara probably fifteen, twenty times, and from what I remember, she keeps to herself. She's reserved. Nice, polite, always helpful, but not what I would call talkative or sociable," Joe explains his personal impressions to Jones. Jones looks at me to confirm.

"He's not wrong. On campus, she's probably only really close to one person. Me. Outside of me, she has a friend group, but it's mostly people in her program at school. The same core group of people in all her classes. She doesn't date, she doesn't really go to parties. The few times she has gone to parties has always been because of me, when she thought I was shutting myself in too much. And even then, I'm right there with her, and she sticks to me like white on rice at those kinds of things," I explain.

"Alright, so not a lot of interpersonal connections?" Jones looks up at me after scribbling some more notes in his pad, I shake my head in response. "Alright, so who would you consider questionable if she doesn't really interact with people?"

"There's a guy in her program that's always in competition with Clara, and she *always* beats him out for everything. She even got the most prestigious internship over him, and he was pissed. Like super pissed. He's more than a little bit of a misogynist. He's definitely confronted her before."

"Name?" Jones asks.

"Preston Pierce," I tell them.

"Okay, anyone else?"

I proceed to tell them all about the people on my list and running through all the reasons I don't think they were really viable suspects, but I figure I should mention them just to be on the safe side. And then I get to my last theory.

"I looked at all those files, I've looked at them a million times. Clara knew something was going on and she was trying to find a connection. It has to be the same person, it's the only thing that makes sense, so it has to be someone who has been on campus each year that a girl went missing. So that's students, employees, professors, teaching assistants, that kind of thing. I have a hard time believing some pimple-faced eighteen-year-old was skilled enough to pull something like this off."

"So you think someone on campus?" Jones asks.

"Yes. Someone Clara probably would have never looked twice at being a danger. Or any of the other girls, for that matter. An employee would have a valid reason to be around them."

"We think so too, Kenz," Joe tells me.

I really did expect Jones to protest Joe validating my theory, but instead he's just going over his notes and jotting more things down.

"Do you know anything else, have you gotten anywhere with all the new information? Any leads, anything at all?" I ask Joe.

Joe sighs pretty big before finally answering me. "Not exactly. We've started running through all the information, independently verifying things. We've had to contact families since not everyone was reported missing. We are trying to get DNA samples from family members, but these kinds of things take time," Joe explains.

"DNA samples?" My stomach bottoms out. "But wouldn't you need something to compare it to?"

Crickets. The room is full of crickets. No one says anything. After a few seconds, Joe and Jones look at each other and Jones finally nods and Joe turns back to me.

"We've had someone looking through old files, people who have been found but not identified. Just trying to rule out that no one who is missing has shown up somewhere else." Joe starts.

"But someone has, someone has been found" I whisper.

"Yes, there's a Jane Doe that was found a few hours outside of Raleigh, no one identified her, and DNA was run but no matches. The general description fits height, age, weight, that kind of thing. All just general information. We just want to make sure, you know, rule out everything." Joe gives me a small smile that's clearly meant to reassure me. It doesn't.

"Fitz..." Jones mutters. They exchange another look.

"There's some concern, Kenz. You were right, the similarities are overwhelming, it looks like a pattern. These kinds of things, they don't normally end with, with well—"

"People who are alive?" I finish for him.

"Yeah. I'm sorry, Kenz. I really am. Like I said, we don't

know anything for sure, but we're going to run the DNA ASAP and get some answers."

"And if it's one of the missing?" I ask.

Joe doesn't say anything. Jones closes his notepad and looks up at me before making things clear.

"If it's one of the missing women, then the chances for the other women go way down. You should prepare yourself."

CHAPTER TWENTY

"FALLEN" BY SARAH MCLACHLAN

"*Prepare yourself.*"

The words keep ringing in my ears. It was always a possibility, but one I would never really let my mind wander off to, only in my nightmares. But in just a few seconds, the far-off possibilities suddenly look a whole lot more like reality. I don't know what I would do if she weren't on this earth anymore.

Living through another death. I probably have the same amount of memories with Clara as I did with my brother, if not more. Losing her would be devastating, the loss of another sibling essentially. Would I survive it? My parents are proof that you can survive something but at the same time not go on living. Is that what my future looks like?

As I'm leaving the police station, the voices telling me goodbye and they will be in touch all sound like they are coming from a million miles away. Like my head is underwater in the bath while someone in the room talks to me. I know they are there and talking, but no clue what they are saying. I don't really even care what they are saying at this point. No. I'm stuck on two words.

The daze I've been in as I walk through the station clears a little as soon as the crisp, cold air hits my skin. The shock of the temperature change has me realizing I didn't zip up my jacket or put on any gloves, so the cold is biting at my skin. Midway through pulling my gloves out of my jacket pocket, I hear his voice.

"You didn't call." The accusation is heavy in his voice.

You can do this. Be cool, I tell myself. I count to five before I finally lift my head and let my eyes meet his. He looks so nonchalant, just leaning back on a metal bench that no doubt is freezing the back of his thighs through his jeans. He's clearly waiting for me. How did he even know I was here?

"What?" I ultimately decide playing dumb is the best way to save face here.

"You didn't call me," Will repeats in the exact same tone and intonation as before. Like a recording, an exact replica.

There's an unspoken standoff between the two of us. Finally, Will sighs before leaning forward and putting his elbows on his thighs and clasping his gloveless hands together. I wonder if his fingers are as cold as mine.

"I would have come with you," he says. I must have a confused look on my face because he clarifies. "If you had called, I would have come to the interview with you. I would have wanted to be there with you."

"It wasn't a big deal, I was just sharing the information you already have." I shift my weight before meeting his eyes again. "There wasn't any need to bug you."

I feel his eyes boring into mine. He sees right through me, I'm sure of it. There is no way he doesn't know that I'm upset.

"What happened?"

"Nothing—"

"Don't," he interrupts. "What happened?"

"I answered some questions and met Joe's partner, like I said, nothing to write home about."

"That's how you want to play this?" he retorts on a huff.

I shift my weight back and forth on my feet a few times, hoping that it comes across as me being cold and not like I am squirming under his questions. I take the opportunity to cup my hands in front of my face to try and warm them up with my breath, and with any luck, keep Will from being able to get a good read on my emotions.

"Kenzie."

"Look, I'm sorry, okay, I just wanted to get it over with and I wasn't really in the mood to call you and talk about everything. Come on, you have to get that, right? It's embarrassing. Did you honestly expect I was just going to pick up the phone and be like 'Hey Will, wanna come down to the police station with me?' I don't think so." The words rush out of my mouth so fast I have no chance of stopping them.

I can tell Will doesn't know what to say to me now. I don't think he thought I was just going to come out and address the giant elephant in the room. That I tried to kiss him and he took a big giant pass.

Will narrows his eyes and takes a moment to stand up before addressing the situation as well. "You don't need to be embarrassed, there's nothing to be embarrassed about."

"Yeah, okay," I scoff.

"I'm serious. You've been through so much in such a short amount of time, of course it makes sense that you would be looking for comfort, we were finally getting somewhere with the case and you were happy. There's nothing wrong with that."

"That's what you think happened?" My eyes feel like they are going to pop out of my skull with how wide they are opened.

"It is what happened," Will declares.

"Okay. Sure."

"Kenzie." He takes a few steps closer to me. "What do you think happened?"

"Well, seeing as I'm the only one who gets to decide what I was feeling or why I do anything, don't you think it's a little more than what I *think* happened?" I retort.

There's a pause. It seems to go on forever.

"You're right," he says.

"I'm sorry, what now?" I say in disbelief.

"You heard me." He sighs. "Now tell me what I'm missing."

I don't want to. I don't want to tell him the truth, I don't want to tell him that I like him. How he makes me feel. How he's the silver lining in this hellish scenario.

"It doesn't matter," I tell him.

"It does if you are going to go in for police interviews without calling me," he argues, bringing us back to the beginning of this godforsaken circle.

"I didn't need to call you. I told you, it wasn't a big deal."

"I heard you the first time. I still don't believe you."

"Well, maybe I don't care what you believe."

"Kenzie."

"Will."

We stand there about two feet away from each other in a stare down. I break first.

"What do you want me to say?" I ask.

"The truth."

"Fine. I like you, okay? Like, *like you* like you."

Will looks genuinely shocked, but I still manage to steam-roll forward.

"Outside of that first day when we met, and I thought you were kind of a douche, but even then, I thought you were hot. You know, that whole hot guy asshole vibe thing." I wave my hand in the air like I'm swatting away an errant thought. "But then after that it was different, you were different. And I liked you. And I get it, you're not interested and it's not a good time. Apparently my friend is probably dead in the middle of nowhere and I'm standing here outside arguing with the guy I like because he doesn't like me back. Who does that? Could I be any more self-obsessed?" The guilt starts crawling up from my toes, quickly becoming suffocating.

The tips of Will's boots enter my vision as my head hangs down in defeat. He's so close I can almost feel the body heat coming off of him. Out of the corner of my eye, I can see Will lifting his hand to reach out to me before he hesitates.

"I don't know where to start," he says quietly.

"Nowhere. It's fine. I'm fine," I lie.

"Kenzie, did they say something in there to you about Clara?"

I guess Will is just going to stumble right on by the declaration of my feelings. Thank God.

"Not exactly," I whisper.

"Then why—"

"They're collecting DNA. There's a body. I think an old body from what they said, but they want to check it against the missing women's DNA. Something about it being consistent. And how I should prepare myself."

"Fuck." Will stops hesitating and reaches out for my hand. How in the world his fingers are as warm as they are is beyond me, but there's a sharp sting that comes with his warm fingers hitting the skin of my cold ones.

"Yeah," I whisper.

"I'm sorry, Kenzie."

I take a few moments to absorb the comfort he's giving me before throwing my walls back up and trying to protect my newly shattered heart against a different kind of trauma. I move out of the space Will and I are sharing.

"How did you know I was here?" I ask, trying to get my head straight.

"I didn't," he says, letting me take the space I need.

"Then how are you—"

"Sitting out here waiting for you?" he asks.

I nod.

"I have some information I needed to turn over to the police and while I was dropping it off, they were kind enough to let me know you were already here. I took it upon myself to wait."

"Information? What information? You handed over everything at the diner." I demand.

"I turned over all the information I had at the time. I had new information."

I barely have the time to open my mouth to demand the information before Will keeps going.

"I told you if this became an official police case, that I would be turning over everything to the police. I'm just doing what I said I would."

"Fine. What information?" I demand.

"Once King had everyone's name, she did a little digging on her own. She managed to get access to a couple of their email accounts and found some emails that fit the same pattern as with Clara. So I turned them over."

"Oh." I deflate a little. Not really new information, more like confirmation of the information that we already had. Nice to have but not really moving anything forward in any way.

"I've also been going over all the footage they have gotten so far from the library."

"You have footage, like real footage?" My body perks up at the thought of real information, something for me to do.

"This is ridiculous. You're freezing. Come back to the office, or fuck, pick a car and we can talk with a heater on."

He's not wrong. I am freezing my ass off. But I know if I sit in my compact car with Will, his presence will overwhelm the space and I will be even more uncomfortable than I am now.

"The truck," I tell him.

"Good." He turns and starts walking toward the parking lot as I fall in step behind him. That's when I notice he has his key fob in his hand and I can hear the beep of his truck in the distance and the engine roar to life. He's warming up the truck. Why can't he go back to being a douche? Him being a jerk would make this all so much easier.

When we reach the truck, he doesn't head for the driver's side. No, of course, he goes to the passenger side and opens the door for me. Our eyes meet as I pass him on the way to the front seat. It only takes a few seconds for Will to be in the truck with me, but I need those to try and convince myself he is a jerk and to let it go. It does not work.

"Footage?" I prompt.

"Joe sent over the footage they were able to get from the library, apparently they upgraded their system a couple years ago so everything is on digital and it's backed up for a fairly decent period of time."

"So twenty-four hours rerecords on VHS tapes?" I joke.

He laughs.

"I don't know how some people still use that nonsense, but no, it's digital. I scanned it and so did King, we both agree that there is no one there consistently over the corresponding time stamps for the emails. It was a long shot, but we had to look."

"Wait. What?"

"This guy has been covering his tracks all along, there was no way he was hanging out at the computer terminals sending blackmail emails in front of a camera so that all we had to do was match time stamps with security footage. We figured it was probably close enough to the library that he was able to tap into the Wi-Fi but far enough away not to be on library surveillance."

"So what, like in a car or something?"

"That's what our thought was," he agrees.

"Let me guess, the library doesn't have security cameras on the parking lot?"

"Oh, they do. The angles aren't great, and it's clear it's not their main concern, the outside cameras are mainly focused on entry points."

"I guess that makes sense." I sigh. "So, did you see anything?"

"Yes. We both found two cars that sat in the back of the parking lot, almost completely out of the cameras' field for long periods of time. But it's so far in the distance from the camera that we can't see inside the car or really get meaningful information about the cars other than they both looked like four-door cars in a dark color."

"Not exactly helpful," I commiserate.

"So early this morning I hit the surrounding businesses that might have any angle on the parking lot and I finally hit pay dirt at the little mom-and-pop taco place."

"You're kidding?" I'm stunned. Did he really just say we got lucky and have a real lead? Because it's sounding a lot like we might have just gotten a lead to work off of.

"Not kidding. I turned the footage over while I was there. I got the full plate of one car and a partial on the other. One of the plates came back as stolen, but the partial has a list we are going to have to sort through."

"Oh my god." I stare at Will in shock. "That's like a real lead. Like actual, *real* progress."

"Not done."

"Continue, continue." I motion my hand, trying to get him to hurry up. I should have never been avoiding him, I could have been working on this all along, how much further along would we be if I hadn't been such a coward?

"King said that one of Clara's files is so encrypted that she can't break it. Well, she said she probably could if she had an unlimited supply of Starbucks double shots and wasn't on a timeline. She decided this was too time sensitive, so she's taking the file to a friend who should be able to open it or at least help out a lot," Will explains.

"Okay, I trust King. If she says she needs help, then I'm all for it," I tell him.

"Good." Will nods.

There's a silence that seems to start small before it starts to build up in the cab of the truck. Ultimately, I'm the one who decides to break it.

"Will, I will never be able to say thank you enough for everything you are doing for me and Clara, I don't even know if I could put into words how grateful I am that you are helping with this."

"I know you're grateful, Kenzie, you don't have to say anything," Will tries to reassure me.

"I'm sorry about the other day. I shouldn't have put you in that position. I don't know what I was thinking. I would never want to make you uncomfortable, and of course, you aren't interested. I just, I wasn't thinking, I just, I dunno, I wanted to. I got caught up, and I shouldn't have, and I'm sorry." Clumsiest apology ever.

"Kenzie, you don't have anything to be sorry about, and it's not that I'm not interested—"

"Will, don't. It's okay. Clara is all that I can think about right now. She needs me. She needs us. So I just want to, I dunno, pretend it didn't happen or something." I lift my eyes up slowly to meet him, trying to will myself a backbone to hold up under the scrutiny.

Will doesn't say anything for a while. He looks like he is going to a couple of times, and his right arm keeps twitching like he wants to reach out, but ultimately, he holds himself back.

"Kenz—" he starts.

"Can we just put it behind us and move forward for Clara?" I'm close to begging. I'm sure my cheeks are red with my embarrassment. Hopefully he thinks it's the heat from the heater blowing at full force.

"If that's what you want, we can put it aside for now," Will says simply.

"Okay, good." I pause for a few moments before forging ahead on our new status quo. "Could you email me everything you have so far?"

"Already done."

"Okay, well then, I guess that's it," I say on a shrug.

"I guess so."

"I really am sorry," I say quietly.

"You didn't do anything wrong, I promise, you didn't do a single thing wrong, Kenzie," he tries reassuring me again. And with that, it is time to go our separate ways. With any luck, the next time we meet it won't be this level of uncomfortable and I won't feel the urge to run and hide under a pile of blankets at the end of it.

CHAPTER TWENTY-ONE

"SCHOOL'S OUT" BY ALICE COOPER

I spend the rest of the afternoon going over all the information for the millionth time, although this is the first time that I have media to go through. I have to admit I don't know how cops spend time going through surveillance footage on a regular basis, it's literally the most mind-numbing thing in the world to do. Besides, unless you really know what you are looking for, it is hard to tell what is just normal everyday people going about their lives and who is the bad guy. Unfortunately for the rest of us, bad guys seem to look like everyone else. It would be so much more convenient if they would just wear signs around their necks or something.

I spent hours watching the footage last night, and if Will hadn't included the helpful hint to not watch it at speed but rather to speed it up, I would have gone crazy. Hell, I did go a little crazy. I even nodded off a couple of times. It's easy to see how things could be missed when going over this kind of footage.

I did finally find the cars that Will was talking about yesterday at the police station. I totally get what he was saying about how it was hard to really tell anything about the cars other than they were four-door cars that were dark colored. I have no idea how he managed to get license plate numbers off them, I had it zoomed in and my face pushed up against the screen and I don't think I could tell you more than a number or two off of them. But then again, Will does this for a living and he has King in his corner, maybe she was able to get it.

I even spent some of last night going over my list of suspects. Or rather nonspecific suspects. I went down some sort of social media rabbit hole trying to find references to the jerk Clara was always competing with or the professor she didn't like. And then I made a big mistake. I looked for current social media posts. I started with Jenny's name because she has the more visible case compared to everyone else.

For the most part, everyone was really supportive, you know the standard thoughts and prayers and people trying to spread awareness about Jenny being missing. Some people were even sharing little anecdotes and stories about how nice she is as a person and how everyone loves having her around. I'd say eighty percent was nice and positive.

But the other twenty percent. It's like a cesspool of cretins. The absolute worst of the worst internet trolls. People speculating about all the possible things that could be being done to her right now, it's like some weird bizarro fantasy torture porn or something.

After that, I just kept going from being so angry I wanted to scream to being so disheartened by humanity that I wanted to cry. I don't understand how anyone could be excited by the idea that some young woman they don't even know could be out there somewhere suffering a horrible fate. It's disgusting.

The only positive about the whole thing is on some of the posts about Jenny there are some mentions of Clara and the other women. The word is slowly starting to get out. This is a case of missing women. Foul play. People are aware now, they can be on the lookout and take precautions to keep themselves safe. It isn't much, but it is something. Something I can be proud of and hopeful that it will bring me one more step closer to getting Clara back home where she belongs.

Which brings me to now. Slightly defeated, slightly hopeful, more than a little afraid. So I do the only thing I can think of. Sitting on my couch for the millionth time staring up at my Wall of Crazy. Everything is starting to blur together, but at least this time I'm comfortable. I still haven't managed to get out of my pajamas. Flannel pants and a hoodie with a cup of hot cocoa while wrapped in one of those overpriced fuzzy lap blankets from Target is my idea of the ideal way to spend a morning. Granted, it would be better if I was watching *The Holiday* for the millionth time instead of staring up at the world's most depressing wall, but that's life.

Thankfully my phone picks this time to start beeping, effectively saving me from falling back down the rabbit hole of despair. Determined to be positive, I stumble off the couch in search of my phone.

Don't ask me how it ended up underneath the sofa, but sure enough, that's where I finally find it.

WILL: **You awake?**

Me: **Yep. Sleeping isn't one of those things that happens a lot around here anymore.**

I miss sleep.

Will: **I'm sure. So I have an update.**

Me: **Okay**

Will: **King is headed over to my place to go over some information.**

Me: **Did she get that last file open?**

Will: **She didn't say.**

Me: **Did she already meet with that guy?**

Will: Look King isn't exactly forthcoming with things except in person.

Me: Oh.

Will: Do you want to come meet with us, that way you get information as I get it?

Me: Really?

Will: Yeah, I don't want there to be any miscommunication between us.

I would rather us both get the information at the same time.

I DON'T KNOW what to do with that. It's kind of nice that he's thinking about my feelings on the matter. And the truth is, I know I overreacted yesterday. My feelings were already bruised from the rejection, I couldn't help but come down on him for not telling me everything immediately. He really didn't do anything wrong at all. But even in spite of that, he's still trying to make me feel better.

I really do wish he was more of a jerk. It would be easier to stop liking him if he could just be an asshole.

ME: I really appreciate that, Will, really, thank you

Will: Of course.

She's meeting me over at my place, do you want me to pick you up?

Me: Are you not at home?

Will: No, I'm at home

Me: Then it makes no sense for you to leave only to head back to your place, I'll just drive myself

Will: Do you remember how to get here?

Me: Uh, not really. I was mostly asleep the last time we drove to your place.

Will: LOL

Alright I'll just text you the address and you can follow the GPS

Me: Sounds like a plan.

It only takes a few seconds for Will to send me a pin to click on with his current location so that Maps can give me directions. I wait for the app to plot the fastest trip to Will's place, which as it turns out, is not exactly the quickest trip in the world. It's at least a thirty-minute drive. I swear one of the things that drives me batty about North Carolina is how you can't get anywhere in any sort of straight line. Even some of the highways out here feel like back roads.

Since it's going to be a trek up there, I need to get moving, I'm pretty sure King isn't the kind of person who is just going to stand around waiting. No, she seems more like the type to do what she sets out to do and leave a trail of dust in her wake as she goes back home.

Still aiming for continued comfort, I slide on my favorite pair of well-worn jeans. The denim is a little thicker because it's not a stretchy material and while the waistband has a nice comfortable fit to it, the rest of it is probably about a half size too big. Basically, the perfect amount of comfort, especially for a trip in my car. A T-shirt and a hoodie complete the look, and two minutes and a messy bun later, I'm out the door.

It turns out Wednesday night at nine p.m. is not a time that anyone is out on the road. And while I always appreciate not

having to combat traffic, it feels more than a little creepy to be out on the road by myself in the dark, surrounded by the giant pines everywhere.

I've never been a big fan of driving in the dark. It's just not my thing. Hell, driving isn't really my thing. I don't trust other drivers. Or the weather.

The quiet in the car is really playing into the creepy sensation that's starting to take hold. And of course, that's the moment that Mother Nature decides my life hasn't been challenging enough lately and the sky opens up.

I know they say it rains in Seattle all the time but I often wonder if these same people have never visited here before. I can't remember a week that went by where there was not some kind of rain, and more often than not, it's more than one day with rain. It never stops. And it always seems to happen when I am driving. I'm like a magnet for rain.

Reaching over to grab my phone off the passenger seat so I can turn on my upbeat driving playlist, I notice there are flashing lights up ahead.

"What now?" I wonder out loud.

By the time I get my playlist started and classic rock starts pumping out of my speakers, I can tell that the flashing lights are construction.

"Always with the fucking construction," I mutter under my breath.

With these small two-lane highways, construction means one side of the traffic isn't moving at all while traffic on the opposite end goes forward using our lane. Basically, hurry up and wait. There may not have been traffic when I started this journey, but there is sure as shit a backlog of cars starting to build up behind me.

I take this opportunity to try and relax. Reaching over to turn up the volume, Alice Cooper starts piping out through my speakers. Before I know it, my head is moving up and down and

I'm doing my full-body shimmy while belting out "School's Out."

It kind of feels like school is out. I haven't been going to classes and I've all but given up on graduating with my entire focus being on getting Clara back, everything else has just flown out the window.

I'm not sure what catches my eye when I am moving around in my seat singing my little heart out but something does. It feels like a cold chill running through my entire body without any warning and without any definable reason.

It's that shudder that crawls up your spine and ends at the base of your neck until the tingling sensation triggers a full shoulder shiver. My brother used to call it someone walking over your grave.

Looking around, I don't see anything. My car inches forward as it looks like it's finally our lane of traffic's turn to go. I don't see anything weird at all. There are people out on the road doing construction in the rain, but they are all actively doing something. It's not like anyone is standing on the side of the road, giving me the creeps.

With a quick glance up, I check my rearview mirror and something just feels wrong. There's a car two cars back, one that I'm positive was pulling out of my apartment complex at the same time I was. It's dark outside, so I can't make out a ton of detail about the car, but one of the headlights is brighter than the other one and I remember thinking it was a weird quirk as I was leaving the parking lot.

As the cars start to move forward and more space is being put between the cars, I can tell this is definitely the car with the weird headlights. I've never seen a car with lights like this before, so there's no way this is just some kind of coincidence.

But why would someone be following me? I mean, there's no way, right?

I keep trying to convince myself I am being paranoid, but in the back of my mind, I can't help but wonder if I'm right.

I bring both hands up to the wheel, focusing on driving and abandoning my classic rock dancing. A quick glance to my phone sitting in the cup holder on the center console tells me that there is a turn coming up that I'm supposed to take.

This is going to be the test I need. Will lives out on land, there are few houses out there, not even really a neighborhood, just a smattering of homes around big swaths of land. So the chances that someone would be taking this obscure exit while also coming from my apartment complex is basically next to zero.

Here's where I find the truth.

My breathing speeds up in my chest. I can feel my chest rise faster and for shorter times as my anxiety starts to reach the pinnacle. I'm trying to resist the urge to tap my foot, not wanting to accidentally hit a pedal not meaning to.

As I get closer to the turnoff, I start debating in my head about whether I should use my turn signal or not. Part of the reason I hate driving so much is that you can't trust people to follow the rules of the road, and there's something about flipping the handle up or down to signal a turn that gives me such satisfaction. I don't think I have *ever* not signaled for a turn in my life.

I decide not to. My anxiety makes it almost painful as I slow my car just enough to take the turn safely in the rain. As soon as the turn is finished, I hold my breath and wait as my car continues down the road.

One Mississippi.

Two Mississippi.

Three Mississippi.

I think I make it, I think I'm wrong, no one is following me. I'm just being paranoid as I keep my eyes glued to my rearview mirror.

Four Mississippi.

Five Mississ—

Wait. Is that him? I squint just a little, while keeping my eyes glued to the rearview mirror. It doesn't take long for me to realize that the car behind me is, in fact, the car with the weird headlights.

Panic starts to completely take over my body. I can feel my heart beating in my chest hard against my sternum.

I think to myself, *What do I do?* I've never been followed before. I've never been in any kind of dangerous situation unless you count Chanel starting drama in person on campus, which, let's face it, is not actually dangerous, just annoying.

Will's face flashes in my mind, he would know what to do. I'm already accelerating down the dark road in an effort to avoid this guy. I lean forward to grab my phone out of the cup holder and feel the restraint of the seat belt push against my chest. I look up just in time to see that the road is curving. The phone slips out of my hand and down to the floor beneath me as I grab the steering wheel to have more control as my car goes into the curve in what is turning out to be a decent rainstorm.

I know I'm not supposed to brake in these situations, it makes it worse. I think. Don't you hydroplane or something? I really should have paid more attention in physics class. Either way, I resist the urge to slam on the brakes and as I'm going through the curve, I feel the back end of my car start to fishtail. My heart feels like it's up in my throat, but thankfully I don't spin or anything crazy as my car keeps eating up the pavement between me and Will's house.

I have no idea how far away I am.

"Fuck." I don't have my phone. I have no idea how far I am from Will's house or even how to get there. I can't pull over to get the phone, that would just be asking for trouble and leave me as a wide-open target. What if it's the guy who took Clara?

I briefly let my mind imagine what would happen if it is

him. Would he kill me or would he take me to where he is holding Clara? At least then I would know if she is alive.

"No! Focus!" I tell myself.

I put my foot down on the gas and start looking for a turnoff or somewhere I can hide so that I have the time to look for my phone. But nothing jumps out at me. The lighting on this road is shit, with my headlights being the only light source working against the increasing rain.

In a Hail Mary effort, I lean forward in my seat and once more feel my seat belt start to pull me backward. My chest just starts to make contact with the steering wheel as I take one hand off the wheel and start trying to feel around underneath me for my phone.

Just as I feel my fingertips brush against it, I feel my car lose grip on the road. It probably only takes milliseconds for me to lose control and my car veers off the road, but in those seconds, everything feels like it is slowing down.

I can see the individual raindrops as they are making contact with the windshield, the trees as they are illuminated by light coming from my headlights, and lastly the high grass surrounding a small ditch running the length of the road that I hadn't noticed until just this second.

And once more, that feeling of dread invades my body. As soon as the car hits the ditch, it starts to roll, and I know I'm fucked.

If this car crash doesn't kill me, there is a good chance whoever is following me will.

At least this time he won't be able to cover his tracks.

CHAPTER TWENTY-TWO

"CAR CRASH" BY OUR LADY PEACE

My body comes to consciousness abruptly at the crack of thunder. It takes a few moments for me to open my eyes because everything just feels wrong. Confusion floods my thoughts and an unexplainable feeling of panic. But the real motivator to get moving and open my eyes is the fear that is pumping through my blood. In fact, in this moment, fear is the only thing I'm a hundred-percent sure of.

My eyes take longer than they should to open. It feels like when you sleep way too long and they are caked closed. Only the sensation is different, almost sticky.

Even in the dark, I can tell my vision is blurry. A flash of light illuminates the area in front of me but it takes a while for me to realize it is lightning, gone as quick as it comes, leaving behind only the confirmation that my vision is a hot mess.

Before I even feel the pain, I feel pressure. My head feels like it's heavy, but oddly, it's mostly a full sensation at the top of my head with a fullness that makes me think my face might be swollen. But the strangest pressure is coming from my chest. It feels like someone is sitting on my chest, but oddly, there isn't any pain or discomfort from the pressure on my back.

Bringing my hands up to my face to see if it is in fact swollen allows my body weight to shift, bringing a sharp jerk of whatever is across my chest, startling me.

"What the hell?" I murmur to myself while bringing my hands down to my chest and find a strap across my chest holding me in place.

I'm upside down. How the fuck am I upside down? Well, that explains all the pressure I'm feeling, my face probably looks like a tomato with all the blood rushing to my head. With that figured out, I go back to trying to figure out what's wrong with my eyes, and sticky is exactly the right word. My face is wet, all over wet. But not all of it feels like water, no, some of it feels thick and sticky.

My pinkie finger brushes up against something embedded in my face, and the pain is startling. It kind of feels like when you step on a pebble and it gets stuck on the bottom of your foot, except different, sharp. It takes a few seconds to get a purchase on whatever it is and pull it out of my face, which only unleashes more sticky liquid down, or rather up, my face. Blood. It's blood.

Another flash of lightning lets me see my rosary pooled at what is apparently the roof of my car, to be exact. I'm upside down in my car.

How the fuck did this happen?

There's a hole where the memory should be. The only things left behind are panic and fear. Trying to rationalize that it makes sense I would be afraid if I was about to be in a car accident doesn't really work. Something tells me it's more than that. The more I think about it, the more I think I shouldn't be in this car.

My vision is finally starting to clear up or maybe my eyes

are just getting the opportunity to adjust to the pitch black, so I decide it's time to go.

Fumbling around trying to find the release to the seat belt takes more time than I would expect, I guess being upside down really messes with the way your brain perceives your physical location. As soon as I hit the release, though, nothing happens. The mechanism doesn't pop out and my weight is still resting on the seat belt, keeping me attached to the seat.

"Think, think," I whisper.

The door. I should try the door next. As soon as my arm starts to cross over my body, I feel this sharp and sudden overwhelming pain. It feels like someone is wrenching my arm out of the socket. The pain is so intense and sudden that I start to get dizzy and feel like I'm going to pass out. Clutching my arm against my chest, I try to hold on to consciousness while realizing how much trouble I'm really in.

A few seconds pass before I realize I have a knife in my glove box that I could use to get out of the seat belt.

There's no way I can reach the glove compartment with my left hand, so with the only option being my injured right arm, I take a deep breath and push through the pain. Tears start welling up in my eyes and a cold sweat breaks out along my skin as I finally feel my fingers wrap around the cold steel of the knife.

I take another deep breath, knowing what comes next is bound to hurt just as much.

It's not like the movies where I could just swipe through the seat belt and suddenly be free. No, it's a lot harder than that. I've been hanging upside down for who knows how long, I'm clearly injured, and my body is quickly getting weaker and weaker the longer I'm in this cold and wet car. What must have been minutes pass by as I struggle to saw my knife through the tightly woven fabric of my seat belt.

The last swipe of the knife has me propelling down to the

roof of my car with no way to catch myself. The shock of hitting the roof echoes through my body and leaves a wake of pain in its path.

I should be feeling better about this. I'm making progress. But honestly, I only feel worse.

My body hurts worse than when I woke up and I feel way more panicked now that I am free than I did when I was pinned down. It doesn't seem logical.

I let myself just lie on the roof for a few minutes before I realize that my body is starting to shake and my teeth are starting to chatter against each other. The urge to take a nap is starting to take hold and the fear I had been battling up until this point starts to take a back seat.

Get up. You have to get up. I lift my head up to look around. I know I just heard a voice, but I can't see anything. And the only thing I can hear right now is music coming out of my radio. I think I imagined it. Either way, it feels like good advice.

Rolling over takes time, as I try to protect all the areas of my body that are aching. The palms of my hands keep landing on top of little pieces of glass I assume are from the windshield, I think a few have actually embedded themselves into the skin. When my hand finally hits the cold wet grass, it's startling.

I no longer want to sleep and the fear is starting to take hold again. I'm still on my hands and knees as I make it out of the car and look around.

Now that I'm out, I can tell I obviously crashed, and the lighting is better so I can get a better idea of what's going on and where I am. Even with more light, I'm struggling to figure out which direction to go, I see headlights coming toward me and that's when everything in my body shifts.

A cold sweat breaks out against my skin and my heart starts pumping harder and I can feel my pulse in my ears. I probably have a head injury and my body is definitely battered and bruised, but I know I can't head toward the road and those lights.

There is no doubt in my mind, not even a little, that I need to move in the opposite direction.

I start dragging my body toward the tree line, at first feeling the wetness of the grass saturate through my jeans even more before I'm able to get into an upright position. I give thanks that I didn't wear flimsy shoes, my leather boots did a good job protecting my feet in the crash, and I get the feeling I'm going to need that protection as I start hobbling into the trees.

I risk a quick look back when I see the lights stop moving next to my upside-down car.

The only thing I know for sure is that whoever this person is, they are in a car similar to mine and that in no way should I call out to them for help.

I start moving faster into the woods, trying to be as quiet as I can, hoping beyond all hope that whoever was in that car didn't see me limping into the woods.

But I don't have that kind of luck. I hear the door slam shut, bringing about a second wind I didn't know I had in me.

The woods are densely packed, which I'm grateful for because I'm having trouble keeping myself both upright and moving forward. I keep tripping over roots or things on the ground, mostly because my legs feel like they are made of cement and it's hard to lift them high enough to get clearance. I keep my left arm as outstretched as possible to keep finding trees to hold me upright while I keep my right arm tucked into my side, trying to protect the shoulder from being jostled any more than it has to be.

I quickly pause to catch my breath, letting me hear someone starting to enter the woods behind me.

Fight, flight, or freeze. I've heard about it a million times. My body wants to freeze, to simply stay still to avoid the pain. My brain, though, is screaming, *RUN*.

Knowing there is no fight in me, I start moving forward as quickly as I can. Even knowing I am being chased, I can't help but to chance a look back. I can't even tell where the tree line begins, let alone make out the shape of a body.

I finally start building up a hobbling rhythm as I stumble through the woods. I know I'm making too much noise. I know I am probably the easiest person in the world to track right now. The grunts alone are leaving a sound trail to follow as I stumble around.

Fuck, I don't even know which direction I should be running, just that I should be running.

And that's when I hear it. A voice. It's close to me and moving closer. My head is pounding and I can't make out what the voice is saying, but I know I don't have a chance. Whoever it is is getting closer and there is no way I can possibly get moving fast enough to outrun them.

So, I do the only thing I have left in my arsenal. Drop.

The impact of my knees hitting the ground is rough, but I don't take the time to absorb it, instead I start moving behind a tree and feeling around on the ground for a stick. My hand finally makes purchase on the wet, uneven bark of a branch. Even though I'm right-handed, I know there is no way I am going to be swinging a branch with my right hand so I take hold of it in my left. The glass still embedded in my palm stings as I grip the branch and wait to make what is probably going to be my last stand.

I start holding my breath, hoping they will just pass me by.

The voice is getting closer.

And clearer.

It's my name.

Whoever it is is saying my name.

"Kenzie!"

There's no fear this time though. No fear at all. Relief.

I can see my breath as I let out the breath I had been holding.

I try to call out, but it takes a few seconds and takes clearing my throat a few times before I'm finally able to call out.

"Out here." It's not what I would call loud, but the rain is starting to die down, so there is a good chance they heard me.

"Thank God," I hear the voice exclaim and I hear the sounds of underbrush crunching down as whoever it is makes it to me.

As soon as I see his face, it's like everything hits me like a semitruck. Will. Clara. The killer. Someone was following me. I crashed my car trying to get away. Oh my god, did someone really just try to follow me into the woods? Denial hits me like a strong slap in the face as I tell myself it was just Will in the woods looking for me. He probably got worried when I didn't show up and went searching for me, found my car, and then set out to find me, Or at least that's what I try and rationalize.

My breathing starts to slow as I start talking myself into this scenario. Until I finally realize, Will came from the opposite direction. I definitely wasn't the only person in these woods, but there is no way Will could be both in front of me and behind me at the same time.

Will crouches down in front of me as I start to hyperventilate. His eyes are scanning my body and I can tell he's all business as he catalogs what are probably a substantial amount of injuries. He leans forward to take my arms in his hands, I feel the involuntary flinch as I anticipate the pain in my right shoulder. He hesitates.

"I would ask if you are okay, but it seems like a silly question. Deep breaths, Kenz. In. Out." I start following his instructions while staring up at him. "Good, that's good, just like that."

"Will, someone was behind me, following me," I plead with him to believe me but he's already nodding.

"I know, I saw your car. There's another car abandoned next

to it. I didn't see you on the road, so I figured you went into the woods. I took a shortcut," he explains. "Come on, we need to get you out of this rain, I already called 911. They should be here shortly and we can get you checked out."

I can tell he's trying to keep me calm by not harping on how close I just came to being in real trouble. But at the same time, I can see him scanning the woods in thirty-second intervals, and when I follow his arm down the length of his body, I notice that he is resting his hand on something on his hip.

Will has a gun. How did I not know that? Of course he has a gun, he used to be a cop. But he's never called attention to it before. He's trying to keep me calm while being prepared to defend us if he needs to. He's right, we need to get out of these woods.

I let Will help me up as gingerly as he can manage, and I can see him grimace when I cry out from the pain in my shoulder as we start moving through the woods. When we finally clear the new tree line, I look back and realize how close all this could have been.

The fear is still there, but the feeling of safety that Will provides is overpowering it.

As I make my way to the truck, I can't help but wonder if this is the kind of fear Clara felt when she went missing.

If it's the kind of fear she's still experiencing.

CHAPTER TWENTY-THREE
"IN THE PINES" BY CAUGHT A GHOST

The red and blue lights from the police cars are starting to make me dizzy. It didn't take long for them to show up after Will and I made it out from the woods. Once he got me settled into his truck with the heater on, I could tell he wanted to go look for whoever else was in the woods, but he stayed glued to my side.

When the cops showed up, they showed up in force. One car quickly became four and people started fanning out into the woods to see if they could find anything. The ambulance wasn't that far behind them.

Which is how I end up sitting in the back of the ambulance, waiting for everyone to decide what is going to happen next. I try to keep my eyes down so the bright rotating lights from all the emergency vehicles don't kill my eyes, but I'm not successful at all. Every new voice or loud noise has me searching the tree line for the bogeyman coming out of the trees.

I've already told the cops everything I know up to this point so now I'm just waiting to see what happens next. Even though more and more of my memory is starting to come back, everything still feels fuzzy around the edges. I'm becoming more and more certain that I have some kind of head injury.

Searching the crowd, I finally find Will, and after only a few short minutes, he starts heading over to me.

"I take it you earned yourself a first-class trip to the hospital," he says, trying to lighten the mood.

"You can ride with us if you want," the EMT tells him.

"Take the truck," I retort immediately, leading to a confused and, dare I say, even a little hurt look on Will's face. "I don't want us to be stuck at the hospital, it will be faster if we have a way to leave," I explain.

"Oh, yeah, of course, I'll follow you guys," he says before turning to walk away.

"Will," I call after him.

"Yeah?" he says after turning around to face me. I kind of love that about him, he always makes sure I know I have his full attention when he talks to me.

"Did they find anything? The car? Anything at all?" I ask, silently begging the universe for answers. The look on Will's face tells me everything I need to know. They don't have shit.

"I'm sorry. By the time they got here, the car was gone. I gave them the license plate number I saw when I was driving by, but the car was reported stolen a couple of days ago so it's not really much to go on." He looks regretful.

"Oh. Okay." The urge to comfort him is strong, and I can't help it. "You saved me, Will. If you had hesitated even a little bit instead of coming after me, who knows where we would be now."

"I just don't like that he's still out there and he clearly knows who you are. You're a loose end for this guy, and I don't want him to get anywhere near close enough to try again."

"You and me both." I try to give him a reassuring smile, but I'm sure it ends up looking more like a grimace. "I'll see you at the hospital."

ABOUT A BAZILLION TESTS later and more imaging of myself than any one person could ever need, the verdict is in. I'm broken. That might be a little dramatic. One cracked rib, surrounded by what they called severely bruised ribs from the seat belt, basically code for it's going to hurt to breathe for a while. My right shoulder was dislocated, no surprise there. Thank God for painkillers because the sound my shoulder made when they put it back in place was nothing short of disgusting. To no one's surprise at all, I have a concussion. As for the rest of me, well, it's not pretty. There are tiny cuts all over my face and hands from the glass in the car. Not to mention all the bruises that are starting to fill in nicely, turning me into a molted mess of blue and purples.

The hospital bed is uncomfortable, people keep coming to check on me, and the lights are entirely too bright for my eyes. I want to go home more than I have ever wanted anything in my life. But I'm stuck here until they give me the okay. Apparently even though I didn't throw up, the fact that I had some memory loss and had a hard time maintaining consciousness basically means they want to watch me for a while. I get it. I really do. I just don't want to stay anymore.

Will hasn't left my side basically the entire time. He stood outside the rooms where I was x-rayed and CAT scanned and he hasn't been more than a few steps away from my room.

Even now I know he's right outside in the hall, because while I can't see him, I can definitely hear him. I'm pretty sure he is talking to King. I know I shouldn't be listening in on his conversation, especially since he left the room to make sure it stayed private, but I can't help myself.

Besides, he's talking about me, that gives me a free pass, right?

"I don't want to leave her on her own. Not until we have a

better idea of what is going on and who was following her." He sounds agitated. More so than I have heard him before.

"She said the first time she saw the car was when she was leaving her apartment complex, so whoever it was definitely knew where to find her. The real question is, what was he planning on doing? Was he just planning on following her, and then he took advantage of the accident or was his intention always to go after her?" Well, that's not unsettling at all.

Why was this guy following me? Was he trying to figure out what I know? Does that mean he knows I'm the one who has been pushing this forward, that I'm the reason we were able to make all those connections and now the cops are after him? Somehow that doesn't seem like a good thing.

"The police have her phone, but I want to get her laptop. I want to know if this guy has been keeping tabs on her from the beginning or if this is new because the cases are all being connected. I looked at all the mentions on social media and Kenzie's name isn't mentioned once, so unless you are a cop, there's no way he should know that she's been at the center of everything."

He's right, of course. No one should know about me. Outside of the first couple of days when I was asking around, there haven't been that many people to talk to about Clara on campus.

"Have you mentioned anything to anyone about Kenzie?" There's only a short pause. "Right, well, can you send me his information? I want to check him out just to be on the safe side." Another pause. "Thanks, King, I just want her to be safe. She's really banged up and in no position to defend herself, so the sooner we put a face and a name to this guy, the better."

It's funny. I feel both reassured by Will's desire to keep me safe and also a little terrified because he's absolutely right. I can't defend myself. And as of right now, any random person on the street could be the bad guy. And with that, I suddenly don't like being in this room by myself.

It's nearly four in the morning by the time the ER doctor comes in with discharge instructions and I couldn't be more excited. If there is one thing I have learned about emergency rooms is that they are full of random people, and when you are being hunted by some unknown person, that's enough to drive you crazy.

"You shouldn't be alone for the next day or so," the doctor says for what is probably the third time.

"I know," I say yet again.

"I'll stick right next to her, doc. No worries," Will pipes in.

The doctor turns to look over Will before finally nodding, apparently having decided that Will will do for taking care of me.

"You need to take it easy too. No strenuous activity for the next couple of days. You are going to be sore, probably increasingly sore for the first couple of days, so you want to let yourself heal. Definitely move around, you don't want to get stiff, but stick close to home and avoid any heavy lifting, especially with that arm." He motions to the arm I'm still semi-cradling against my body.

"Got it, take it easy, I can do that," I lie through my teeth.

The doctor rolls his eyes, clearly being wise to my plans of getting right back to my normal life.

"You are also going to want to take deep breaths. It's going to hurt, and you aren't going to want to do it, but if you don't, you risk developing complications from the broken and bruised ribs." He explains.

Figuring I don't have anything to lose, I give it a try. Feeling the air rush through my nose and start to fill up my lungs is fine at first, and then it feels like ribs are being ripped from my chest for a moment. I quickly release the breath while cringing from the pain.

"Yeah, hurts. You're looking at about six weeks for full recovery but breathing will get easier with time," he assures me.

"If you say so," I mutter in disbelief.

"Well, that's it, you're free to go. Take care of yourself." With that, he's gone without a second glance back.

"Well, that was abrupt," I try to joke.

"It's busy out there with the rain and everything," Will explains.

"So, you don't mind giving me a ride back to my place, right?" I say with a grin.

Will's expressions shift from being calm and concerned to full of darkness.

"You can't honestly think you are going back to your apartment," he says incredulously.

"Of course I do."

"You were literally just chased through the woods, you can't be left alone with your head injury, you can barely use your dominant arm, and you can't take a deep breath without collapsing in on yourself. There is no way you are going back to that apartment by yourself."

"So what do you suggest then, since you seem to know everything?" I ask.

"I'll take you back to your apartment," he says, and I must look like the cat who caught the canary because he quickly follows it up. "But only to get your laptop so we can hand it over to King and pack you a bag."

"Seriously?" He just stares at me. He doesn't even look like he's breathing. He's just staring at me with the no-nonsense look on his face. "Where exactly am I supposed to go then?"

"You've slept in my guest room before, no reason why you can't do it again," he explains.

"Will—"

"No. Whatever argument you have, it doesn't matter. I'm not leaving you out there by yourself to get picked off by this guy. He was at your apartment complex, Kenzie. He knows where you live. What's to stop him from trying again? At least my house has security, King even vetted it, so I know you will be safe there. Until this guy is caught, I'm not going anywhere. And you aren't going to be alone. It's not worth the risk."

"Will, I know you're worried and everything, and trust me I am too, but don't you think that with everything it's going to be awkward or weird?" I plead.

"No. It can be awkward and weird later. When the threat has passed. And you're still alive to argue with me or ignore me or whatever you want."

Water starts to build up along my tear line at having someone in my life who wants to protect me like this. Well, it's something I didn't realize how much I wanted.

But one thing is for sure, I'm going to hold on to it for however long it lasts.

"You win," I tell him. "Let's go home."

CHAPTER TWENTY-FOUR
"BACK TO YOU" BY THE MAYRIES

I feel the sunlight on my face long before I open my eyes. It is honestly more than a little disorienting since I have blackout curtains in my bedroom. What can I say? I'm a girl who loves her sleep.

Opening my eyes is nothing more than a mistake as the sunlight seems to sear the interior of my brain. After a lot of blinking and trying to shield my face from the abrasiveness of the light, I look around the room trying to figure out what is going on.

It takes a few moments to remember the events of last night. Going to see Will to get new information from King, almost dying, not being able to stay at my own apartment for the foreseeable future. Fuck, my life is a hot mess.

I don't know why it never once occurred to me to ask last night, or I guess early this morning, what it was that King was coming over to explain to Will. I try to think back to remember if there was any clue about what she might have found. I remember something about more files being so encrypted that she wasn't going to be able to open them on her own and she wanted to reach out for help. Maybe she was able to get them opened, and she was going to tell us what was on them. Will would for sure know what was going on.

So, I set out to find Will. Only, of course, that doesn't work out as planned.

I roll out of bed the exact same way I always do. Like muscle memory. Only this time, I almost collapse to the floor while doing it. My entire body feels like it has been run over by a steamroller. I can't help but wonder if there is any part of my body that isn't bruised.

I barely manage to catch myself using my left arm to grab hold of the bed, which, of course, means my torso makes contact with the bed as I am falling. Bruised ribs are no joke. I don't know how I even forgot that they were messed up, because the searing pain that follows is intense. Every breath feels kind of like little needles inside my chest.

By the time I manage to get upright with my feet steady underneath me, I have already abandoned my plan to get dressed before going downstairs to find Will. It sounds too painful. Will can just deal with my puppy pajama pants and ripped-up T-shirt. I am beyond trying to impress anyone at this point. Plus, he has seen worse, I looked at myself in the mirror at my apartment this morning and saw just how rough I looked before I showered and packed a bag. Not a pretty sight at all.

I am actually pretty good walking down the hallway. One foot in front of the other, no teetering, mostly just soreness. But the stairs... the stairs are a whole different beast. Every step down jostles my torso and my ribs. Not to mention the shock impact on my poor knees as one leg has to support my whole body weight as I maneuver down the stairs.

I find Will sitting on the couch in the living room, hunched over with his elbows on his knees, looking at a laptop sitting on a coffee table. If he had a hard time sleeping last night, he certainly doesn't look it.

Clothed in what I am starting to think of as his uniform,

dark-blue jeans, black compression shirt. The only difference is this time he isn't wearing the boots. He isn't wearing shoes at all, just a simple pair of black socks. Probably more for warmth than anything else.

So basically, Will looks put together, and I look like a train wreck. A train wreck breaking out in a cold sweat after the going downstairs excursion.

"Hey," I say slowly as I continue to maneuver myself into the living room.

"You're up," he replies without looking up.

Looking around the room, I briefly consider sitting next to Will on the couch before quickly deciding against it. The couch looks so comfy, the kind of couch you can sink into and take a nice nap and not wake up sore. Basically, if I sit in it, there is no way I am going to be able to get up anytime soon.

Instead, I go for the accent chair that looks like it has way more structure than the couch could ever hope for. I should be able to get out of it later without needing any help.

"Yep," I finally reply. "What are you up to?"

"Just going over everything again, trying to make sure I didn't miss anything."

"Have you heard anything from the police yet?" I ask nervously.

Will finally looks up and the wince that crosses his face is gone so quickly that I probably would have missed it if I had been blinking. I'm guessing the bruising is worse than it was last night. There's a reason I didn't look in the mirror when I made my pit stop in the bathroom.

"Actually, yes," he tells me as he leans back into the couch. "They found the car that had been following you last night, only a couple miles away too."

"Really?" I say, unable to keep the excitement out of my voice.

"It's not a big break, he set the damn thing on fire. If there was any evidence in that car, it's long gone, and even if there is something left behind, it's going to take forever for them to recover it." He sounds pissed.

"Oh. Alright then, anything else?"

"They did some interviews. The construction crew remember the car, your description of the uneven headlights was very helpful. Everyone remembered the car. Unfortunately, it was nighttime, so no one got a good look at the driver. The only thing everyone agreed on was that it was a man. So not exactly helpful, but confirmation of your story. I think they are going to try and pull any surveillance footage of the route you took; they were able to recover your route from your phone."

"Well, that's good, right?" I ask, trying to find anything to be optimistic about.

"Only if they can trace him back to the beginning. We already know what kind of car he was in, and it was stolen and already recovered so unless the backtracking leads up to a video of him physically getting into the car, the footage probably isn't going to do anything."

"Right, that makes sense." My head is starting to hurt again. "So basically, the cops confirmed my account but we don't actually have anything new to go on."

"Exactly." I can tell he is trying to figure out how I'm doing because he's analyzing my every movement, or rather, lack thereof. "How are you feeling?"

"What's worse than like shit?" I ask.

"Death warmed over?" Will says with a smirk.

"Sounds about right."

"Well, you made it downstairs on your own, which is honestly kind of impressive. I thought for sure you were going to need help down the stairs."

"Oh, really?" I narrow my eyes at him.

"No judgment, I've laid down my bike before and while nothing was actually broken, my body felt like a walking bruise. I didn't go upstairs for a week because those stairs just weren't worth it," he explains.

"Oh."

He chuckles.

"So about last night," I start.

"What happened last night should have never happened, I should have gone and picked you up. I don't know why I didn't consider that someone might be watching you. Kenzie, I'm sorry." He genuinely looks torn up about it.

"Oh my god, Will, no. You have nothing to be sorry about. It didn't make any sense for you to leave your house, pick me up, drive back, and then have to drive me back to my apartment and then drive back here again. It wasn't practical. I don't think anyone considered that I might be a target. Joe certainly would have said something if he thought I was in danger."

"He's pissed, by the way."

"What? At me?" I feel my heart rate start to pick up as I consider the possibility that Joe is mad at me.

"No, not at you, at himself. He's been calling to check on you every couple of hours. I wouldn't be surprised if he just refuses to go home until he figures this all out."

"But it wasn't his fault either," I argue.

"While I agree with you in theory, in practice we almost lost you, and that's not something either one of us is willing to even entertain the idea of," he explains.

"Oh, well, okay then, that's kind of sweet." Will chuckles again. I'm really starting to love the sound of his chuckle. "Anyway, I was just wondering if you could tell me why I was going to your house in the first place, why King wanted to talk."

The smile leaves Will's face quickly. I think somber is the best word to describe his expression.

"Did she get the files open?" I ask.

"No."

When he doesn't say anything else, I let the silence hang

between us. There is clearly something he doesn't want to tell me, or that he is worried about telling me. Whatever it is, I can wait him out. But thankfully I don't have to.

"Kenzie, the DNA was a match. To the first girl who went missing."

There's a buzzing in my ears that seemingly came out of nowhere. I just sit in my chair rigidly, trying not to breathe in too deeply and staring at Will. The few pieces of hope I have been carrying around with me are starting to flicker out of existence.

"The cops, they're sure?" I can't keep the silent plea out of my tone.

"The cops haven't released it yet." I must have had a questioning look on my face because Will rushes to explain, "King doesn't exactly do well with waiting. Or playing by the rules, for that matter. I assume she has been monitoring communications between the police. She got confirmation last night and wanted to tell us in person since she isn't exactly supposed to actually know anything yet."

"Oh."

"The autopsy was done a while ago. She was found months ago, so most of the work has already been done outside of identifying her."

"How did she die?" I ask as a single tear slides down my face.

"Homicide." Will leans forward and rests his elbows on his thighs again before clasping his hands together.

"How did she die, Will?" I ask again.

"Kenzie..."

"How?"

"Are you sure you really want to know this?" he asks.

"Yes."

"Okay. The coroner wasn't exactly sure. She had a lot of blunt force trauma to her body, but she was also shot in the head as well as strangled. Both happened at or around the time of death, so they aren't sure of the exact mechanism of death."

"Jesus." I'm suddenly glad I haven't eaten lately because the nauseous feeling that is settling in my stomach is borderline overwhelming. "Did, um. Uh. Was there any, I guess, evidence that they found?"

"There was a partial fingerprint, not enough to use in a trial but it could be used to rule someone in or out."

"So no suspects then?"

"No. I'm sorry."

I nod. And keep nodding. Trying to absorb this new information.

Is this the fate that Clara is going to have? And Jenny? Is this what all of them who came before went through? Another cold tear rushes down my face as I try not to imagine this poor woman's last moments.

"What was her name?" I ask.

"Lauren, it was Lauren."

"Lauren." It feels so final. "She was the first."

"Yes," he confirms. "You okay?"

"No." I don't even bother trying to lie about it. I am not okay. I don't know if I will ever be okay again.

Death is one of those facts of life. And I have been exposed to death more than once. Losing my brother was horrible. And the aftermath was just as bad. But no one set out to kill him. It was a tragic accident. The culmination of a million little choices made by countless people that ended in tragedy. Was it horrible? Yes. Absolutely. Could it have been prevented? Doubtful.

But this. This wasn't a million different choices by countless people. No. This was a choice by one person. One person bent on taking the life of another. And then who apparently decided to do it again. And again. And again. And who knows if they will ever stop.

"I'm so sorry, Kenz," Will says, trying to bring me some level of comfort. I know he means well, but I can't take it right now.

"What's next?" I ask as I quickly wipe the tears off my face, ignoring the pain coming from my lungs and shoulder.

"Kenz,"

"What's next? Where do we go next?"

"You don't have to do this—"

"YES. I do. What. Is. Next," I repeat.

There's a long pause before Will finally gives me with an answer.

"I was planning on talking to the guy who King had reached out to for help."

"Why?" I ask.

"Because I want to check out anyone who had any kind of knowledge of our investigation." I raise my eyebrows, my skepticism slightly showing. "I'm not taking any chances."

"Will."

"You can look at it one of two ways: one, I'm looking for any connection no matter how small to Clara, or two, I'm keeping you safe. The sooner we find out whoever is behind going after you, the sooner we find Clara."

"I'm not opposed to keeping me alive, Will. I just kind of wonder if you really think investigating everyone we have ever talked to about this is going to yield us any results."

"I'm not losing you, Kenzie. I'm not. It's not happening. When I took this case, I told you I would find Clara, and I will. But I am not going to lose you in the process."

The look on his face is so intense. The way he is looking at me is different than before. It's obvious he is worried, that's a given, but there is something else underneath it.

"Will, I'm fine. I'm right here. I'm not going anywhere, and I promise I'll follow whatever ridiculous instructions you have for me to keep myself safe while we figure all this out, okay?" I try to reassure him.

"Kenz, you have no idea the things that went through my head last night. When you didn't show up, I had this feeling in my gut something was wrong. King was already here waiting, and she felt it too. By the time we were out on the road looking, you had already crashed." He lets his head fall forward before running his hand over the top of his head. A quick shake of his head and he's back to looking at me, utter devastation written all over his face.

I can't help it, I get up. Too quickly.

I go to move toward him, to comfort him, but my brain, or I guess my heart, must have forgotten the catalog of injuries and pain I am lugging around with me.

Will is on his feet before my grimace fully takes over.

"No, don't, stay. Sit down, don't hurt yourself," he says while gingerly holding on to my left arm, trying to guide me back to the chair. I let him. It hurts more than I am willing to admit to myself.

"Will, I don't know what to say." I pause. "I hate that you're this upset. I'm okay, I'm going to be fine, everything is going to be fine." I try to reassure him as he kneels down in front of me.

"Kenzie, when I saw your car upside down in a ditch, I panicked. I'm always the cool headed one, but I was out of the truck faster than my brain even realized I had done it. And then to see that asshole's car there alongside yours, where he clearly bailed out and was going after you." He shakes his head like he's trying to clear the memory out of his head.

I reach out and take Will's face in my left hand, feeling the prickly scruff. He covers my hand with his own.

"I kept thinking I was going to get to you too late. I had to guess what to do. Should I take off into the woods and hope I caught up with him before he got to you, or drive around to the other side of the woods and hope to meet you before he caught up?" He swallows hard. "I knew if I made the wrong choice, it meant losing you. I was so scared, Kenzie."

"I was too," I whisper.

"When I finally found you, I was so relieved, and then I saw the shape you were in and I was back to being in full panic. I don't ever want to find you this hurt ever again," he says quietly.

"I knew you," I say quietly back. Confusion muddles his expression. "In the woods. I knew you. Up until I saw your face, I didn't know anything. I was afraid, I knew I was running from someone, but I didn't know why, or who, I didn't even remember the crash. It took me minutes to figure out I was upside down in a car." I breathe in slowly before continuing.

"But when I heard your voice, I wasn't afraid. And when I saw your face, I knew you. I knew I was safe. I knew who you were. And everything came back. I knew everything was going to be okay," I tell him.

"Look, about before, I know we should talk about it, clear the air, but right now I just want to keep you safe," he says.

"We can do that. It can wait. I'm not going anywhere," I assure him.

"And you'll stay here, at least until you're better?" he asks with a twinge of pleading running through the question.

I don't hesitate.

"I'll stay."

CHAPTER TWENTY-FIVE

"1979" BY SMASHING PUMPKINS

"You're not going." Will is standing at one end of the counter in the kitchen of his house repeating himself over and over. Like a broken fucking record.

"And again, that's not your decision to make, *Will*," I say for what feels like the millionth time.

"Kenzie, I'm fucking serious. There is no way in hell you are coming with me. You have two choices. You can stay here alone with the security system fully armed, locked inside or I can call King to come hang out with you while I'm gone. Pick one."

"No."

"No? Just no?" Will says incredulously.

"Yep."

"You can't be serious."

"Of course I'm serious. I am going with you. I want to talk to this guy."

"But you don't need to talk to him. I will talk to him and I will tell you everything we talk about. Hell, I will even Face-Time you while I am there, so you can watch the conversation if you want."

"Don't you think that would be a tad on the awkward side?" I ask with a raised eyebrow.

"Yes!" Will slams his hand down on the counter. "Of course it would be fucking awkward. But you're acting like a lunatic right now and at this point, I am willing to do anything to get you to see reason."

"It is *not* unreasonable to want to be a part of the investigation that almost killed me and has my best friend *missing*!" I yell back.

"That is exactly my point! *Almost. Killed. You.* You are literally hobbling around the house. You sound like you're dying when you walk down the stairs, but for reasons passing all understanding, refuse any help. I'm ninety percent positive your head is still killing you since you keep turning off all the lights and squinting every time there is light."

"No one needs that much sunlight," I argue.

"You do hear yourself right now, right?" I huff. "You are seriously trying to make the case for too much sunlight to cover the fact that you're recovering from a pretty serious concussion?"

"Look, I'm going whether you take me with you or not, so wouldn't you rather just take me with you?"

"You're insane. Seriously insane. This guy probably doesn't even know anything, I'm just crossing his name off the list since he is one of the people who knows about our investigation."

"Well then, it's not dangerous and I can go," I argue.

"I'm not taking you."

"Thank God for Uber."

"No."

"Yes."

"No."

"I can do this all day, Will."

"I noticed." He sighs. "Why can't you just stay home? I'll be there and back before you know it, I can even pick up food.

From anywhere you want. Pick your poison and I'll get it. Sky's the limit. As long as you stay home."

"Not even a little bit tempting. I'm going."

Will throws up his hands and walks out of the kitchen toward the living room. I can't help the chuckle that escapes me. I'm pretty sure Will didn't hear, but I try and stifle it down just the same. It's kind of nice having someone this concerned about me.

It's only been about a day since I've been home from the hospital, but he's always around. Do I need anything to eat? Do I want any medicine? What about helping me down the stairs? He's hovering. And I should hate it.

But I don't.

It's weirdly attractive.

Maybe it's just because outside of Clara, I've never had someone this concerned with my comfort and safety. Years of a relationship with Collin and he was never like this. Not even when I came down with pneumonia.

I follow Will's path through the kitchen and into the living room, only to find him staring out the window, looking at his truck in the driveway.

"You really would call an Uber, wouldn't you?" he asks without looking at me.

"Wouldn't it be better if I went with you? You could watch me all you want; I promise I will do whatever you want. If you say stay out of sight, I'll hide. When you say duck, I'll stop, drop and roll." He chuckles.

"That's for fire."

I shrug. "Fire, gunshots, same thing. Stay in motion and get down, right?"

Will turns to face me.

"You might be the most ridiculous person I have ever met in my life."

"Hey!" I say in mock outrage. "I will have you know I'm a

fucking delight."

Will full on laughs out loud. I smile back at him.

"Fine. But there will be rules."

"Okay, lay it out." At this point, I'm willing to agree to anything just to be a part of this.

"Number one, you have to listen to me. I promise I won't ask you to do anything that isn't necessary for your safety, but I need you to listen."

"Done."

"Number two, you have to tell me if you are in pain. No hiding, no pretending, no acting like you're fine when really you've broken into a cold sweat and your eyes are tearing up," he says with a pointed stare.

"You caught that, did you?" I say with a joke.

"Kenzie."

"Fine. Fine. Okay, I'll tell you."

"And you will ask for help or at the very least let me help you when I try."

There's a pause while I consider my options here. What can I say? I'm terrible at accepting help.

"Kenzie," he says flatly.

"Okay. I agree to your terms."

"Then we should get going, no sense wasting daylight."

"Who are we going to see again?" I ask.

Will freezes.

"You just spent a half hour arguing with me and you don't even know what you were fighting to go do? Are you kidding me right now?"

I shrug.

"I knew it had to do with Clara so I knew I wanted to be there, that's really all I needed to know," I rationalize.

He looks incredulous. Like he can't believe he just spent all this time arguing with me. He might even have a vein starting to pop out on his forehead. It's quite possible I'm driving him crazy.

"We are going to see King's contact. She told him the bare-bones basics about the investigation when she asked him for help with the last encryption. He's one of the few people who knew anything about you being involved, so I want to just talk to him and get a feel for him. Maybe he's not the crazy guy in the woods."

"You don't really think he's the guy in the woods, right?"

"It's not high on my list of possibilities, but I don't discount this kind of thing anymore. Better safe than sorry," he says.

"You were a Boy Scout, weren't you?" I ask.

"Why do you ask?" he asks suspiciously.

"No reason, you just seem like one of those *always be prepared, never leave a stone unturned* kind of guys," I explain.

"I feel like I should feel insulted given the way you just said that, but yes. I was a Boy Scout."

"Of course you were."

"Alright, alright. If you're done teasing me, can we get going?" He motions toward the door.

"After you," I say with a smirk.

I DON'T THINK I am able to contain my surprise when we end up back on campus. King's contact is a student?

I guess I shouldn't be too surprised. Clara is one of the biggest badasses I know and she hasn't even graduated yet. I'm also about ninety percent sure that King doesn't have a college degree either and clearly, she knows what she is doing.

"He's a researcher," Will explains.

"Researcher? Not a student or something?"

"He's a full-time university employee, working on a doctorate or something."

"Oh. So, he's not like a TA or something; Clara wouldn't have had him for class or anything?"

"He's definitely not a TA, and I don't think he knew Clara," Will clarifies.

"Why do you say that?"

"I would have thought he would have told King when she explained everything, don't you think?" he asks.

"Yeah, that makes sense." It does make sense. If he knew Clara, of course he would speak up, right? If not, it would be pretty suspicious if someone made a connection to him down the line. "What's his name?"

"Michael. Michael Davis."

"Ah, a two first names guy."

Will chuckles as he pulls his truck into the closest space to the computer science building.

"Stay there, I'm going to come help you down." He doesn't even wait for me to answer before he's out with the door closed and hustling over to my side of the truck.

I'm not above sending him a small glare so he knows how much I hate being the broken girl who can't get out of a car without grunting. But I'll let him help, because as much as I hate to admit it, this trip is already taking a lot out of me.

Turns out breathing is really important when it comes to having energy to move around.

After Will gets me out of the truck, we head into the building, me at a much slower pace than normal and probably at what is considered glacial speed for Will.

He never complains once.

He honestly just kind of pretends it isn't happening. I think he's trying to let me have my dignity.

He seriously needs to stop being so fucking likable. I'm never going to get over this crush on him if he keeps this up.

Once we get inside the building, I take a deep breath. I never would have expected that breathing in the colder, drier

air of winter would be so painful on my aching lungs. Sometimes it still feels like I am hanging upside down in that car,
being held in place by the seat belt. Not at all comfortable.

I follow Will as he walks glacially slow for me down a few
hallways deep into the building, he seems to know where he is
going. I've been in this building probably a hundred times over
the last couple years, but I always get turned around. The halls
all look the same, signage doesn't seem to be something they
believe in, and everyone walks around with their heads down
or with headphones in, so it's impossible to ask for directions.
Eventually you just accept you will be lost.

Not Will though.

We finally arrive at a room with a sign on the window that
says LAB FOUR. Personally, I think the lettering could be
bigger.

Will knocks.

I had forgotten that some of the labs you need to use your
ID to get in or have someone let you in and then you have to
sign the sign-in. Apparently, a few years back a group of kids
tried to make off with thousands of dollars' worth of high-end
computer equipment. After expulsion, thousands in fines, and
a pretty sizable jail sentence, everyone else now has to swipe in.

Will looks all business while we wait for someone to open
the door.

As much as I want to chat with him about what we are
going to ask this guy, everything hurts too much. Primarily
breathing. So instead I try to look as determined as Will and
less like a hunched over dying person.

The guy who finally answers the door is the definition of
nondescript white guy. He looks like everyone and no one all at
once. Not a single distinctive facial feature. Not a graphic tee
with a funny saying, not even Chucks with writing on them.
Not a name brand, signature scent, or interesting quirk with
this guy. Interesting.

"Michael Davis?" Will inquires.

"You the PI?" he replies, not really answering the question.

"So I'm told. King should have told you I was coming."

"Come on in." He opens the door and ushers us in before pointing at the sign-in sheet. "You have to check in."

Will bends down to fill in his information and when I start to step forward, he shakes his head.

"I took care of it," he assures me with a look.

I look back at the sign-in sheet, trying to resist the urge to check.

"No bending," he whispers, low enough that only I can hear.

With that, I feel my cheeks start to tingle as they undoubtedly fill up with pink at my embarrassment. Will reaches forward to squeeze my hand ever so quickly before turning to go back to talking to Michael.

It takes me a few minutes to fully check back into the conversation going on. Will is all business though. He's already briefly introduced me before moving on to his questions.

"I know you had previously spoken with King about our investigation but I was hoping you could answer a couple of questions for me as well." Will broaches the topic. He's firm but not aggressive.

"Sure." Michael shrugs.

"Great. First, I wanted to see how the decryption was going. I haven't had a chance to speak with King today so I figured I would ask since I'm already here." Lowball, easy question. Good strategy.

"Oh yeah, sure, of course. It's really fascinating actually. We haven't been able to open anything yet, but definitely been making some progress. The coding and the math are a thing of beauty. King tells me an undergrad here wrote it." He looks excited and super animated when he brings up Clara. "Man, I want to meet this girl. I was actually going to show it to one of the professors here, she would be great to have on our team." He looks over at me and then back at Will. "I would have cleared it with King first, of course."

"So you didn't know Clara?" I ask.

"No, King showed me a photo, and she looks familiar, but honestly with the number of people who are in and out of these labs, I'm not surprised she looks familiar." He explains.

"Well, as you know, Clara is one of several women who have gone missing in the last couple of years." Will pauses, and I look over at Michael to see his reaction. He seems serious. Not shifty. Just attentive. "Kenzie here is Clara's roommate, and there have been some incidents lately, so I'm just going around checking out everyone with any information about the investigation. Just trying to knock possibilities off the list."

Will is pretty affable about the whole thing. In fact, he didn't even ask a question. Just a suggestion.

"Oh totally, totally. Well, I've only spoken with King about it, no one else. I've basically been living in this lab for the past week, so I haven't really had much of a chance to venture out into the land of the living," he chuckles. I believe him. I'm not sure why, but he just doesn't raise any alarm bells.

"Okay, great. Do you think it's possible anyone overheard you and King speaking?" Will asks next. A question without any blame. Interesting.

Michael pauses to think about it.

"I'm sure it's possible. Truthfully, when I'm in here, the whole world kind of fades out, I don't really pay attention to who else is here. You need a key card to swipe in or you have to sign in on the sheet, so I always just assume if you are in here, you're supposed to be."

"I've worked with King more than a few times. I'm very familiar with the zoning out," Will says on a smile. Michael smiles back.

They exchange a few more pleasantries while I kind of look

around the room. Without moving at all, of course. There are a lot of workstations. Some of them are clearly for singles, some of them are designed for what looks like more of a team approach. There are even some areas with whiteboards and tables to spread out on. I could see how this place would get busy and someone could easily overhear what other people are working on.

"Well, thank you for your time." Will starts to get ready to leave.

"Yeah, no problem. I'll have some time tonight, so I'll be working on that file later." He tells Will.

"Well, good luck. I think everyone is interested in what's on there," Will responds.

And with that, Will motions for me to head toward the door.

I'm exhausted.

I don't know how. I'm literally just standing there trying to follow a conversation. But the reality is my body is beat the fuck up.

As soon as we are outside the lab and into the hallway, Will's face shifts to one of concern.

"You holding up okay?"

"Yeah," I lie.

"I was going to run over to the admin office and see if I can get a copy of all the entry swipes the last three days..." He hesitates. "But you look like you need a break."

"I'm fine, Will, really." More lies.

"Kenzie."

I'm starting to sweat. The energy it is taking to keep me upright and engaged is way more than I was prepared for. I just need to cool down and then I'll be right back on and ready to go.

"I just need some fresh air. You can walk me out to the

benches right outside the building and I can sit and wait for you so you can get the information," I offer.

He looks skeptical.

And worried.

"We can just go home and I can get King to get it later," he suggests, giving me an out.

"No really, it's fine. I don't mind waiting, really." I really don't want to be the giant baby here, especially after I basically demanded to come along for the ride.

Will finally nods his agreement and we start walking. Even so, I can tell he doesn't feel great about it.

He needs a distraction.

"He seemed genuine," I say.

Will nods.

"He didn't set off any of my spidey senses," I joke.

"Yeah, me either. King vets the people she works with anyway, it was always going to be a long shot."

"But you think maybe someone overheard?"

"I think no one in there pays any attention to anyone else, so yeah."

"Hence the logs?"

"There isn't really going to be much to do with them if we get them, but maybe we can cross people on or off the list once we have some names to work with," Will explains.

I think he's just looking for some way to be productive and not feel helpless in this situation. I get the feeling.

Before I know it, we are outside and Will is helping me to sit on the bench. The cool air against my skin already feels better. Not great on my lungs, but at this point, the overheating is taking priority.

"You sure you're okay?" Will asks with a worried expression.

"I'm sure," I assure him.

"You'll stay right here? No going anywhere?" He's looking around the building, seemingly cataloging everyone outside.

"I promise. Right here. No further," I say with a smile.

Will shakes his head. "Be right back," he says before he hustles back into the building.

Sitting on the bench, I can't help but watch all the students just going about their lives. Going to class. Stopping by the lab to work on a project. Heading to a study group or for office hours. How mundane it all is. How for granted everyone takes it.

It's Friday afternoon and people are all leaving the building for the day, but not Clara. Clara would still be in one of the labs working on her latest problem. Sometimes I had to boot her out of here. Remind her to eat and sleep. Melancholy floods my system as the crowds start the thin as people head out for the day.

I was spending so much time in my head and watching the abstract students going about their lives that it never even occurred to me to look a little closer to home.

I never noticed him watching. I never felt the unease tingle on the back of my neck to tell me someone was watching. And as the sun started to get lower, I didn't notice when he started moving closer.

In fact, it wouldn't be until he was right next to me that I even noticed him at all.

CHAPTER TWENTY-SIX

"IMMIGRANT SONG" BY TRENT REZNOR, ATTICUS ROSS, KAREN O

I felt someone sit down next to me on the bench. At first, I didn't think anything of it. I've been on this campus for four years, and outside of my recent brush with death, I've always felt so comfortable here. People approach you all the time. Do you know where *x* building is? Here's this flyer for a frat party on Friday night. Do you want to sign my petition to get the school to adopt more green initiatives? There is always something.

Five seconds after they sat down, though, I knew something was wrong.

Very wrong.

"You just couldn't leave well enough alone, could you?" a man's voice says, coming from my left side.

The chill that ran down my spine was my strongest one yet since this whole thing started. Without even realizing I was doing it, I turned my head to get a look at him.

"Don't look at me," he says with an unmasked tint of malice.

I was going to ignore the directive.

As far as I was concerned, we were out in public.

Sure, the sun had begun to set and darkness was starting

to take off. The student body population had since died down to a drizzle, and those students that were left were all in a hurry to get where they were going. It was Friday afternoon, and the weather was about to shift back down in temperature.

Either way, I was still in public, so while this guy was definitely giving me the creeps, I still felt like I had a good chance at being okay.

Until I felt something cold touch my skin.

I may have come outside to cool down, but my body was frozen now.

Every possible scenario began running through my head.

Was it a knife?

Or was it a gun?

If I made enough of a scene, would he still take a shot at me before making a run for it?

If I went along with what he wants would I end up another name on the missing list until someone discovers my body at some later date?

Fear has taken hold, so I listen and stop trying to get a good look at him. All I know so far is white male, college age, and I think brown hair.

"That's it, now look ahead." He spoke to me the way shitty dog owners speak to their dog. Condescending and slowly. Jack ass.

I listen.

"You really just don't know when to stop, do you?"

I'm not sure if he really wants me to answer, so I just sit quietly. One of the hardest things I have ever done. Keep my mouth shut. I want to scream at this guy. I want to beat the crap out of this guy. But until I know what is in his hand, I am going to play this game.

"You know you aren't the only one who just couldn't help herself." He pauses, almost like he was doing it for added drama. "Clara certainly couldn't leave well enough alone either," he whispers.

I feel my body jerk into complete stillness.

Something that apparently greatly amuses him since he chuckles afterward.

"Look at you, even after everything, you come all the way out here to keep poking around, not caring that you look like some battered spouse. I would have thought the other night would have taught you a lesson. I let you live and this is how you repay me."

"Fuck you." I couldn't help myself.

"Ah ah ah. That's no way to talk to the guy who is going to give you everything you wanted."

Confusion floods my body. I want to argue, I want to question him. But the metal object that was once just resting against my side, is now pushing against the skin. I can feel my skin pushing inward, enough for pressure, but not enough to break the skin.

"I thought you wanted to see Clara again. That's what all this was about, right?" he taunted me with his singsong speech pattern. "Well, I'm about to make all your dreams come true."

"Where is she?" I demand.

"You're about to find out," he replies as he shoves the object further into my side.

Not a knife.

No way it's a knife. It would have definitely already cut through my clothing and for sure broken some skin by now.

It's got to be a gun.

I file the information away while still trying to come up with a plan.

The more information I can get out of him, the better.

How to do that without ending up as one of his victims, however, is another story entirely.

"Here's what's going to happen next. You are going to get up.

Slowly. We are going to walk to the parking lot. You are *not* going to call any attention to yourself. I'm sure you can guess what's going to happen if you decide not to comply." He pushes the gun harder into my side.

I count my blessings he is pushing on the left side and not the right where most of the injured ribs are. If he was on the other side, there is no way I wouldn't be screaming by now.

"I think we both know you are going to use that whether I come with you or not, so why would you think I'm going to go with you?" I retort.

"Because I have something that you want."

"Prove it," I demand.

He laughs. Just straight up laughs. It's beyond unnerving. Every cell in my body is freaking out, and my eyes keep darting to the door to the building, willing Will to walk through the doors and find me. The door doesn't open. And I just sit in silence while I wait for his Joker laugh to be over.

"Maybe you aren't as stupid as I thought," he says at the end of a laugh.

I can feel him shift around on the bench, but the pressure on my side from the gun never lets up, if anything, it increases. After a couple of seconds of movement, I can feel him place something on my knee.

Just before I cast my eyes down to see what he brought out; I hear her voice.

I would know her voice anywhere.

Even if all I can hear is a scream.

He has the volume turned way down, so there is no way anyone would really hear it unless they walked by pretty close, but the fact is there is no one anywhere near close enough to even get a hint of the sound coming out of what I assume is his phone.

I cast my eyes down quickly, and it's almost a close-up shot of Clara's face. Like a camera was only inches from her face is what it looks like. Until she reaches up to wipe the tears out of her eyes and I realize there is no way there is a camera that close to her face. It's a zoomed-in shot.

I can't see anything in the background. There is nothing identifiable anywhere. I keep trying to catalog the images as quickly as possible in case there is something to go off of later. If I make it through this.

But the fact is I can't even see her entire face, it's so zoomed in. There's even a decent amount of image distortion from being zoomed in too much. He's being careful. Too careful. He planned this whole thing out.

Which makes me think he has an exit plan. And that my chances of getting out of this alive are decreasing.

"Where is she! Where is Kenzie? You promised! What did you do!" Clara's voice screams. It's bloodcurdling. Dread fills my entire body, as well as panic. She thinks something has happened to me? I'm so confused? What is happening right now? When was this recorded?

Out of the corner of my eye, I see his finger come up to the screen and stop the video. I should have been taking the time to memorize everything about him, if his nails were well kept, his skin tone, if he had any scars, anything to identify him later.

Instead I'm just frozen.

The harsh reality, that whatever is happening to Clara, or whatever happened to Clara, I am being used as some kind of pawn to torture her emotionally or to get her to do what he wants.

My stomach turns and I resist the urge to vomit, it is strong.

I have to get to her. Nothing else matters.

"Now then. Are you going to be a good girl or are we going to have a problem?" he asks, using that condescending tone again.

The logical part of my brain says no. It's screaming at me not to go anywhere this guy wants me to. To take a chance at being shot. My chances diminish the further away I get from people.

But the rest of me. The rest of me wants to get to Clara. The rest of me is ready to put anything on the line to get to her. Even if it means I don't make it out of this alive.

It's not even a choice.

I stand up slowly, not wanting to spook him.

"That's a good girl." He chuckles.

If he keeps talking to me like a dog, I'm going to have a hard time not blowing everything and punching him in the face.

Taking as deep a breath as I can without causing myself to double over in pain, I start moving forward. Given my injuries, I'm already walking at a pretty slow pace to begin with so I don't even bother trying to walk any slower.

I'm torn about whether I want to call attention to my situation. If I do, I might live through this, and the bad guy could get caught. But where would that leave Clara?

I keep moving.

He moves closer to me, more off to the side so it looks like we are walking side by side together. He's trying not to call attention to us.

The gun never leaves my side, though, and I can tell he's having a harder time concealing it. I'm sure he had this all planned out perfectly in his head, but in reality, it might not be as easy as he anticipated.

With only a few more steps to the parking lot, I take the chance at trying to get a look at him. I manage to get a decent glimpse of his side profile. Definitely white. No tan. No color at all. But not quite pale. He has a beauty mark on his right cheek since he's on my left. And I can tell by his profile that his nose is either crooked or has been broken in the past. Either way, it's a noticeable characteristic.

I file it away in my brain.

"I don't know where I'm going," I say as I stop at the edge of the parking lot.

"Not much farther." He pushes the gun against my side harder, like he's trying to indicate for me to move forward. "Second row, sixth car back."

I sneak another look before I start moving again.

He looks familiar.

I know I've seen him before.

I'm sure of it.

I don't know him though. He isn't friends with Clara, he's not one of the people in her core group that she collaborates with, I definitely don't know his name. But I know his face.

I wonder to myself how many times I have walked by this guy. How my brain must have filed away his face like some kind of facial recognition software. Even though I don't know his name, knowing I recognize him makes me think it will be easier to identify him later if I manage to get out of this. Anything to cling to a shred of hope and positivity.

At the second row, my body is starting to falter.

I don't know if it's fear or if it's my injuries catching up to me, but my speed has taken a dive and my vision is starting to get blurrier. I'm about positive the adrenaline is the only thing keeping me moving forward and not aware of the amount of pain I'm really in.

I start counting the cars.

One.

Two.

Three.

Four.

Five.

It's black. Of course it's black. There's no license plate on the back. No bumper sticker or window decal that I can see. Windows have a good tint to them, enough for me to think they are straddling the line of legal and not.

It's a Ford Focus. Great. One of the most popular cars on campus.

I hear the pop of the trunk before I see it bounce upward.

"I think you know where this is going," he taunts before shoving his gun in my side again. I'm going to have a barrel-sized bruise there if I live through this.

"You've got to be kidding me," I say incredulously. "There is no way my broken-ass self can climb into the back of a trunk. I can barely fucking walk. And do you honestly think no one is going to notice my battered self crawling into the back of a truck? Are you some kind of moron?"

My head swivels to look at him straight on. Yes. I was right. I know that face. I start cataloging it more in my brain, trying to cement the image for later.

He shoves me. Hard.

"Bitch." He says every man's favorite insult.

I feel the sharp impact of my hips hitting the back bumper of the car. I'm guessing the bruising from the seat belt in the accident didn't help matters because I can't keep the yelp in.

I feel more than see the movement out of my peripheral and I know instinctively he is about to hurt me.

I brace myself for whatever is going to happen next, knowing I just have to get through this. I just have to make it through this part before I can get to Clara.

It never comes.

No.

Instead, I hear the voice of an angel.

The man who I thought I would call dad. The man who was going to walk me down the aisle.

"Freeze. Police." It's loud. And clear. No nonsense. Aggressive and sure, but not emotional.

The man next to me does. He freezes. If only for a second.

I'm trying to imagine the scene from above, and I realize Joe can't see the gun. He's coming up on my right, and Creepy is on my left where the gun is hidden by my body.

Running through the scenarios, I realize this means Joe isn't going to shoot right away.

"Do exactly as I say or I swear to you, not only will you never see Clara again, but you won't even find the body," he whispers menacingly.

This is my last chance. I need to get as much information out of this guy as possible before shit hits the fan. Who knows if he will talk to the police.

"I said freeze. Put your hands up slowly where I can see them and take two steps away from the girl." Joe shouts instructions as he continues moving toward us. His voice getting closer and louder as he goes.

"I can help you, I know him, he'll listen to me," I bargain. "Just tell me where Clara is and I swear I'll help you."

He wraps his free hand around my arm, the motion being blocked by my body before he starts trying to maneuver himself and me behind the side of the car, out of the line of fire.

"You are going to stand right there while I get in this car," he says menacingly.

I realize his plan. Use my body as a shield, get in the car and drive away before Joe has a chance to shoot him or backup arrives.

This is going bad quickly.

If he leaves the scene without me, chances are if Clara is alive, she won't be for long. He's going to cut his losses and run. I can feel it in my bones.

With no other option, I decide to chance it.

I lean back and try taking a step back.

There's a look of shock that quickly passes over his face, like he can't believe I would have the audacity to challenge him.

"Final chance, Kenzie. If you don't do this, I promise Clara will be nothing but a sad story that follows you for the rest of your life. Nothing but a memory. You'll always wonder what happened to her. If I don't make it out of this, I would hate to think what my partner is going to do when I'm not keeping him in check," he leers.

"Stop moving now. Release the girl and step out from behind the car." Joe is getting really close now.

A partner. A partner. I never even considered a partner. I doubt anyone has. My mind races with all the possibilities and suddenly the outcomes aren't looking so great. Making a choice with only a split second to decide and literally having lives on the line is a situation I would never wish on anyone. I can feel the tears start to flood my eyes as I make my choice.

I take another step back.

In only a few short seconds, I will be able to reach out and touch Joe. Safety is at my back but danger still lurks in front of me.

Shock turns to rage on his face. Pure rage. I know it's a look Clara must have seen when she was with him. Animalistic. It's the face of a monster.

He's made his choice too.

I see it flash on his face before time slows down.

The smirk starts to take hold, even in the midst of all that rage, as he lifts the gun to point at my chest as I continue moving back.

"Drop the gun!" I hear the sound of a bullet before the sound waves carrying Joe's last command fully integrate into my brain.

Time freezes.

I don't know who fired.

One of us is dead.

It's a matter of who.

And that's when I feel it.

The splash of hot liquid hitting my body.

I look down at my hands and see the red.

My vision blurs.

I barely register his body crumpling in front of me or the feeling of hands gently taking hold of my arms and starting to move me.

I lived.

But will she?

CHAPTER TWENTY-SEVEN
"TRAGEDY" BY BRANDI CARLILE

W*hat comes next* is the thought that keeps running through my head as everything around me keeps moving but I seem to be frozen in place.

It only took Joe seconds to fully put himself between me and the body of the man who had taken my best friend.

Seconds that seemed to be never-ending.

Watching Joe remove the gun and check the pulse of a man who clearly was missing part of his skull was surreal at best.

I couldn't stop looking at my hands and the splashes of red all over them. I knew my clothes and my face were probably also covered as well.

I'm certain that things moved fast after that, Joe moving me off to the side out of view of his body, sirens being heard in the background, Will running toward me, once more sitting in the back of an ambulance, the crowd that comes with a crime scene. It all happened in flashes. Like miniature snapshots in my mind.

The thing I remember the most is not speaking. My brain was working, albeit more than a little confused, but no matter how much people were talking to me and asking me questions, I couldn't seem to respond out loud.

Will never left my side, just kept reassuring me everything was going to be okay, that I was in shock but that we were going to figure everything out when I was ready.

I don't know how much time passed between the shooting and when I finally found myself sitting next to Will in an interview room with the police. It was a much friendlier room than the last one. No metal ring on the table to attach to prisoners.

The involuntary shaking had just subsided, but I want to get it over with. All the questions. Questions I'm sure are going to be asked a million different ways over a long period of time.

Thankfully, Joe is in the room, even if he isn't the one asking the questions.

Detective Jones walks into the room, looking every bit as haggard as I feel. Either he isn't getting a lot of sleep or his stress level is at an all-time high.

"Miss Sharp." His voice is more on the kind and cautious side.

"Jones," I whisper back.

"I was hoping I could ask you a couple of questions before you head home, while everything is still fresh in your mind," he explains.

I shrug, and Will squeezes my hand. The hand I am currently holding his with in a death grip. The same death grip I've kept since he sat next to me in the back of the ambulance. It is my anchor helping to keep me together.

"Can you tell me what happened in your own words?" he asks softly with his notepad out and ready to write down anything I say.

This will be the first time. The first time I will say anything about what happened.

It pours out of me slowly. Every once in a while, a tear

slowly trails down my cheek. No one interrupts me or asks any questions. They all just let me get everything out first.

When I am done, it is my turn for questions.

"Who is he?" I ask.

"A graduate student, he was a teaching assistant for the computer science department. We've already been able to find some links with some of the missing women, so we are pretty positive at this point this is the man we were looking for in regards to all the other missing women," he tells me.

"His name?" I ask.

Jones hesitates. I don't understand why. I'm sure his name will be plastered all over the news, there was certainly more than enough camera crews at the scene.

"Jonathan. Jonathan Nash."

I run the name through my brain, trying to remember every conversation I ever had with Clara about people she interacted with, I try and remember every random person who introduced themselves to me when I was visiting her while she was working on projects for hours on end. I come up short.

"I don't know him," I say. "Well, I know his face. I recognize his face, but not the name."

"That's not out of the norm, a lot of times the perpetrators of these kinds of crimes fit in, they don't raise any alarm bells," I can tell he's trying to make me feel like this isn't my fault, like there is no way I could have known.

I don't blame myself. Not for him, at least.

There is no way I could have known that this guy would have turned out to be a lunatic and that he would go after women on campus. There was no way Clara could have known, and chances are she did know his name. Chances are she spoke to him, smiled at him, maybe collaborated with him in a lab.

No, the blame I hold for myself is that he's dead, and she's missing.

"Did you watch the video?" I ask.

Jones looks over at Will and they have some sort of silent conversation between them.

"Yes," he finally answers.

"I only saw a few seconds of it. Was there more?"

"It was a ten-second clip on a burner phone. Our techs aren't optimistic about tracing the origin."

My heart sinks. I was counting on an IP address or metadata to show where it was taken. Anything to show where Clara was when the video was taken, or at least where he was when he put the video on the phone.

"So she's still missing? There's nothing to go on?" I ask.

He hesitates.

"What about the partner? Did you find anything on him or his car or phone, anything, anything at all about the partner?" I continue pushing forward for information.

"Kenzie," he starts slowly, and immediately I know I'm not going to like what comes next. "There wasn't a partner."

And if my life wasn't already a shit show, this is when it officially becomes the twilight zone.

"Yes, there was, he said so, he told me. I was there. I heard him."

He keeps looking over at Will.

"Don't look at him. Talk to me," I declare, still not letting go of Will's hand.

"Kenzie, he would have said anything to make sure you cooperated with him. Our techs have looked at the phone, checked out the car, we've even had someone at his residence and as of right now there is nothing to even suggest the slightest hint of a partner." He sounds so sure of everything he is saying.

But I know he's wrong. I know in my gut he wasn't lying. I don't know how I know, but I do.

There were moments in our interaction where he didn't

seem as sure of himself, especially when we were more out in the open.

But when he brought up the partner, there was conviction in his voice. There is no doubt for me. There is a partner. I knew it as much then as I know it now.

"Then where is she? Where is Clara?" I demand as my voice starts to grow louder.

"We don't know."

"So not in the apartment?" I question.

"No."

"She wasn't held there then?" I ask.

"It doesn't appear that way, no."

"Then he obviously had somewhere else. A second location he took her to. Who's to say evidence of a partner isn't there?" I say with a slightly mocking tone.

"Kenzie, I'm not saying we aren't going to look into the possibility, and if evidence comes up to support your theory—"

"It's *not* a theory," I seethe.

"We will, of course, certainly investigate any evidence that points us to anyone else involved in the crime." He sounds like a robot, just giving me the canned answer.

"I'm evidence! I'm a witness. I'm telling you, there is a partner."

"Again, we have nothing to go on in regards to a partner—"

"You have got to be fucking kidding me. Even you have to admit we never figured out showed up at the registrar's office to withdrawal Clara, the supposed uncle. What if that's the partner?" I let go of Will's hand to throw my hands up in the air.

"Looking at the surveillance footage, there is no way to tell if the man claiming to be Clara's uncle is Jonathan Nash or not. There's no reason to think it isn't. Kenzie, I promise, I am going to look into every avenue that comes up, I swear it to you," Joe finally pipes in.

"Joe. You don't even know where she is. She's out there

somewhere and even if you are right and there isn't a partner, he's dead. He's not going to be keeping her alive. She's on a clock," I implore.

Joe looks down and takes a deep breath. And that's when I know the ground is about to drop out from beneath me.

"Honey, I'm sorry, but right now, we don't think Clara is alive. We think most likely he knew people were starting to get closer, especially you, and he was cleaning up loose ends." Joe explains slowly with sadness in his voice.

"Why? Why do you think that?" I whisper.

I know he wouldn't be saying this if he didn't believe it. He wouldn't just tell me that he believes my friend is dead without having something to back it up.

"We found Jenny."

I start shaking my head.

"No." I won't believe it. I can't. "No."

"I'm sorry. She hadn't been dead for very long, probably only a few hours before he went after you. We are searching areas all around where we found her to look for Clara, but right now there's no reason not to believe he followed the same pattern with Clara as he did with Jenny."

"You're wrong. I know you're wrong. I would *know*. I would know if she were gone. He said. He said the partner was going to take—" My voice breaks, and I can't hold back the tears.

Will wraps his arms around me gingerly, clearly avoiding my injuries. I don't want to lean on him. I don't want to accept this. I can't.

Looking at Joe, he looks crushed.

"I really am so sorry, Kenzie," Joe says quietly. "We are going to follow every clue we find. I will chase down everything myself if I need to, so we can bring you the closure I know you need."

Closure.

Closure doesn't exist.

AFTER WHAT SEEMS LIKE FOREVER, Will and I are finally leaving the police station. I'm in a daze. I can't believe after everything; this is where we are.

That they are all just giving up.

I don't believe any of it.

Clara is alive.

I know it with every fiber of my body.

But as much as I know it to be true, reluctantly I have to admit I kind of understand why they would believe that she isn't. Finding Jenny was surprising, and honestly not a good sign of Clara's fate.

I'm even more ashamed I forgot about Jenny. During the past twelve hours, all I was thinking about was Clara. When Jonathan and I were in the parking lot, I never even considered Jenny. I never asked about her. I never wondered what was happening to her.

I had tunnel vision.

Clara was my only thought.

And I feel horrible.

Jenny had a family. One who loved her.

Friends who were on campus passing out flyers trying to find her, just like I was trying to find Clara.

And I didn't even try. I don't have anything to share with them about Jenny.

"Come on, let's get you back to my house," Will says quietly when I stop moving toward the parking lot.

I shake my head. I can't.

"No. I want to go home." My voice is monotone. Like there is no room for emotion left in me.

"Kenzie, I promise I will take you back to your apartment tomorrow if you want, but not tonight. You need rest and someone with you," he explains softly.

"No. I want to be closer to Clara. And you all insist the threat is over. I want to go home. The last place I knew for sure she was." My voice is still monotone but tears leak from my eyes.

There's a pause. Like he's weighing his options.

"Okay."

And with that, we start moving again.

Arriving back at my apartment is soul crushing. Every single square inch of my apartment is filled with memories.

Conversations about nothing.

Tears shed over our pasts.

Hours of advice about boys.

Countless movie nights with ice cream and popcorn.

The endless attempts by Clara to get me to understand her life's passion.

And every other small mundane moment in between.

"I'm going to stay here with you tonight if it's okay. Just in case you need anything," Will says.

I nod.

"I'll take the couch."

And that's when the phrase that has been repeating in my head over and over again all night long finally makes its way out.

"What comes next?" I ask.

"Anything you need," he replies simply.

"No. Really. What comes next? Literally."

His eyes search my face for a while before he answers.

"Well, I'm sure there will be more questions. Memorials and funerals, probably some on campus. It won't be easy. It will take time. But eventually, life will keep moving. You'll go to class, graduate, start your life. You'll carry this with you always, but life keeps moving, even when we don't want it to," he says gently.

"I don't think I can," I confess.

Will walks me over to the couch and sits down next to me before taking hold of my hand again.

"I know you don't, but you can, you will."

"No. You don't understand. I don't want to. I don't want to go back to class. I don't want to graduate. I don't want to be on campus. I don't want any of it. None of it matters anymore."

"That's okay, you can take a break, step back, figure out what comes next, it's normal. You've been through something horrible, it's completely okay to reassess what you want to do now."

The thing is I don't know what I want, I only know what I don't want. And I don't ever want to be on campus again. I don't care about graduating anymore. I don't want to teach. I don't want to apply to graduate school. I don't want any of this life of academia that Clara loves so much.

But Will is right about one thing. Life keeps going. Bills still need to be paid. I still need to eat. The world keeps turning.

"I can't afford it," I whisper.

"Can't afford what?"

"Time," I say simply. "I won't be able to make rent or pay my bills."

"Oh."

"Yeah." I look around the apartment. "I won't be able to stay here." My voice cracks.

"Come work for me," Will blurts out.

"What?" I must not have heard him right.

"You said you don't know what you're going to do next, but you need time. I can give you time. You can help me get the office together just like we talked about. You have good instincts and I could use someone who will push back against my stubborn ass. Plus, I can help you while you heal."

I know he's talking about more than just the injuries on my body.

"Will, you don't have to do that." I meet his eyes and they look so sincere. Not an ounce of pity in them.

"I know. I want to. I can teach you what I know, and you can stay for a long or short as you want, but at least you can get back on your feet," he explains.

"Will," I start.

"Plus, it would be nice to have you around. We could get to know each other. Maybe we could help each other." His eyes search mine.

The idea is beyond tempting. Will is the only person in the world right now who brings me any sense of safety and security. But more than that, he calms my broken heart.

I think about the people he works for; I think about the cases that might come across his desk. I think about the friends and families who must come to him for help. Exactly like how I came to him for help. I never want any of those people to feel like I do in this moment.

But more than that, I still believe Clara is out there. I believe there is a partner. I don't care what anyone says. Will made way more progress than the police did. And if he can teach me how to investigate, maybe, just maybe, I have a shot at finding Clara, when clearly no one else is going to be looking for anything more than a body.

"Yes," I say with conviction.

"Yes?" A look of hope crosses his face.

"Yes. I want to work with you."

He smiles at me softly, and I know then my life is going down a path I never suspected.

But I know it's the one I was meant for.

EPILOGUE

"GOODBYE, DEAR FRIEND" BY DEER TICK

Will is right about one thing.

Life keeps going.

The days keep passing.

Sometimes it feels like someone pushed the fast-forward button on the world but I was still standing still.

Sometimes it feels like I am rushing through it all but I can't keep up.

Time is constant. But perception is the fickle part.

Weeks have passed, and the flurry of activity has begun to settle.

At first there were questions.

Questions all the time.

Police. Reporters. Neighbors. Students. Friends of the missing.

Everyone had questions.

I answered those from the police. And those of the loved ones.

To everyone else, it was a sideshow. A car wreck that you slow down to look at on the highway.

I didn't entertain those questions.

Answers came too. Not enough answers.

Police did their jobs, and Joe kept me updated every step of the way.

They tore apart the life of Jonathan Nash. As unremarkable as it was.

Everyone had a theory about why he did what he did.

But he was dead and some answers we would just never get.

They did manage to find where he kept the missing women.

Most nights, I wish I didn't get the answers to the questions I had about that.

The description of the room.

Where they went to the bathroom.

What he mostly did to them.

The pieces of themselves they left behind.

It's the kind of thing nightmares are made of.

But there were no bodies.

Just Jenny.

She left this earth with his hands wrapped around her neck. Apparently, the same way the first woman was found.

The terror she must have felt as she felt her body start to slip away, only able to see his face above her own.

Police believe at this time that all of the women are dead. Even if no other bodies have been recovered. That the night he went after me in the woods, he must have panicked and started getting rid of loose ends.

I *never* want to hear women described as 'loose ends' ever again.

I avoided campus as much as possible.

Never going back to class.

I withdrew from the university. My adviser and the administration were very kind. After all, I was the almost victim of a serial killer. No one knew what to say though. Just a simple "we're here for whatever you need," and of course, that I could come back whenever I was ready.

I would never be ready.

I knew that.

Which brings us to now.

The sky looks like my soul. Gray and overcast, rain leaking from the sky, much like my tears do at night when I'm alone.

The weather is warmer. Further proof that time keeps moving forward, no matter how unready I am.

Today is the day I have been dreading. The last time I will need to be on campus.

It's the day of the memorial.

They waited. I suppose, hoping that more women would be found and more closure could be brought to those who knew them. Eventually though, people wanted closure, even if it wasn't really real.

Everyone holds white candles in their hands, by some miracle, they stay lit even against the drizzle falling from the sky.

People go up to the dais and talk about how loved these women were.

Clara's professors talk about how smart she was, how much promise she had, how they will always remember her as one of their best and brightest students. The kind of student that makes them love being a teacher.

I listen to it all.

I resist the urge to scream out that she's still alive.

I've seen how people respond to that over the past few weeks. I can't stand the looks of pity and the whispers about how sad it is that I just can't accept reality.

So instead I just stand in the back and listen to people remember. My hands in my pockets, the rain on my skin. My fingertips rest just on top of the metal that means everything.

As everyone bows their head in a moment of silence, I pull out Clara's locket from my pocket and place it around my neck. While everyone else is praying for those they have lost, I'm making a vow.

A vow to find her.

No matter how long it takes.

I will never give up.

And I will carry this locket next to my heart until I can put it around her neck once more, where it belonged all along.

WANT MORE KENZIE SHARP

Continue the search for Clara with Kenzie while she learns how to become a private investigator alongside Will. Can they work together to find the answers she needs?

SHARP BETRAYAL

Coming June 2022

BONUS CONTENT

Want to see how everything ended with Collin or get bonus scenes from this book or the next?

Sign up for my newsletter for the latest bonus content

Newsletter

HANG OUT WITH KATE

Sign up for my newsletter to get the latest news, some exclusive content, and even some surprise bonus scenes.

If you want to check out my reader group on Facebook to hang out and talk about not just my books but books we love in general, come check us out here.

For more ways to connect
    Website: www.kateanders.com
    Instagram: KateAndersBooks
    Twitter: KateAndersBooks
    Facebook: Kate Anders
    TikTok: KateAndersBooks

ABOUT THE AUTHOR

Kate was born and raised in Texas, and after almost a decade as an army wife, settled in North Carolina. She lives with her husband and their four dogs: Anders, Khaleesi, Patrick, and Charlie. Kate spends a great deal of her time reading new books from all over the romance genre, binge watching TV, practicing cooking, and obsessing about all things nerdy.

SEASON OF JUSTICE

In 2020 alone more than 540,000 people went missing, with more than 340,000 of those being children. So many of these cases will never get any media coverage. Many of these families will go without answers.

Like many people during the pandemic, I started listening to podcasts. One of my favorites has been *Crime Junkie*, a podcast that talks about a variety of cases, some that are even decades old. While I was listening to this podcast an overwhelming theme that kept coming up was people just disappearing one day. Sometimes families knew right away, sometimes it took days or weeks. Sometimes the police were invested right from the start, in other cases it would take months. But the overwhelming consensus seems to be the sooner the better.

I have always wanted to write a book, and this is where I had my moment of inspiration. What happens if no one believes the person in question is missing? What if that person has no family to propel the investigation forward? Would that person ever be found? Would anyone even look?

I know I am one of the lucky ones. If I ever went missing,

my husband and parents would move to mountains to find me. But not everyone has that. I want to highlight organizations that help with real life versions of the events in my book. So for this book I picked Season of Justice. It's the non-profit organization started by the people who make *Crime Junkie*. The goal of this organization is to help law enforcement and families help solve cold cases. So if you are so inclined, please consider donating to Season of Justice.

Season of Justice
 www.seasonofjustice.org

ACKNOWLEDGMENTS

First and foremost, thank you to my husband. He has been my biggest cheerleader for our entire marriage. I could wake up tomorrow and tell him I wanted to go to space and he would be like, let's figure out how to do that. So when I said I wanted to write a book he was like let's plot it out. He checks in on my progress everyday, texts me all the time while he's at work that he's proud of me, and he takes an interest in a genre that isn't his thing. Without him I am certain I would have never pushed through to write the book let alone publish it.

Next, is my mom. There has never been a time in my life where books did not play a major role, and that is 100% because of my mom. There was never a time when I didn't have access to as many books as I wanted, no matter what else was going on in our lives. She fostered my love of books right from the beginning. I have carried that with me through my entire childhood, into college, and now with pursuing my dream of being an author. Without my mom I know I would never have written this book.

I had a great group of people help to get this book to the finish line. Super, big thanks to my editing team over at My Brother's Editor, who stepped in and saved the day at the last minute. Also to my amazing cover artist, Murphy Rae. I was so nervous about getting a book cover, worried I wouldn't love it, but this is the cover of my dreams, so thank you so much for that.

The last couple of years have been tough for me, medically

speaking. Setbacks seemed to be around every corner. I have had an amazing medical team over at Duke University and an even better support system at home. So for everyone who took care of me while I couldn't take care of myself, thank you. To my husband who went to every PT session, and literally helped me relearn how to sit up and walk again, you will never know how much that meant to me. To my mom who would do lego sets with me as I regained the use of my hand, thank you. Like most people, I'm a work in progress, and I'm forever grateful for the people who are supporting me through it.